CORONATION SOUVENIR

Edward Arno

The Victory Rose Press
LOS ANGELES CA

Edward Arno/The Victory Rose Press
Victory Boulevard
Burbank, CA
www.edwardarno.com

Publisher's Note: This is a work of fiction. Names, characters, places, and incidents are a product of the author's imagination. Locales and public names are sometimes used for atmospheric purposes. Any resemblance to actual people, living or dead, or to businesses, companies, events, institutions, or locales is completely coincidental.

Book Layout ©2013 BookDesignTemplates.com

Library of Congress Cataloguing in Publication Data:
TXu001069212
Coronation Souvenir/ Edward Arno -- 1st ed.

ISBN 978-0-9996465-0-2

In Memory of
Bessie and Harold Dewhirst

A good traveler has no fixed plans, and is not intent on arriving.

—LAO TZU

CHAPTER ONE

The Watcher

The moon slid behind the growing darkening clouds. The ghosts and demons of children's dreams readied themselves to visit the minds of the innocent. From the darkness of an unfinished semidetached house, the watcher's bright piercing eyes stared out into the empty cul-de-sac. Decorations for Queen Elizabeth the Second's Coronation hung from the lampposts and specially erected poles, casting shadows across the road. The streetlights had not yet been connected, and illumination from the newly occupied houses on Crowhurst Road created a strange shadow on the road. Paper banners and crowns had been taped to the windows, adding color to the illumination. The glass panels of the front doors sported pictures of the Queen. High on the brick wall between some of the semidetached houses hung wooden shields with the House of Windsor crest. Union Jack flags stuck out from behind the shields, and red, white and blue triangle shaped flag bunting had been strung across the road from house to house. It was May thirtieth nineteen fifty-three and the country was excited with anticipation for this great event.

A trench several feet deep lay open in the round center, which joined the arms of the T-shaped cul-de-sac. The silent watcher had learned the hard way not to tell anyone what he had seen. Black circles ringed his unblinking eyes, because he was kept awake by the fear of what the night might bring. He felt the blood trickle down his back, the thin cotton shirt stuck to the open welts. He kept things to himself, always remembering what his father had said, 'big boys don't cry' even though this is what he wanted to do. His innocence was destroyed. As a dog ran down the road, the watcher receded into the shadows.

The constant thump of the mechanical hammer, followed by the release of steam, from the Austin Motor Company's pressing plant filled the night with noise. A symphony to industry, which most residents living in the area had long ago ceased to hear. It was when the silence was longer than a few minutes that the local residents began to listen and wonder what had happened. The watcher listened to the mechanical orchestra as it played on. Only the new inhabitants were disturbed, annoyed and irritated until it became part of their lives' sound track.

A drunken construction worker, unable to find his way home, staggered down the center of the road and fell into the trench. The watcher inhaled and held his breath, only releasing it when the man hauled himself out of the trench and tottered off to find somewhere to sleep in one of the unfinished houses. The bunting flags flapped as a breeze traveled down the road, applauding the night's arrival.

Heavy footsteps made the eyes of the watcher vanish. They continued to watch from the grey division between darkness and light to see two men carrying a large bundle wrapped in sackcloth material. One man was rotund, about five feet eight inches in height, constantly puffing on a cigarette sticking out of the corner of his mouth. The other was taller, skinny and very nervous, looking around as he carried the end of the bundle. They were dressed in Birmingham City workmen's uniforms. The rotund man's uniform belonged to someone several sizes smaller. The night watcher looked on as the men passed his location, they were unaware of his presence. Reaching the open trench, they dropped the bundle into the hole, making a loud thud. They stopped and stooped down, waiting to see if someone would come out of the houses to investigate the noise. A dog barked at an argument, which was growing louder from one of the occupied houses, only to stop after a few banging doors. To the residents of Crowhurst Road, a loud thud, slamming door, or barking dog was the tympani to the ongoing industrial symphony.

The watcher pressed against the rough wood of an unfinished window, and observed more intently the escapades of this night's performance.

The men waited for a few minutes then picked up the shovels left by the real workmen and began to fill in the trench, covering the bundle. They labored in silence. The dog returned and wandered onto the wooden makeshift stage that had been erected for the celebrations. He growled at the men filling in the trench. The rotund man picked up a stone and threw it at the dog, which ran off yelping in pain.

The wind started to pick up and blew the banners hanging around the circle. The bunting clapped. The two men placed the shovels quietly on the ground and retraced their steps up the road to one of the finished houses. The watcher sank into the darkness as they passed. Then sat on a cold toilet seat waiting to be plumbed into a house. He wrote frantically what he had just seen in the white spaces of a small Bible he took out of his pocket. His eyes strained from the lack of light.

The street grew silent once more. The watcher moved to a different unfinished house to see more clearly the wind create small dust swirls, which danced with the flags and banners. Keeping to the shadows, he crept to the trench and peered in. The men had filled it almost to the top of where they had buried something. A train whistle made the watcher retreat into hiding, this time not to reappear.

CHAPTER TWO

The Souvenir

The young man stood looking at the yellow front door of Number Thirteen Crowhurst Road.

He hopped from one foot to the other, contemplating if he should walk down the pathway and knock on the door. This wasn't his normal demeanor. James Pidgley would normally take control of a house viewing not giving the estate agent a chance to speak. This time it wasn't just about building the family empire. This purchase could jeopardize the harmony and feelings of his family. Checking his appointment book to see if he had the right date, June the first, two thousand and three. After a few moments, he turned to walk away. The front door suddenly opened, and an overanxious estate agent called to him, "Can I help you?"

He turned back and stuttered, "Err."

"You've come about the house," she continued, "Please let me show you around."

Ms. Elizabeth Friedman was bleached-blonde and several pounds overweight. Her drawn lined face gave the impression she needed this sale. As she had no ring on her finger, he assumed she must be divorced. From the state of her shoes, the heels worn down and the side stitching breaking apart, he knew her life had gone down hill. The tone of her voice indicated she had something to prove, and she didn't care how she accomplished the task. He liked that in a person, but he was no push over when it came to buying property. His research into the house and Ms. Friedman had been fruitful. She had lived in the neighborhood all her life. Therefore he felt she must feel herself best qualified to sell the house. He observed as she wiped her sweating hands on the back of her skirt. Flicking several strands of hair from her face, then she gave her professional smile, trying to hide her coffee-stained teeth.

James walked down the un-weeded garden path and approached Elizabeth with some trepidation. Was he doing the right thing? His father would have said no, he thought, but his brothers would say yes if the price were right. He had incredible respect for his father, a quiet, soft-spoken man. But this was a bargain, and they were in the business to make money. He would fight with his conscience and maybe his family later.

Elizabeth held out her hand to shake the young man's hand. "Elizabeth Friedman, are you the young man who called and said you wanted to view the house?"

"Yes," replied James. Confident, as she looked him up and down. Coughing politely he regained her attention.

For him time was money. Shaking her hand he became conscious of his own soft manicured hand. Her rough hard skinned hand shook vigorously.

"Oh yes," she said, "Please let me show you around. You must understand the house has been empty for nine months, since the last owner died." James gave her a quizzical look. "He didn't die here, I might add."

He noticed she had focused on a small white thread of cotton on his lapel. Picking it off the suit, he held it between his thumb and index finger before letting it go. They watched as it floated off into the light breeze. He checked to see if there were any more cotton threads on his suit. Elizabeth stepped aside so that he could enter the house. She was as he expected desperate and she was playing into his hands. It would be like taking candy from a baby, he could even get the purchase price lower than he first thought.

James entered the dimly lit hallway. Letters and free newspapers had been neatly piled together on the floor. A strong smell of dampness permeated the stale air.

"I'll leave the front door open to get some fresh air into the place," said Elizabeth. "If you would like to turn to the left and enter the lounge, Mister..." He didn't reply, but entered the lounge, as she had called it. The room was large, running from the front to the back of the house, and it was dirty. The coal fireplace situated in the middle of the room still had ash in the grate. Soot fell from the chimney as a bird dislodged it high above in the chimney pot. He looked around the room. The orange, yellow and brown colored nineteen sixties carpet was stained. The path of compressed pile revealed where people had walked. The metal window frames had begun to rust from years of condensation. The putty holding the panes of glass had become cracked and in some place were missing.

He had expected someone else to accompany them during the viewing. After all she was in a house alone with a strange young man. Surely her colleagues had warned about this reckless act. Since the disappearance of an estate agent in London several years earlier, he would have thought she should never be alone with a single male client. It made him feel very uncomfortable, and he hesitated on continuing the viewing.

As Elizabeth passed him, he relaxed. He noticed a button missing off her blouse and the small tear in her skirt. Her tension and over eagerness on their meeting told him she was not only desperate but in a hurry. She had a pretty face, although too much makeup for his taste. But he wasn't here to date her.

She was standing at the far end of the room looking at him. He gave her a smile, showing the white teeth he was so proud of.

"This area here is used as a dining room. I can imagine a large table sitting at least ten people. Do you have a family, Mister...?"

"No."

"Well I am sure you can image yourself at a table with twelve of your friends, eating an exotic feast that your wife has prepared. How your friends would enjoy themselves on *picade* duck and roasted pheasant.

Although I don't know what a *picade* duck is, let alone how to cook it, but it sounds exotic."

He coughed behind his hand hearing the nervous desperation in her voice.

"Oh, I am sorry I really don't know why, but this house certainly makes my imagination work," she said apologetically.

"That's okay. I know places can do that. Is this the kitchen?" He walked through a doorway into the kitchen. The fake wooden cupboard doors hung haphazardly from their hinges. The work of a wandering cowboy installer who was out to make a quick penny by doing a shoddy job that at first looked good but soon fell apart. He opened one of the cupboards black mold was growing inside. Elizabeth appeared behind him and peered over his shoulder to look into the cupboard.

"We admit the kitchen does need some work, but it could be made to look very nice. Maybe your wife would have some ideas for it."

"I'm not married."

"Oh!" retorted Elizabeth surprised.

"I want this house as an investment." He knew she would squirm at this, as he would now haggle about the price.

He looked at the square porcelain sink a relic from when the house was built in the nineteen fifties.

"I see," replied Elizabeth, she continued, "Through this door we return to the hallway."

James entered the small passageway, which led into the main entrance hall. To his left he noticed a door under the stairs. He opened it, forcefully blocking Elizabeth's way. The hinges screamed as though in pain. He peered into the darkness and wondered what secrets were hidden inside. Elizabeth pushed against the door, and he moved out of the way, letting it close. Elizabeth fell into the passageway. She gathered her composure and pushed past him.

"I think I should go first, just in case there is any problem," she said with some forcefulness. He let her pass. As they entered the main hallway again, a stream of fresh cool air blew in through the open front door. The noise of workmen just outside could be heard.

"They are digging up the road, I am sorry about the noise," said Elizabeth as she started to ascend the stairs followed by James. She grabbed the handrail tightly. He saw the white-knuckled grip of Elizabeth's hand on the handrail.

"Are you alright Ms. Friedman?"

"I had a fear of falling while climbing stairs since my childhood."

For the first time James felt a chill travel through his body and he shuddered. He grabbed the handrail, not wanting to tempt fate. He was superstitious to the ridiculous, according to his mother. He would never walk under a ladder and on seeing a black cat he would either cross the road or walk the other way. This was not the action of an aggressive businessman according to his brothers. He would always reply, "What has walking under a ladder and a black cat got to do with business practice?"

On the landing at the top of the stairs, five white-painted doors stood closed and imposing.

"There are three bedrooms and a bathroom," said Elizabeth, leading the way to one of the doors. Opening the door and entering, Elizabeth continued, "This is a small single bedroom, good enough for a child."

"Or a small adult," said James.

"Well, yes," said Elizabeth, showing some irritation in her voice. He could tell she hated being interrupted from her tone. To him it was obvious she didn't like smart-ass comments as it undermined her confidence.

"The next room is the master bedroom, with its own gas fire." She opened the door and stood aside to let him enter a room full of dust and cobwebs.

Dead flies had created their own cemetery on the windowsill. It had been a massacre. The dried black bodies were piled several deep. The opening of the door had created a draft, and a few of the flies fell onto the carpet.

"The master bedroom, like the rest of the house, does need a little painting," ventured Elizabeth, feeling it was better to be open about the problems of the house.

The price was dropping by each room. Giving a little nod he continued to look around the room.

From a side-glance he could see Elizabeth standing in the doorway looking at him. She had positioned herself as if she was posing for a fashion magazine. The problem was her ankles.

James was looking at every detail in the master bedroom and stood up after examining the gas fire. He smiled at Elizabeth standing in the doorway. She was in deep thought staring at him and didn't acknowledge the smile. Her expressionless look unnerved James, and he hoped she wasn't analyzing him in the way his mother said woman of certain age did.

He pulled back the rotting net curtains to look out of the window. The dead bluebottle flies cascaded to the floor. A bluebottle fly Niagara Falls! The dried dead bodies bounced as they hit the carpet. Then others followed, bouncing off the ones already there. As James turned from the window, his feet crunched on the corpses. He looked down at the dead bodies and stepped carefully over them. Standing in front of Elizabeth, he saw she was in a trance and took a few seconds to bring her out of it to face him eye to eye.

"It needs a lot of work."

"Yes," was all Elizabeth could reply, blushing a deep red.

Noticing her embarrassment, he said, "Shall we look at the next room?"

Elizabeth led the way back onto the landing. James closed the door. The doorknob came off in his hand.

"Oh I'm sorry. I keep meaning to fix it."

"Don't worry, it will only knock a pound off the asking price," with a twinkle in his eyes as he said it. Elizabeth looked at him and realized he was joking. She gave her girlish giggle. He replaced the knob and closed the door.

"Next room, I think." Passing the middle door, Elizabeth moved on. "This is a good-size bedroom, which looks out onto the back of the house." Opening the door, they both were taken back by the black-painted walls with a thin gold stripe that ran all around the room at about four feet from the floor. "I think this must have been the last owner's daughter's room."

"Interesting," said James.

"I think she was a very disturbed young lady. She didn't even go to her father's funeral and hasn't been back since." James had hardly stepped into the room before he left it, closing the door as he did. This created a surprised look on Elizabeth's face it was such a quick inspection.

He felt uncomfortable in the room. There was something sinister about someone painting their bedroom walls black. He personally advocated that every room should be a bright light color. But how could anyone sit in a black room and not get depressed, he thought.

Elizabeth opened the door to the left, saying, "This is the bathroom. It does have a shower curtain fitted above the bathtub and a connected shower head to the faucet."

The atmosphere had changed. He saw the tension form on her face. Entering the bathroom, he looked straight at the fitted shower curtain falling from the wall. The toilet bowl had a large black crack running from the top to the bottom. Elizabeth poked her head in and remarked, "Sorry! It looks like something died in here," then retreated onto the landing.

James quietly mumbled, "Yes, my grandmother died in this bathroom, alone." But Elizabeth was out of earshot.

Mildew was growing everywhere, and the smell of stagnant drains saturated the air. He left the room quickly, closing the door behind him. Not wanting to relive the great loss and pain his family had felt at his grandmother's death.

Elizabeth moved to the top of the stairs and was about to descend. James went to the middle door asking, "What's this room?" He opened the door on a cupboard housing the hot and cold-water tanks. Elizabeth joined him and peered into the cupboard. "It's just an utility closet," she replied, and turned back towards the stairs. He crouched down, and by the foot of the hot water tank he lifted a loose plank of wood measuring four inches wide by ten inches long. He put his hand inside and pulled out a small black book. Elizabeth turned to see if he was behind her and caught him taking out the book. "What have you found?" she asked.

"Just an old book someone left behind," replied James. Elizabeth took one step on the landing towards him when the noise of someone entering the house downstairs caught her attention.

Someone shouted from the hallway, "Does anyone have a phone?"

Elizabeth turned and looked down the stairs. One of the workmen who were working in the road had entered the house.

"Pardon?" she said. "This is a private residence."

The workman came to the foot of the stairs and looked up. He was a stocky man with a head of flaming red hair, and he was wearing a red tank top and very dirty, tight blue jeans. He smiled at her. It was such a beautiful smile, Elizabeth's left leg lifted off the floor. James standing behind her, realized that whoever had spoken to her had stirred romantic feelings inside her. He had seen his own sisters react the same way when they found a man interesting.

Using his hands when he spoke. "Sorry to bother you, Miss. I need a phone to call the police. We've just dug up a body in the road."

"Oh," said Elizabeth, becoming flustered on hearing the workman saying, "Miss." She continued, "Err, please, please use my mobile." She descended the stairs, and taking her mobile out of her handbag, gave it to the workman. Smiling, he went out into the garden with Elizabeth at his heels.

On the landing, James placed the book he had found into his pocket, replacing the wooden plank and closing the closet door. He started to walk towards the staircase but stopped and turned back towards the second bedroom. Opening the door, he entered and went over to the window. He peeled back the net curtain and looked down onto the triangular back garden. The house might have been empty for nine months, but the back garden had not been tended for several years. It was overgrown with weeds, and someone had thrown garbage and other rubbish into it as well. A brick shed was attached to the house, its door swinging uneasily from its hinges.

James let the net curtain fall back into place. He stood still, looking down at the shed. Someone was there watching, his inner senses told him. No one appeared, and for the second time that day he dismissed his instincts. Maybe he was losing his touch. Looking around the room before leaving, he checked at the window again. The shed door was no longer swinging, but tightly closed.

Back on the landing, he closed the door and descended the stairs. At the foot of the stairs, in front of him, was another closet door. He opened it, but found only the gas and electricity meters—neither registering any activity.

Outside in the road he could hear a commotion. Leaving the house, he closed the front door behind him. Walking up the garden path, he closed the yellow gate behind him. It was this type of action that his brothers would have made fun of. He just liked things to be neat. He looked at the small crowd that had gathered around the hole dug in the round center, which joined the arms of the T-shaped cul-de-sac.

Elizabeth peered into the hole and became unsteady when she saw the skull and bones unearthed by the workmen. As he approached, the workman went to her aid, holding her firmly in his arms as she gathered her composure. Seeing that she was okay, he looked into the hole. A skull and several bones protruded from the disturbed earth. It was impossible to tell the sex of the person. He returned to Elizabeth and asked, "Are you okay, Ms. Friedman?"

Elizabeth said weakly, "Yes, I shall be fine in a moment," and she searched her handbag, taking out several dolly clothes pegs. They were old looking and hand made. James smiled to himself, recognizing his ancestors' workmanship.

"I found them in the house. I really don't know why I kept them."

"I haven't seen washing line clothes pegs for years, the gypsies use to make dolly pegs you know?" said the red headed workman.

She nodded then found a clean white handkerchief edged with pink embroidery and wiped her eyes.

The workman guided her to a milk crate they had been using for their tea breaks. A half filled white tea mug stood by the side of the milk crate. He bent down and picked it up, looking into Elizabeth's face as he did. "Would you like some tea, Miss?"

Blushing again, Elizabeth replied, "It's Missus actually, but I'm divorced, and a little water might help. Thank you."

"Right you are, then."

The gathered crowd turned and watched a police car slowly enter the cul-de-sac as though going to a picnic rather than a possible murder scene. An overweight police officer stepped out of the car and wandered over to where the small crowd stood. His uniform was too small for him, and he bulged in all the wrong places. The stains from several meals already consumed that day were evident down the front of his shirt.

"Now then, who reported finding a body?" he asked.

"I did," said the workman, who had returned with a cup of water for Elizabeth. "John Townsend, that's me name, officer. And I'm single," he added, smiling at Elizabeth. "The body is over here." He walked over to the hole in the road and pointed into it.

The police officer said, "It's not in the library, then?" and laughed embarrassingly at his own joke.

John answered, "No, it's here," in a slightly irritated tone and again pointed into the hole.

The police officer strolled over and, bending down, peered in. On seeing the bones, he cried, "Christ!"

"Unlikely," said James, just loudly enough for Elizabeth to hear. She gave her girlish giggle. This was followed by an even louder laugh from John Townsend.

The police officer straightened himself up and spoke into his communicator, "Control, this is four-five-one. Over."

"Four-five-one, Control over," said someone at the other end of the wireless transmission.

"Control, there is a body in the ground. Repeat, there is a body. Over," said the police officer.

"Four-five-one, are you trying to be funny?" said the voice from Control.

"No Control, looks like it's been in the ground, under the road, for several years, but there is a body. Over," replied the police officer.

"Four-five-one," said the voice at Control, "I will dispatch a crime scene team. Cordon off the area and secure the crime scene, and keep any witnesses there. Over."

"Will do. And we thought it would be a quiet day! Four-five-one and out," replied the police officer.

A few children had arrived home from school and joined the crowd of onlookers. They pushed each other towards the hole until one, an acne-faced boy, almost fell in. The police officer went to the trunk of his car, removed blue and white tape, and began to rope off the area around the hole. He then replaced the tape in the trunk and, upon closing it, turned and walked over to where the workmen, Elizabeth, James, and others were. "Who found the body?" he asked again.

"We did," replied John Townsend. "Me and Dave here."

"Okay, well, you stay right here," said the police officer and turned to Elizabeth, asking her, "Who are you?"

"The young lady let me use her phone to call you guys," answered John Townsend.

"I see," replied the police officer. "And why are you here? Do you live on the road?"

Elizabeth, gaining her strength, said, "No, I don't live here. I'm the estate agent for Number

Thirteen, and I was showing Mister... Err..." She paused and looked at James.

He turned and looked at her, smiling, "Pidgley; James Pidgley."

"Mr. Pidgley," continued Elizabeth, "around the property, when this nice workman Mr. Townsend came in and asked if we had a phone he could use to call you."

"Okay then, let me get your names and addresses, just in case we need them, and you can be on your way," said the police officer. Both Elizabeth and James gave the police officer business cards. He took them, looked at them, and was about to say goodbye when he was interrupted.

"Could I have one of them?" John Townsend asked Elizabeth. She gave him one. He placed it in his wallet without looking at it.

"Officer, by the way, my mate Dave has just remembered something."

"What?" asked the police officer.

"You tell him, Dave," said John.

"Well, I..."

"Before you start, what's your name?" interrupted the police officer.

"Dave Boscombe." He was a man in his late sixties, his head covered with a haystack of white hair. His skin, especially on his face, was like hard leather from the many years of working outside.

"Good. Now continue and be quick about it."

"I was a young lad when this road was built. I had just started to work for the city. Me Dad was already working for them and he got me the job. It was just before the Queen's Coronation."

"Yes?" said the office impatiently.

"Well, we had a trench which ran right across the road just where that hole is now, and one night someone filled it in," said Dave.

"Okay" said the police officer, even more impatiently. "What happened next?"

Dave continued, "Well, we had been told to fill it in as quickly as we could for the Coronation, so we didn't check to see if anyone had put something in the hole. We just put tarmac over it."

"You're telling me that some fifty years ago you dug a hole here, and no one has ever dug the road up since?" said the police officer.

"I don't think anyone has, but they'll know for sure at the depot. They keep records and things, and it's all computerized these days," said Dave.

Elizabeth then asked, "Do you need us any more, officer?" The police officer looked at her and James and shook his head. They walked back towards Elizabeth's car. "I'm really sorry this has happened," said Elizabeth.

"Why? It's not your fault," said James. "Now, about the house."

"Oh, yes," said Elizabeth, preparing herself for the worst.

"I'm very interested. Let me talk to my partners, and I will get back to you tomorrow, if that's okay," said James.

"Yes, that will be fine. But I shall understand if they are not interested."

"Oh, we are interested. We may have to work on the asking price, given the condition of the house."

"I understand, and I'm sure the owners will too. I know we can come to some agreement," said Elizabeth, trying to keep her excitement under control. They shook hands, and Elizabeth went to the front door of the house to make sure it was locked before going over to her car. She looked back at James, waved and got into her car, then drove down the road, passing the arriving crime scene vans.

James sat in his car and watched the police arrive. He then took the small, well-worn book from his pocket. It was a Bible. He opened it and looked at the inscription on the inside cover. The nameplate was from an old Baptist church Sunday school. The Bible had been presented to Matthew Thomas Pidgley. He ran his fingers over it before he closed the book and returned it to his pocket. He began to chew his lower lip as he looked again at the police activity. Then he started his car, drove down the road, and turned left.

CHAPTER THREE

Family

James stood looking into the glass panes of his parents' front door to check his appearance. He needed a haircut, and was sure his father would make a comment about him looking like an old hippie. He searched for a comb, but couldn't find one in his pockets. He ran his fingers through his inch-long hair. For James, his appearance was important he believed it conveyed his personality. First impression were important was what he had been taught. To him if you let that impression slip it showed you were shallow. Maintaining the image meant a lot to him even in front of his family. He rechecked his hair and instinctively looked at his shoes to see if they were polished. Only today, he had forgotten he was wearing a new pair of black and blue sneakers.

The purchase of the Crowhurst Road house had disrupted his routine. He hadn't had time to prepared how he was going to sell the buying of the house to the family. After speaking with his brothers Donald and Bryan about the property, he didn't feel confident. Donald in his usual way had listened to what he had to say and agreed if their father were on board they would purchase. Bryan on the other hand had reacted as he always did, confrontational. He always claimed he was playing the devil's advocate. James knew this was just his way of being difficult, if not jealous. James felt Bryan saw himself as a hard-nosed businessman and James as a wimpy boy. This was the problem between them and the cause of many company meeting arguments. Bryan wanted to build their property empire quickly taking unnecessary risks. James wanted to build slowly and a little cautiously. Today he would have to face his father, hoping to avoid rejection and this scared him. Not because he was frightened of the man but because the last thing he wanted to do was hurt him.

He put the key into the door, as he had every Sunday since leaving home four years earlier. It was the only time he used the key. On other visits, he would knock, to his mother's annoyance. The family ritual of Sunday lunch together had continued, even though several of his siblings had families of their own. The whole family turned up, and James knew it was more love than a sense of duty that brought him back every Sunday.

He stepped onto the hall carpet, with its autumn leaf pattern, and heard his mother ordering his younger brother to get on with chores. James smiled to himself. He remembered his mother doing the same to him. He closed the front door, almost crushing the flowers he had bought for her, making his way along the hallway filled with the smells of cooking and her favorite potpourri. He stopped and listened at the door to the front room, behind which he heard his father's deep voice. Nervously he began to bite his lip. He loved his father, but knew how stubborn he could be, especially about things he didn't want to confront. James smiled at the thought that he really was like his father.

The kitchen door opened with some force, and Paul, at eighteen the youngest of the ten Pidgley children, appeared. James froze, caught like a child doing something he shouldn't. He bit his lower lip harder. Composing himself, he gave Paul a nod.

"How's it going, James?"

"Okay. Who's arrived?"

"Dad and Bryan are in the front room, Mom, Eileen… Oh, Sol hasn't come, and Jane is in the kitchen."

"Bryan got to dad first did he?"

"Err not sure what you mean. I don't know where Anne is, and the others haven't arrived yet."

James had asked both Donald and Bryan not to talk to their father about the property. It was typical of Bryan to corner their father first. James hoped he wouldn't talk negatively about the property. If he had, Bryan would just smile and say it was business nothing personal little brother.

"I'll go and see Mom," said James, opening the kitchen door. The kitchen wasn't very big, and it was impossible for the whole family to be in the kitchen at the same time. Sarah, his mother, was standing at the sink, washing a bowl of cherries. He stood looking at her. As always she was wearing her favorite primrose colored knee length dress. The white apron had been pulled tightly around her body so the dress remained clean. She turned to pick up a dishtowel and saw him. "James, you made it," she said, and blew him a kiss.

"Good morning or is it afternoon?" he said, and gave her a kiss on her cheek, adding, "For you," as he presented her with the flowers. He could smell her scent that had comforted him over the years.

"Why the flowers? What have you done?" she quipped.

"Nothing," he replied, protesting his innocence.

Eileen, the eldest child in the family and married to Solomon, was standing by the stove. "You need Mom to be on your side against Dad," she said. "You always bring flowers when you need that."

"That's not a nice thing to say," said Sarah.

"Maybe," replied Eileen, "but it's true mother. If he had done something wrong, it would have been chocolates!"

"Is that true?" asked Sarah. James said nothing, but gave a disapproving look at his sister behind his mother's back.

The door to the garden opened, and Mary, her husband Colin and their three-year-old son Thomas arrived. Mary was the fifth child of the Pidgley clan and had married Colin when she was pregnant with Thomas. Sarah stopped washing the pans and gave Mary a peck on the cheek and then pretended to headbutt her son-in-law. She stooped down to give little Thomas a big kiss.

Thomas asked, "Are we having chocolates for dinner?"

"No, why do you ask?" questioned Sarah.

"Because I heard Auntie Eileen say Uncle James had given you chocolates," replied little Thomas.

They laughed, and Eileen said "Later I will find some chocolates for you, but only if you eat all your dinner."

"Okay," said Thomas, and continued, "Where's Grandpa?" He then ran out of the kitchen into the hall, followed by his mother and father.

Sarah went back to the sink and began to wash up the pans stacked to the left. Eileen took the flowers, placed them on a chair, and looked for a vase. James stood by helplessly, wondering what to do. The front door bell rang, and James excused himself to answer it. In the hallway, Paul had beaten him to it and was already opening the door. Peter and his wife Rose stepped in. Peter was older than James by one year and had recently married Rose Wood. She was a pretty girl he had met at a New Year's dance several years earlier. Peter now acted as though he were an old married man, and tried to order his brothers and sisters around. He and brother Bryan owned a used-car dealership and had for many years been at the mercy of the family jokes. Although they never really did anything illegal, some of the sales could be thought of as P.T. Barnum said "one sucker born every minute."

Paul, who had stepped aside to let them in, closed the front door and started to tell them who was where and doing what. Peter looked past him, and seeing James, gave him a nod. James nodded back and gave Rose a smile.

"You okay, Little Brother?" asked Peter.

"Yeah," replied James. "Why do you ask?"

"Well, you found that body."

"I didn't actually find it. Some workmen did."

"But you were there."

"Well, yes, but don't mention it to Dad. I don't want the idea of a dead body to put negative thoughts in his head before I tell him about the house."

"If that's what you want," said Peter, turning to see his wife being propositioned by Paul, who was leaning over Rose so that she couldn't get by him. Peter clipped Paul on the head, helped his wife to pass the protesting brother, and entered the kitchen.

Paul and James watched them and laughed. Paul raced after them. James heard the top step of the stairs creak and looked up to see his sister Anne. She was the family's ninth child and three years younger than James. She had been listening at the top of the stairs, and now, with a smile on her face, descended. Anne was not the most popular child in the family, regarded by her siblings as positively evil. Her nickname was "Daft Ada," a play on the evil Darth Vader from the *Star Wars* movies. She had been known to cause many arguments and set one family member against another. As a little girl, she would try to destroy her siblings' toys, and she once put chili powder in Mary's pretend makeup, so that when Mary and her friends played grownups, they had covered their faces with the burning spice. Several weeks later, the truth came out, but only after their father Matthew had threatened to give Peter a beating for playing such a bad practical joke. When asked why she hadn't told them before, she replied, "No one asked me." The relationship between Peter and Anne had never been healed, and even to this day they disliked each other.

"Anne you look pleased with yourself."

"Not really but they do say knowledge is power."

"What do you mean?"

"Nothing, is dinner ready?"

"Almost, I think it is time to set the table." James held the kitchen door and let Anne pass him.

The children of the family gathered in the kitchen. Bryan appeared from the dinning room, a smug smile drawn across his face. Seeing James his smile grew in to a nervous laugh.

James knew by Bryan's reaction that his father had already been told about the property.

"You told him then?"

"Oh it came up in our conversation."

"Sure and pigs can fly. I asked you not to, but I forgot you have a big mouth."

"Meaning what?"

"You have to put the knife in."

"Look I have the right to talk to dad about the properties we are buying."

"Sure, convince yourself Bryan, just remember two can play your game."

"Whatever, one day little brother you will grow up." Bryan emphasized the word 'little'.

James loved his siblings and often found it difficult to understand why they felt the need to be so spiteful. More often than not, he found himself playing the diplomat when he would really like to have said what he felt. Of course his older brothers had said this was a sign of his weakness. James felt it showed a great deal of strength. In his mind, great businessmen were also great diplomats.

Sarah, the matriarch, had just finished washing the pans, which was a signal for the Sunday ritual of laying the table to begin. Ever since they were small, each Pidgley child had been given his or her own particular task in this ritual, and it always started the moment Sarah wiped her hands after washing the cooking pans.

Peter looked at the others and then went into the dining room, walking over to the CD player and very carefully removing a CD from its plastic box. He pressed the button on the machine and the tray slid out. Placing the CD on it, he gave the tray a little tap. The tray slid in as quietly as it had appeared. He looked at the CD cover: "Les Yeux Noirs – A Band of Gypsies." It had become the family's favorite piece of music for the Sunday ritual. The violins sprang into life and calmed the tense atmosphere. The door from the kitchen opened and Paul entered, carrying a well-ironed tablecloth. He placed it carefully on the table, removing the bowl of shining glass fruit and placing it onto a side table. He picked up a crystal apple to see if the imperfection was still there. He had told the others it was a grub caught in time!

Back in the kitchen, the others were getting on with their tasks. Anne was wiping the William Morris-patterned placemats, while Elizabeth sorted the knives and forks.

Sarah slid her hand into James's and took him into the laundry room. "What's the problem?" she asked, stroking her son's head as she had done since he was a baby. James said nothing, just enjoyed the feel of his mother's touch. "Come on, I know you have something on your mind."

"It's nothing, really. I want to buy a house, and Bryan thinks Dad will be angry, that's all."

"Why would your father be angry? Don't you and your brothers buy houses for a living?"

"It's Dad's old home." Said James, putting his head on his mothers shoulder.

"Oh, I see," replied Sarah. "Do you think it's a wise thing to do?"

"Mom, it's a bargain, and we can rent it for a few years and then sell it at a profit. As a shareholder of our company, Dad will not be angry with that. Also, he doesn't have to go to see the place."

Peter appeared at the door carrying small side plates. "Come on, James, we need the dinner plates."

"Sorry," said James. He gave his mother a kiss and then went back into the kitchen. When James entered the dining room, Peter was arranging the side plates, and Mary was getting in his way trying to put the spoons on the table. James picked up the dinner plates, with their different famous houses painted on each one, and placed them on the mats. As a child he had hated Sunday, but now, because the whole family was together, he really enjoyed the whole ritual. His appreciation of his siblings and the importance of the family meant something. It harked back to the days when his ancestors traveled from one place to another, then gathered around the campfire at night to eat and tell stories.

The music played in the background as the routine continued. Donald had not yet arrived, so Eileen placed the serving spoons, which signaled the end of the ritual. They each in turn looked at the empty place on the table where the carving set should have been and awaited the arrival of their father to carve the meat.

Mary became very agitated; "Donny's not here! Where is he? We can't start without him. It'll mean bad luck. I know it."

"Another one of your stupid superstitions Mary, at you age," taunted Anne.

"We all have superstitions," cried Mary.

"I don't," replied Anne, a superior smirk on her face.

"Don't be so stupid Mary," said Eileen, then continued, "James please get the carving set."

"Oh no. Oh. Donny should do it. He's always done it. Let's wait until he comes," whined Mary.

"If we wait, the food will get cold and dry, and you know how Dad hates cold, dry food," said Eileen.

James placed the carving set on the table and turned to face the others. "Ready," he said, "Let's get the food."

"Oh, oh, this is wrong," said Mary, beginning to tremble, her whole body shaking.

"Mary, stop it, you're becoming hysterical," said Anne very loudly and raised her open hand to slap Mary on the face.

James stepped in between Mary and Anne and closed his eyes expecting to be hit by Anne.

Mary's husband, Colin entered from the kitchen and looked at his wife then went to her. Seeing how upset she was, he put his arms around her. "What's the problem, my sweet?"

"Donny's not here, and James put the carving set on the table. Colin, it's bad luck, I know it is," said Mary.

"It's okay. Nothing's going to happen, my precious, not now that I'm here, your little hubby."

"Yuck. I think I'm going to throw up," retorted Anne.

Mary placed her head on Colin's shoulder and began to sob.

"Don't cry, Mommy. Uncle Donny will come," said Thomas, grabbing his mother's leg to comfort her.

"For heaven's sake, I wish you would just stop all these histrionics!" said Anne. "You are upsetting little Thomas."

"Just leave it, Anne. She has always been the one for drama. I thought she would have made a good actress," said Bryan. "Let's get the food before we upset Dad and Mom."

They left the dining room one by one, to return carrying plates of food. Mary and Colin stood holding each other as the others placed the food on the table. Little Thomas jumped up and down, clapping his hands and giving a little squeal at the sight of each dish. The table soon filled with food. As Eileen put the gravy boat on the table, Paul, with inept eagerness, clapped his hands and said, "Ready."

"Oh," sobbed Mary, grabbing her husband even tighter.

"Your wife never grew up, Colin I may be the youngest girl but she is the real baby of this family," said Anne.

"Let it go Anne, not everyone can be as resilient as you," said James.

"Always the family diplomat James, it really must be boring for you."

"I'll ring the gong," said Paul, and promptly left the dining room. James quickly followed not wanting to get into a heated discussion with Anne. In the hall Paul picked up the hammer to ring the gong, a brass disc that had been his grandparents' and may have been their parents' before that. It was the duty of the youngest child to bang the gong once he or she reached the age of three, and Paul had been doing this since he was that age. James watched him, a tinge of jealousy he had only had the opportunity for one year.

A key could be heard turning in the front door; they both looked up as Donald and his wife May entered the house. Quietly Donald closed the door and was surprised to see Paul and James standing in the hall with the small gong hammer in Paul's hand.

"Hello Donny, Mary just had a fit because you weren't there for the ritual, but it's all done."

"I'd better go and see her and Mom," said Donald. He gave James a punch on the shoulder.

"You okay?"

"Of course but I am getting hungry." James knew what Donald was alluding too but didn't want to get into a long discussion.

May gave Paul and James a peck on the cheek. At the door, Donald turned back and said, "Don't do the gong just yet."

"I'll give you five minutes then it's gong time," said Paul.

CHAPTER FOUR

Little Black Bible

Matthew Pidgley, patriarch of the family, sat in the front room, which was usually used for visitors. When the children were growing up, they were never allowed in this room. Its furniture had been changed over the years, though Matthew had wondered why his wife had felt it necessary to keep changing the furniture when they never used it.

As he sat in the big winged chair contemplating what Bryan, his third child and second son, had just told him. The Pidgley property company owned by him and three of his sons Donald, Bryan and James had found a house for sale. It was a bargain. The three boys ran the company and so far it had been very successful. There was one problem, as far as the boys were concerned. This bargain was the house Matthew had grown up in as a child, and the horrors of that childhood still remained with him.

Matthew's parents, Florence and William, had given up traveling the roads of England and its vicious uncertainties to settle down and give their children a better chance in life. The prejudices against Romani, or what most people call Gypsies, had really gotten to Florence, and were probably to blame for the loss of many of her children just a few days after their birth.

Unfortunately, his father couldn't accept the change and had made Matthew's, his eldest son's, life a living hell. The constant beatings, starvation, and on several occasions his father even tried to kill him. At seven years old, the welts on Matthew's back had already formed a deep pattern in the child's flesh. The teachers at the school would ignore the blood stained shirt as he was just a gypsy. They expected him to disappear after a few months. When he didn't they continued to ignore the obvious pain the boy suffered. By high school he had learned to hide his thin starved body with its ridges and scars.

Just before his thirteenth birthday his father had beaten him into a state of unconsciousness. Matthew woke in a narrow metal box, the lid sealed shut. He lay there for four days before his father released him.

The memories of what happened in that house still haunted Matthew, but now he had to decide. Bryan had said the boys would abide by his decision. Matthew's father, William, had faced the choice to give up the horses, pigs, and the open road. This was no different. And yet Matthew was having a hard time accepting it. He knew James would be very worried how he would react. It was James who had found out that the place was for sale. He sat with his hands on his chin, his elbows resting on his knees. His stomach rumbled. He was hungry, and the lunch gong was a long time coming.

In the dining room, Mary was chastising Donald for being late when the sound of the dinner gong rang out. Paul jumped up and opened the dining-room door to see his father banging the gong. Matthew looked at him and said, "Are we not going to eat today?"

"Sorry Dad," said Donald. "It's my fault for being late."

"Where is your mother? I'm starving." Matthew entered the dining room and took his place at the head of the table. The Pidgley children in turn took their places at the table, their husbands, wives, and children next to them. James passed by his father and kissed him on the head.

"Hi Pop," he said. Matthew patted his son on the head and gave a little tug to his hair. Finally, Sarah took her place opposite Matthew and looked at her husband. They sat in silence, and each child in turn looked at Matthew, trying to gauge his mood. Matthew stared at his wife. He knew he had shaken the family by ringing the gong. It was the first time he had ever changed the Sunday ritual, and he liked the effect it had on his family. They were not so complacent or smug. It was time for a new beginning. He looked at his wife, a beautiful woman who had borne him ten children and still held his love and affection. He smiled and pursed his lips, blowing her a kiss.

The family members all followed the kiss. Sarah smiled back. Matthew coughed, and their heads sprang to face him. Sarah, bemused, said, "Are we going to eat now or wait until next Sunday?" Then she leaned over and took the dish of potatoes. Matthew began carving the leg of lamb. They passed their plates towards him to receive some meat. All except Anne, who had become a vegetarian, except where gravy was concerned. She always poured an ample amount onto her vegetables.

Donald had just picked up the dish of cabbage when Paul asked, "How was your week, Donny?"

Donald's wife May winced at the use of "Donny," but put her napkin to her mouth to cover up her expression and said, "Donald's been very busy this last week."

"Anything interesting?" asked Paul. Before Donald or May could answer, Anne butted into the conversation "Oh, I'm sure it was a very interesting week to keep Donny busy. Maybe he's bought a new property?"

"Yes, we have one or two houses we are interested in," replied May.

"But I'm sure there was one special house, isn't that right, James?" retorted Anne.

James flinched and looked quickly at Bryan then Donald, hoping one of them would rescue him. It was Sarah, his mother, who changed the subject. "Eileen, is Solomon working today?"

"Err, yes, sort of, I mean he had things he needed to do," replied Eileen.

"Really. I didn't think he did anything on Sunday! What was it he once said? Oh yes, I remember, 'My Sundays are mine and I will never be made to do what I don't want to do'," said Anne sarcastically.

Once again silence enveloped the table. The awkwardness was broken by the clank of cutlery on the china plates, followed by Mary saying, "You're being a bitch today, Anne."

"She never changes," said Peter. Anne gave an innocent smile. The others tried not to make eye contact with each other.

Little Thomas, who had just consumed a Brussels sprout, placed his knife and fork neatly on his plate, turned to his mother, and asked, "What's a bitch, Mommy?"

Bryan almost choked on a piece of meat. Colin, Thomas' father, gave out a laugh before putting his napkin to his mouth. Eileen, who had been able to control the laugh that had been her reaction too, said, "It's what Auntie Anne is." The whole family then erupted into laughter; only Anne kept a long face.

"Out of the mouths of babes..." said Matthew. "Which gives me the chance to bring up a few things." He looked directly at James, who blushed before placing his knife and fork on his plate, wiped his face with his napkin, and turned to face his father, expecting the worst. The others all stopped eating and faced their father.

"Every Sunday you have had this ritual of laying the table, getting the food, coming here for your Sunday lunch. Well, this is the last Sunday we will do it," said Matthew.

Mary, protesting, said, "But Dad...." The look from her father made her stop and take the hand of her husband.

Matthew continued, "I think it is time for change, to get rid of the old ideas and to stop living in the past. Your mother and I would like to see you all together at Christmas and maybe Easter. But from now on, we would like our Sundays to be quiet. Just the two of us and we may even eat out."

Mary couldn't contain herself any more and turned to Sarah. "Mother, is this true?"

"If your father says it is, then it's true," replied Sarah.

"But what are we going to do?" asked Mary.

"Get a life," said Anne. "You may even have to cook a meal for your husband. Now that's a novelty! What do you say, Colin? No more takeout some real home cooking."

"I cook!" snapped Mary.

"Oh yes, I remember one of your meals from domestic science class at school. You almost poisoned us."

"You wicked hateful bitch!" retorted Mary.

"Anne, Mary," said Matthew, "the world is changing. I may not like the changes, but unless we go along with some of the changes, then we will all come to resent it. Some of you may already."

Bryan looked at his mother, then said, "Well, I think it's a great idea, and may I be the first to take you and Mom out for Sunday lunch. We could take a little drive down to Stratford, sit by the river, and have a nice quiet Sunday lunch there."

"What a nice idea," said Sarah. She looked at Matthew and gave one of her special smiles, which always made him feel comforted.

"Colin, what do you think?" asked Mary, posing a question to her husband, but not really wanting an answer.

"Well I...," began Colin, but he was interrupted by Mary. "If that's what you and Mother want, I suppose we will have to go along with it. Remember, we can always go back to the old ways if you want. I'm sure it's going to bring bad luck one way or another."

"Meet 'Miss Negative of 2003," said Anne.

"Maybe some of you would like to go out with each other on Sundays. A picnic or something," said Matthew.

"In that case, I know one thing for sure," said Paul. "Anne will be eating by herself!"

Elizabeth, the eighth child in the family and affectionately known as Lizzie, who had sat quietly throughout the lunch, suddenly said, "As this is 'Let's shock the family day,' I have some news." She paused while her siblings settled down. "I've been offered a new job." Once again she paused. "In America. And I've decided to take it."

Peter, who had always been close to Lizzie, said, "What! Where? When? What job? Why didn't I know about this?"

Lizzie smiled and then said, "In Los Angeles, at the end of next month, same company, but I'll be a vice president."

Matthew rose from his chair and came around the table to Lizzie. She stood up and he gave her a hug saying, "Congratulations!" Everyone began to clap.

"Sol's left me," blurted out Eileen.

"That's nice," said Sarah. "Will he be back in time for tea?"

"No, he's left me, gone off with another woman, Jane Foggsworth from his office."

"Old Foggie from school?" said Bryan. "She was a real dog, a right old slag. She'd slept with every sixteen year old at school by the time she was thirteen!"

Ignoring Bryan's comment, Matthew asked, "When did this happen?"

"Last Tuesday. I came home from work, and all his clothes and things, and most of our furniture, had gone," said Eileen.

"I'm sorry," said Sarah.

"He left a note saying he was fed up with the Pidgley family."

"She's not moving back in with me," said Anne.

"That's the last thing she would want to do," retorted Elizabeth.

"I'm going to sell the house and buy a smaller one in Tamworth. I've already filed for a divorce, did that on Friday."

"Well, if you need anything," said Matthew, "just ask. You know the family will always be there for you."

"That's one thing I can count on. There is actually one thing I could do with some help on right away. If Donny, Bryan, or James know of any property for sale in the Tamworth area, could you let me know?" said Eileen.

"I'll look out for something," said Donald.

"So what's next?" said Anne. "Pregnant again, Mary? What about you, Rose? My brother been able to get it up, to do the thing?"

"Anne, please," said Sarah.

Anne, ignoring her mother, continued, "What about you, Jane? Ready to come out of the closet and tell the world you're a lesbian?"

"If I was, at least I would be something," said Jane, blushing bright red.

"Meaning?" asked Anne.

"Meaning I'm not a screwed-up bitch without a life like you," said Jane, going even redder.

"Call me what you like. I just say what everyone is thinking."

"I don't think like you." Protested Peter.

"That's because you don't think."

"Enough," said Matthew. "Mother, are you sure Anne is one of ours?"

Sarah laughed, "Oh yes, I remember the pain!"

"And she has been a pain ever since," said Eileen.

"What a Sunday!" said Matthew. "That only leaves one thing, for James and me to talk about Thirteen Crowhurst Road."

James sank into his chair and, with a little-boy look, turned to face his father. Matthew knew the other siblings would enjoy the pleasure of seeing James wriggle trying to answer those difficult questions he had planned to ask. Then there would be Anne's sarcastic comments. She would have a ball at James's expense.

Before he could say anything, Sarah said. "I think that conversation should be done in private. Heaven knows what Anne would say if she was privy to it."

"I agree," said Matthew. "So if no one else has anything to confess," he looked at each of his children, "James, let's you and me adjourn to the front room. I think we need to use the furniture a little more before your mother decides to change it." Sarah blew her husband a kiss.

James slowly got up from his chair and walked to the door like a condemned man.

Little Thomas tugged on his mother's dress. "Mommy, what's a 'Lesley Bean'?" The whole family began to laugh as James and his father left the room. Matthew closed the dining room door behind them.

Matthew and James sat in the front room, a cold and impersonal room. The two men, father and son, stared at each other, unsure as to who should speak first. James gave a little laugh, his usual sign of nervousness, and then began to bite his lower lip. Matthew twiddled his thumbs.

"Dad," said James, finally breaking the ice. "About the house." He paused looking directly at his father. "We can pull out of the deal if it's a problem for you, but the profitability is too high to just let it go." Matthew stared at the floor unable to make eye contact. "But," James continued, "If it would really upset you, then of course we won't buy it. We have until tomorrow at noon."

He paused again. "Dad, the problem is that you never really told us what happened, so it's hard for us to understand why you hate the house so much and why it causes you pain."

"James," interrupted Matthew, "it's okay. The time has come for me to let the past go, so you and the boys go ahead and buy the house. I'll even help you clean it. What happened is history. Nothing I can say or do will change that. But now I must let it go, move on with my life and stop it from eating me away."

"Are you sure, Dad?"

"James, it's okay. I don't want to go into what happened, only to say your grandfather made my childhood miserable, and it would be hard to go back to that house and relive those memories. He is dead, buried, and only my mind can recreate the horror. So if I don't let it go, then he has killed me inside."

"Do you hate him?"

"I don't think I hate him, not any more. It's just coming to terms with why he did it or at least understanding why I think he did it."

"I think I understand. Look what I found in the old house under a floorboard in the utility closet." James produced the small black Bible from his pocket. Matthew took the book and slowly flicked through the pages. He then looked at his son and laughed.

"What?" asked James.

"Where did you find it?"

"Under the floorboards in the utility closet."

"What made you look there?"

"Ever since we were little, you've said everybody should have a hiding place. When I opened the cupboard door, for some reason I just knew there was a hiding place there. I think it may have been something you said in one of your bedtime stories. But why do you laugh?"

"It was mine. I suppose it still is."

"What's the writing down the side of some of the pages?"

Matthew again opened the Bible and looked at the very fine pencil writing in the margins. "It's secret writing. I would sneak out of the house at night and watch what the neighbors were doing. Then I would make notes in the margin about what I saw."

"Okay, but what language is it in? Romani?"

"No, English. Remember it's notes; therefore, I didn't use *and*, *the*, *it*, *is*, or even *a*."

"I see."

"I was only a child of eight when I started it."

"If you were eight, then you may have written something down about the body in the ground. You may have seen something."

"I doubt it. All I remember about the Queen's Coronation and the road party is my father getting everyone drunk on home-made brew put into brewery bottles! The party ran for two days."

They both laughed. "Your grandfather knew how to throw a party, and he even made a profit."

"Is that where you learned it from?" Before Matthew could answer, the door of the front room violently swung open. Bryan stood in the doorway looking quite pale.

"There's been a murder, another murder, on Crowhurst Road," blurted Bryan.

"What!" said James. "Another murder?"

"In Crowhurst Road. A woman's body has been found. That's all they said in the radio report."

CHAPTER FIVE

Inspector Smith

The dull rays of a cloud-covered day spilt into the room through the torn heavy black velvet curtains. The body lay as though positioned for a television police series or an amateur production of an Agatha Christie play. The corpse lay on its back with the left arm raised above the head and bent at the elbow away from the head. The left leg bent at the knee pointing to the left, the foot at a right angle to the leg. The right hand was tightly closed over the centre of the chest, between the woman's breasts, and it was very clearly a woman. She was fully clothed except for her right shoe, which appeared to be missing.

The carpet had a light covering of dust over it, and only the footsteps of the police officer who had found the body could be seen imprinted on it. From the doorway, Inspector Mark Smith used a heavy-duty, police-issue flashlight to scan the room. Huge threatening cobwebs hung from the ceiling. The light from the inspector's flashlight crept slowly over the woman's body. From this distance, he couldn't see how she had died. Her clothes looked clean and un-crumpled, with the gold rings on her right hand glistening in the light.

Behind the Inspector, two members of the crime scene unit had arrived. They peered into the room. "I want everything photographed and samples taken of the room before anyone approaches the body. This looks more like a bloody film set than a crime scene. Is she real?" barked Inspector Smith, a twenty-year veteran of the Birmingham City police force.

No one answered, so he pushed past the crime scene unit officers and out into the dull daylight. At forty-eight years old Mark Smith was already planning for his retirement. His solid, no-waist figure had not changed in thirty years. He regarded himself as well built, although he had heard other colleagues call him fat. The only thing to change during that time was his hairline, which had receded. He resembled the classic image of a monk, and some of the senior officers would call him Brother Smith. He had tried many of the over-the-counter hair tonics and hair-growth formulas, only to waste his money and time. He carried resentment towards older full-haired officers on the force.

Outside, in the normally quiet cul-de-sac, the crowd of onlookers was steadily growing. The first of the TV news crews arrived. From the doorstep of Thirteen Crowhurst Road, Inspector Smith watched as the mobile operations room made a wide turn onto the road, traveling slowly, stopping opposite the murder house. It was only the day before that this vehicle had packed up and left the same spot. The officers busied themselves unpacking, preparing for the detectives and others to arrive, making jokes and generally horse playing.

A commercial food wagon arrived and began setting up on the public side of the police line. Several police officers shouted to the owner putting out chairs and tables to "Get brewing up!"

Inspector Smith walked up the path and stood on the pavement. He was amazed how ant-like the officers were. Each one had his or her own tasks, and they seemed to be the height of efficiency. He knew that appearances could be very deceptive. Underneath this glossy image was a lazy, unethical, demoralized group of policemen and women who had learned how to play the game for public consumption. He himself had become complacent after the many changes that had taken place over the years. These days, the criminals seemed to have the law on their side, and with the interference from the European Union, dictating what they can and cannot do, it was becoming hard to get a conviction without a little creative work on the evidence.

A young police officer came out of the crime scene house and looked around for the Inspector. He walked quickly to him, his eagerness brimming over. "The crime scene lads have taken the pictures you asked for, sir. They are going to put some plastic sheeting down to get close to the body."

"Good, do they want my help?"

"Err, no, I don't think so, sir."

"Just tell me when the coroner arrives. I want to be there when he examines the body, if he lets me."

"Yes sir," said the young officer, returning to the house with a larger grin on his face, pleased with his first involvement on a murder case.

Mark Smith looked at the gathering crowd. His thin-lipped mouth formed a sneering expression. He had never really liked the people who came to stare at a murder scene. He often wondered what they hoped to see. He was sickened when he heard reports on the television how, after a plane crash just outside of London; the emergency services couldn't get to the site because gawking sightseers blocked the narrow roads.

He stiffened as he looked up the road and saw his wife's car parking next to the food wagon. Rosemary Smith got out of her bright yellow BMW. Everyone turned and looked at her. There were several wolf whistles from the onlookers. She had Lucille Ball red hair, bright red lips, and two-inch diameter gold-colored earrings. Her lime-green sweater fitted like a glove to the contours of her body. The yellow miniskirt reminded those who could remember of the 1960s. It had to be pulled down with every step she took. She approached a young officer, who immediately blushed a scarlet red while looking at his peers to see who was watching. As she was speaking, he pointed to Number Thirteen.

Mark Smith tried desperately to hide his embarrassment, but he felt the itching build in the anus area and he knew he would be scratching it for the rest of the day. This was his weak spot, and he had many hours of discomfort in the past due to his wife or his mother.

Rosemary arrived at his side, slightly out of breath and hopping on one foot while she tried to pick a piece of paper that had attached itself to her bright red shoes.

"Sorry to bother you at work, my sweet, but your mother has just arrived for a three-week holiday."

"What!" retorted Mark, pulling his graying white y-fronts from the cheeks of his backside.

"Your mother has arrived. She said she had called you last week, and you said it would be okay."

"I don't remember her calling, but it's bloody inconvenient. I have two murders to solve. You, my darling, will have to entertain her."

"Now, my sweet thing, you and I have talked about this before. It was agreed after the last time you had another inconvenient murder. That I would not have to suffer your mother on my own again."

"I would not call a murder inconvenient, at least not for the victim."

"That may be so, but every time I want to do something, my dear husband, someone always goes and gets murdered. It happened, if you will remember, on our wedding night. You stayed here, and I went to the Costa del Sol with your mother!"

"Only because we had paid for the honeymoon, and they wouldn't give us a refund."

"Another inconvenience."

"Where's Mother now?"

"In the car, my sweet one." They turned and looked at Rosemary's car. It was empty. "Oh dear," said Rosemary.

"Bloody hell!" said Mark, his left hand beginning to scratch at his anus.

A small group of policeman had gathered at the food stand. They were laughing loudly. As one of them moved to get a cup of tea, Mark and Rosemary could see Mark's mother, half sitting on a rubbish bin, entertaining the younger uniformed officers. Mrs. Margot Smith was dressed from head to toe in a bright red suede outfit. The jacket had ermine tails hanging from it. She always claimed they were real, but they hadn't dry cleaned very well and now looked tatty. The skirt had stretched over the years of use, and with the extra pounds Margot had put on, now fitted half way up her ample thigh. Her hair had been dyed to match, except for the gold streaks running through it. She claimed she looked like a Goddess and expected everyone to treat her like one.

Mark Smith angrily said, "Get her back into the car. I will talk to you tonight." Rosemary looked at him. He continued, "Please!"

Rosemary started to walk towards her mother-in-law, then stopped and called back to him, "Mark Aubrey Smith, this is going to cost you, my sweet."

Mark nodded and mouthed without being audible, "It always does."

Rosemary returned to her mission, collected her mother-in-law, and steered her towards the car. Margot Smith, looking about her, saw Mark, waved to him, and shouted in her loud Birmingham accent, "Hi baby see you later." She then addressed the crowd of onlookers. "That's my son," she shouted. "He's in charge, such a good boy."

The crowd began to applaud. Mark gestured to his wife to get his mother into the car. Rosemary obliged.

Mark Smith watched them drive away before making his way to the mobile incident room. He went through the pieces of paper in his pocket and found the one that noted his mother's arrival date. He tore it up and let the little fragments fall to the roadway.

Sindhu Jalawan sat behind the telephone console in the crime scene control room. He nodded as Mark entered and gave him a handful of messages. Going through them, disregarding all but two, Mark read them carefully before putting them into his pocket. He walked into the front of the mobile unit and sat down at one of the small desks, picking up the phone and checking to see if it had the dial tone before he dialed a number.

"David, it's Smith," he said, as someone at the other end answered the phone. "Where's the bloody Patho? I need to get this thing moving. It's more like a circus than a crime scene."

Before he could get an answer, Sindhu shouted from the door, "Patho's here."

"He's just arrived. I'll call you later." He put the phone down and made his way to the door. The phone rang. Inspector Smith left the unit as Sindhu called after him, "It's your wife, sir."

He heard Sindhu but chose to ignore him. Crossing the road, he put his left hand out. It felt like rain, but there were no raindrops just black clouds gathering. He hated unpredictable weather, neither one thing nor another. He looked at his fingernails. They were full of dirt from his previous day's gardening and this was his only real pleasure in life.

Reporters and news camera teams had gathered in the garden next to Number Thirteen. At the door, Inspector Smith looked at the officer on duty outside of the house, then at the media, and said very quietly, "Move them," indicating with his head the media people.

The young officer spoke into his communicator as Inspector Smith entered the house. The humid smell of death and decay hit him as he approached the living room. The pathologist was standing on a plastic sheet with a large flashlight looking carefully at the body. He knelt down and looked more intently at the neck of the dead woman. He suddenly stood up and said to his assistant, "Bag and tweezers." He looked at the Inspector and smiled, his brown tobacco-stained teeth filling his mouth. "Interesting, this one, Smith. Have you noticed the room?"

"You mean it looks like a film set?"

"Yes. And the body has been placed into this position. The legs were broken to make them this way." The pathologist assistant handed him a plastic bag and tweezers. He very carefully picked something off the top of the body and placed it into the bag, then sealed it. "I'll be about forty-five minutes, if you want to get a cuppa or something, Inspector…"

Inspector Smith hated being dismissed in this way, but just replied, "Okay," and left the room scratching his anus. He needed to get some cream or the problem would spread. His mother always had this effect on him. He remembered when he was a child at school during one of those abominable Christmas plays. As he stood on stage, his mother kept waving to him. He became embarrassed and began to itch uncontrollably, so much so that the rest of the parents watching began to laugh as he scratched. His mother thought he was such a clever little boy making everyone laugh, as the play was so boring. He was never picked to be in a school play again, and after the show he was sent to see the school nurse, as the teacher believed he had lice or fleas.

In the hallway he looked about and then opened a cupboard beneath the stairs, shining his flashlight inside. It was empty. He began to leave the house but stopped, turned and ran up the stairs, two at a time. At the top he stopped to catch his breath. He was not a man to over exert himself. He looked at the five closed doors. Hesitating for a moment, he finally picked the back bedroom door and opened it. The black walls with their gold stripe and the very dirty carpet surprised him. It was something his wife would do, just to upset him. He could see where the furniture had been placed. From the indentations in the carpet it clearly showed where the bed had stood. The wardrobe, from the marks in the carpet, had been a heavy wooden one standing behind the door. The wall there was still white, the painter of the black unable to move the wardrobe.

The windows didn't have any curtains, and someone had attempted to clean them. Inspector Smith looked out onto the back garden. A reporter with a camera was trying to climb the fence. A police officer appeared from inside the house and dragged the reporter into the garden. A scuffle broke out between them, and two more officers joined the melee. Inspector Smith watched, the sneering smile creeping over his face. He could see the headlines in tomorrow's papers: 'POLICE BRUTALITY AT MURDER SCENE'. Laughing out loud he left the room. Back on the landing, he opened the airing cupboard door and closed it quickly.

He forcibly opened the master bedroom door and stood looking into the room, contemplating a dramatic entrance. The room was empty and clean. Over at the window he looked down at the police trying to move back the public. Looking the other way, he saw a car arrive and park on the public side of the crime scene tape. This was followed a few moments later by another car arriving. A tall lean man in his fifties got out of the first car and stood by it, looking at the police activity. Inspector Smith mumbled to himself "I wonder who he is?"

A younger man from the other car joined the older man. They spoke before moving to the crime scene tape. They spoke to a police officer. Lifting the tape, he directed them to the mobile crime scene unit.

Inspector Smith watched them walk to the mobile unit before letting his attention wander. He stared at the crowd of onlookers. He had read somewhere that a murderer might come back to the scene of the crime to have a look at the police finding the body. He scanned the faces of the people in the street. Could one of them be the murderer? He made a mental note to have a closer look at the crowd.

A commotion on the pathway of the house diverted Inspector Smith's attention. The reporter who had tried to get a better look from the back garden was now being carried, hogtied, to a waiting police van. He called to his fellow media friends, and they in turn took photographs of him being carried by the police. The reporter was laid on his stomach in the back of the police van. The doors were closed, and the van drove off with some speed. Inspector Smith watched it roar away. He also noted the car of the young man who had just arrived also drove away, almost as if it were following the police van. At the top of the road it turned to the right, in the opposite direction.

He could hear someone calling from below, "Inspector, Inspector!" He tensed and went out onto the landing. Leaning over the banister, he looked down into the hallway. A young officer beamed up at him. "Inspector Smith!"

"What?" barked Smith, agitated.

"The owners of the house have just arrived, sir. What should I do with them?" Inspector Smith looked at the officer, winced, and then pulled back onto the landing. "Inspector?"

"Okay, I'll be down in a moment. And keep them out of the house!" He looked at the fourth door and opened it onto the bathroom. The smell of mold and damp permeated the air. He turned the hot faucet on in the sink; cold rust-colored water came gushing out. He waited for it to clear and then washed his face. He looked up to see if there was a mirror. It had been removed, and dirt marks stained the wall. He foolishly looked around for a towel to dry his face. There wasn't one and the toilet roll had one torn sheet stuck to the cardboard roll. Taking a clean white handkerchief out of his pocket, he unfolded it and wiped his face dry. Other officers at the station had made fun of his always having a clean handkerchief, but it was at moments like this that Inspector Mark Smith felt he had the last laugh.

The Inspector left the house and was greeted by the smiling officer. "Where are the owners?" he asked.

"There, sir," said the officer, pointing to Matthew and James, who had entered the garden path. Matthew was trying to close the yellow gate but without much success. Inspector Smith, looking them up and down, believed the first impression was always right. Well his was and he didn't like the look of them. They looked as though they were working class in suits or worse, and therefore shouldn't be treated with any courtesy. The younger of the two men looked like a male model, the type he had seen in his wife's magazines. The type who could wear anything and look as though it was very expensive and had been made only for them. He hated that kind of man.

After years of dealing with every type of criminal he could tell when there was a deep-seated hatred of officialdom. This pair of losers in his opinion had all the hallmarks of troublemakers.

"Smith, Inspector Smith. I'm in charge here, and you would be…?"

"Matthew and James Pidgley. We took possession of the property today at noon." Matthew held out his hand to shake the Inspector's. Seeing the hand, Inspector Smith immediately placed his own into his pocket.

"I see. So you would know who the young lady lying dead on the floor in your living room would be?"

"Well, not without seeing her!" replied James

The Inspector realized the anger the young man seemed to have in his tone.

Matthew put his hand on James's arm and stepped in front of him. "Inspector Smith, we came to see if there was anything we could do."

"Well, there isn't anything, unless you know who the woman is or you would like to confess to the murder."

"Why would I do that?" said Matthew, grabbing James's arm even tighter to stop him speaking.

"Your kind usually has something to do with it when a crime has been committed!"

"Meaning?" blurted out James, having great difficulty controlling the anger building up inside of him.

"Well, Gyppos! That's what you are, aren't you? With a name like Pidgley, you must be."

"We may be Romani ethnically or, as you put it, Gypsy, but my son and I are also respectable businessmen, and I don't care for your attitude, Mr. Smith."

"Inspector Smith. I'm sorry if I hurt your feelings, but in my book, once a Gyppo, always a smelly thieving Gyppo!"

"Once a bigot, always a bigot! And you wonder why so many people call the police pigs." said James. Matthew turned and started to push James up the path. The front door opened, and the coroner's men brought out the body of the dead woman. Inspector Smith, Matthew, and James were forced to step onto the garden as the men passed them.

Inspector Smith suddenly shouted, "Stop!" He unzipped the plastic cover and exposed the woman's face. "Do you know her? Or is she one of your unwanted women?" he asked.

Matthew came close and took a good look at the face, shaking his head. "We don't have unwanted women. All our ladies are desired. I've never seen her before."

James looked. He couldn't believe it. He knew who she was. "Yes, I've seen her before."

"Who is she?" A sneering smile crept over Mark Smith's face.

James looked at his father and then at the Inspector and took a deep breath. "Her name is Elizabeth Friedman. She is the estate agent who sold us this house."

"Really, now, isn't that interesting? I was right! If a crime has been committed, you lot are always involved. When did you last see her?"

"Two days ago, in her office on Staple Lodge Road. I assure you we are not involved in this murder."

"That's what you say. Johnson!" said the Inspector, looking around for the police officer.

"Here sir."

"Johnson, take these persons and get all their information. Find out where they have been in the last week, and what was the last conversation they had with this poor defenseless victim."

Inspector Smith then entered the house, closing the door behind him.

CHAPTER SIX

A Stolen Car

The coroner's men zipped up the bag and carried the body to a waiting van. The onlookers had surged forward in the hope of seeing something, but the coroner's men were used to this kind of behavior and quickly placed the corpse into the van and closed the doors before anyone could see anything.

"If you gentlemen would like to follow me, I'll get your information and you can be on your way." James and Matthew followed him to the mobile police unit. Inside, they sat on one side of a metal desk, which was secured to the floor by big bolts, which James kept hitting with his foot. He tried to move the metal chair, but it too had been fixed to the floor. Matthew looked at James as he tried to get comfortable.

"They've bolted the chair to floor, scared we might steal it," said James, laughing. Matthew gave a smile, then a nervous laugh, which flowed into an uncontrollable giggle.

Officer Johnson looked at them disapprovingly, then took a statement form from the desk drawer and fed it into the typewriter. He readjusted his position on the seat and began to fill it out. "Names?"

"Matthew and James Pidgley."

"No, no, one at a time, please."

"Matthew Pidgley."

"Spell the last name."

"P-I-D-G-L-E-Y."

"Address?"

Matthew gave the address.

James looked around the police unit. It had been very well designed. Most of the other police officers just sat around drinking tea and talking. He was surprised that there wasn't more activity in a murder case. Near the door they had just entered stood a young officer who looked as if he should have still been at school. The officer was answering the phones.

"James, it's your turn." James turned and looked the officer in the face. He then proceeded to answer the same questions his father had been asked.

"When did you last see the murdered woman?"

"Two days ago. She gave me copies of her paperwork, and we agreed to meet today so she could hand over the keys to the house."

"Did you get the keys?"

"No, not yet."

"Is that all?"

"Yes, I think so."

"You mean you don't know?"

"No."

"No, you want to say something else?"

"No, it's all I have to say."

Officer Johnson finished typing and handed James the statement to sign and date. "Thank you. We will be in touch if we need any other information."

"When can we get into the house?" asked James.

"Oh, that's up to Inspector Smith. He's in charge, you'd better ask him."

Matthew and James were briskly shown out of the mobile unit. Once out of earshot, Matthew looked at his son, smiled, then said, "And they wonder why people hate them!"

"Dad, they are just prejudiced. We have lived with that for a thousand years, don't let it get to you."

"But he got to you."

"Not really. I just like to have a go. It's the activist in me."

"Nothing changes. Even with all the laws to stop discrimination, we Romani still have problems."

"You taught us kids that we were better than them, the none gypsies, the *gajo*, and we had to rise above them."

"I know. Look, I have to get back to your mother. She will scold me if I don't. She'll want to know everything."

"Okay Dad. I'll go and see the Inspector to find out when we can get into the house. I must get the keys, too. I have someone wanting to rent it."

"Just be careful with that one. His hatred is very deep, almost psychotic."

"Okay Dad."

Matthew walked to his car. James watched him. He knew it must have been hard for his father to keep quiet when the Inspector started with his comments. James walked down the path to Number Thirteen. The officer standing at the door stuck an arm out to stop James from entering the house.

"Can I see Inspector Smith?"

"I don't know." The officer went into the house, closing the door behind him as he went. He returned with Inspector Smith, who looked James up and down, his nostrils flaring out like a bull about to charge.

"Yes?" he said impatiently.

"We were wondering when we could take possession of the house again."

"That depends, two or three weeks if I've finished with it and arrested the murderer."

"Oh, I was hoping earlier. I already have a tenant for it."

"Well we don't want you to lose money, do we? But I have to collect all the evidence and that could take, as I said, three or four weeks. We'll let you know when you can take possession." Inspector Smith reentered the house and closed the door. James looked at the police officer, who shrugged his shoulders and then spoke into his communicator. James stared at the door for a few moments, then returned to where he had parked his car. He was so absorbed with thinking about the attitude of Inspector Smith that he didn't notice his car was gone. As his thoughts cleared, he began to look for it. He was positive he had parked it behind his father's. He walked up and down the road looking for it, he felt as though someone were watching him from one of the houses. He turned quickly and stared at the house. The yellowing net curtains fell back into place, but he could just sense the dark shape of someone behind them.

He walked back to the police line, checking both sides of the road. He reached into his pocket for his cell phone. It wasn't there! He must have left it in the car. James lifted the crime scene tape, went to the police mobile unit, and knocked on the door. A mature officer opened it. He had a cup of tea and a half-eaten cake in his hand.

"Yes sir?"

"My car has been stolen, or at least it's not where I parked it."

"Sorry to hear that, sir. And when did you park your car? Where did you park it?"

"About an hour ago. I came to see Inspector Smith."

"I see. Well, sir, you will have to report it as missing or stolen."

"Okay, can I do that with you?"

"No, sir. You'll either have to call the police station or go there. This is the serious crime mobile unit, and we only deal with serious crimes."

"Can I use your phone, then? I left my cell phone in the car."

"Sorry sir, these phones are for official business pertaining to serious crimes only." The officer then closed the door. James saw Inspector Smith leaving Number Thirteen and ran over to him.

"Inspector Smith."

"You still here?"

"My car has been stolen."

"Sorry to hear that, obviously by one of your Gyppo young car thieves who squat around here. You'll have to report it."

"I tried to just now, but they told me I had to go to the police station."

"That's correct, Mr. Pidgley. Now you have a good night. Looks like rain." The Inspector went into the mobile unit. Passing an officer, he stopped and talked with him, pointing to James as he did. As the officer approached him, James relaxed, in anticipation of the help that he was about to receive. Maybe the Inspector wasn't as bad as he appeared.

"I have to ask you to go behind the crime scene tape, sir. Inspector's orders." The officer directed James on to the other side of the crime scene tape. This time he was on the other side of the crime scene area from where he had parked his car.

"But I had my car stolen."

"Sorry to hear that, sir. You must report it."

The group of onlookers had moved from the pavement nearest the house to where James was being made to cross back behind the tape. A woman with ashen face, black-dyed hair with a white Alice band holding back a few strands from her face, moved closer to James. She was wearing tan-colored gloves and a gabardine raincoat. She grabbed hold of James's arm. "Did you know the murdered girl?"

James looked at her, and still slightly disorientated by what had just occurred, he just mumbled, "I've had my car stolen."

A man in his mid-forties, who had an unlit cigarette sticking out of his mouth, said, "He's had his car stolen. Stolen by the murderer I dare say!" The small crowd all conferred and agreed with this statement. A shout from the officer at the house, "Get the Inspector!" made the crowd move back to the pavement.

James stood by himself, unable to clear his thoughts and make a decision. He wandered to centre of the road and stood looking back at the police and the crowd. It was as though he were watching a film.

CHAPTER SEVEN

The Coates

The weather was changing. Dark, threatening clouds drew closer together. Rain could be expected at any time, and from the density of the grayness, it would be a heavy down pour. James stood, unable to believe the reaction of the police to his problem. Now he understood why people were so apprehensive about helping them. There was no give and take. The police wanted it all their way or not at all. He gathered his thoughts. He needed to contact his family; maybe one of them could come and pick him up. Checking his left pocket he produced some loose change and in his right pocket he found three cough drops. He had become addicted to them and used them as breath fresheners. Inside his organizer notebook he had twenty-five pounds. Unfortunately, that was in the car with his cell phone

Looking around, he found himself standing in the circular T-junction of the cul-de-sac. It was hard to believe that it had been only six weeks since the skeletal remains of a woman were discovered beneath

75

his feet. The road had been resurfaced and the black tarmac had already started to lose its newness, but the smell still remained. As a child, one of his brothers had told him that if you have a cold, you should smell fresh tarmac. It would cure a cold or the flu. You had to put your nose on the freshly laid tarmac and breathe deeply several times. The problem was, when he had a cold, he could never find any tarmac to see if it really helped.

He hesitated and, looking at each arm of the T-junction, decided to take the right one, as it seemed to have better street lighting. He walked down the sloping road; he felt the eyes of someone watching him. He looked at the houses as he passed to see if he could see any movement of curtains, but there was none. Reaching the circular end of the arm of the T-junction, he peered down the pedestrian alleyway that ran between two of the houses and then down to another road. He turned and looked behind to see if anyone was following him before entering the dimly lit alleyway, the daylight was beginning to fade. He had grown up always being cautious, and he knew now was not the time to lower his guard. He felt he had softened lately, so he formed a fist with his right hand. It was his hearing that would give him the best early warning. As a child, he had been taught by his grandfather to listen and separate the different sounds, and to recognize the threatening ones. He trod carefully to avoid the excrement left by street dogs that roamed in packs, terrorizing the elderly out for a walk and small children playing in the street. There was a street lamp about halfway down the alley. The light high on a pole flicked on and off, sending the alleyway into darkness before illuminating it again. James slowly ventured further down the alleyway.

A voice came from behind him that made him jump, even though he was not normally a nervous person. Something in the voice reminded him of a 1930s movie. It had a gruffness that comes from smoking too many cheap cigarettes. "Mister, mister, I need to talk to you."

James turned and confronted a small, thin, colorless youth, who seemed to have a hard time keeping still, his arms and hands gesticulating constantly as he spoke. His clothes were hand-me-downs and from a much larger man. The youth had closely cropped hair and deep sunken eyes giving him a wild-animal look. "I need to talk to you, mister. I know somethin'."

"Why don't you tell the police?"

"Can't, they won't believe me." The young man continued to move, hopping from one foot to the other as though he were doing an Irish jig. James watched as the youth hopped closer and closer to a large pile of dog excrement.

"Why won't the police believe you?"

"They won't believe, because I lie."

"So why should I believe you?"

"Because, I'll tell you the truth. I only lie to the people I don't like."

"So you like me?"

"Yeah, you look kind, and the police hate you."

"That's true." A few drops of rain began to fall. This made the young man hop even more, and as he danced just in front of the dog excrement, James was amazed at how he kept missing it.

"Well, what do you know?"

"What ya gonna give me?"

"Nothing. If you have some information, tell me and I'll tell the police so they will believe it too."

"If you ain't gonna give me nothing.' I ain't gonna tell ya nothin'." The young man then began to move backwards up the alleyway.

James shouted to him, the distance grew between them. "If you know something about the murder, you should tell the police."

"I don't know nothin' about the murder. I know who stole your car." The young man turned and ran up the alleyway into the darkness, disappearing as quickly as he had appeared. The darkness of the night and the heavy dark clouds now consumed Crowhurst Road.

"Shit!" said James out loud. He continued down the alleyway, the rain became heavier. He began at first to walk faster, eventually breaking into a run. He came out of the alleyway into Edenhurst Road and quickly turned left. In front of him was a dirty red telephone box. He opened the door and stepped inside. He immediately regretted it; the smell of stale urine penetrated his nostrils. He had often wondered why people urinated inside phone boxes, but he had never caught anyone doing it, to ask. He had come to the conclusion it was because there was a lack of public toilets, and now, phone boxes were being removed he dreaded to think where people would urinate when they couldn't get home in time or they were in a drunken state.

He took some change from his pocket, picked up the phone from the cradle rest, and wiped the ear and mouthpiece on his jacket. He listened for the dial tone. The handset was dead. He hit the button several times, but he still didn't get a dial tone. He replaced the handset; he then noticed that the wire connecting it to the coin box was cut. As a teenager, he had messed around in phone boxes, but he would never have cut the wire. What was the point?

He opened the door to leave. The rain was pouring down. The ashen-faced woman who had spoken to him earlier by the crime scene tape stood as though she were waiting for the phone. Her large yellow umbrella sheltered her from the rain. She smiled at him.

James smiled back. She seemed like a frail woman. The thinness of her face and the translucent skin gave that first impression. But judging from the way she gripped the handle of her umbrella, he realized that she had hidden strength. Their eyes met, and she smiled again. James stared intently at her face. She didn't appear to have any makeup on. Her hair was brushed tightly back and tied into a bun. The gabardine raincoat almost reached the ground, the belt knotted immovably in the front.

"Err, sorry, do you need to use the phone?"

"No."

"It's not working anyway!"

"I know. It has been like that for about a year. It's a good thing we don't need the police or an ambulance. I really don't know what we would do."

He felt awkward in the phone box, but if he stepped outside of it, he would become soaked in seconds, as the rain continued to come down in torrents. The woman took one step closer to the phone box and James. She looked to her left and then to her right before speaking, "You shouldn't believe everything Bobby Coates says. Everyone around here knows he lies."

"Who's Bobby Coates?"

"The lad you were speaking to up the alley."

James wondered where she had been hiding when he spoke to Bobby Coates. "He didn't say anything."

"Oh, he will I assure you. He'll find you and tell you lies and then more lies. He can make you believe them, too."

"He said he knew who had stolen my car."

"Oh yes, he might know that. Probably his brother Willie did it. That's what Willie does, I think. Steals cars for the fun. Bobby, on the other hand, lies."

"What does Willie do with the cars?"

"Depends what mood he is in. I'm told he sometimes sells them, and then I've known him to just burn them."

"Where does he live?"

"Don't you know? Number Twelve. Lives with his mom. Dad's still in jail or mental home, not sure which, but he's been there for years."

"Thanks for the information."

"Oh that's okay. I like to help when I can, especially if you are going to be a neighbor."

"Thanks again," said James, not answering her obvious probing. James left the phone box and passed her. He hesitated at the alleyway but decided to go the long way around to Crowhurst Road. He turned around to look again at the woman with the yellow umbrella, but she had disappeared.

The rain was falling very hard, and the pavement and road were now covered with a film of water. James ran to the corner of the road, splashing as he did. He turned and looked up the hill before him. The rainwater was racing down the hill, causing a passing car to hydroplane across the cross street and slide into a parked car, setting off the car's alarm.

James began to run up the hill, deliberately splashing in the water as he went. Each stride seemed to take forever. A dog darted out of one of the gateways and into the road, just missing him. The dog's coat was soaking wet. It stopped and turned to look at James its pathetic face looking for a friend. James continued running up the hill. The dog ran to the other side of the road and up a path leading to a house with a light on.

At the top of the hill James turned onto Crowhurst Road. The roadway was filled with water, as the small drain was blocked with garbage. He jumped into the mini-reservoir and continued splashing his way across the road, the water covering his shoes, soaking his socks and feet. As he ran, he looked down the road to where the police vehicles were. There was no sign of activity, and the mobile café had packed up and left. The news media vans were closed, and the onlookers had all returned to their homes.

He reached the Coates house, taking long striding steps to the front door. The garden was well kept, with no unattended weeds. Standing under the small concrete canopy jutting out from the house, he knocked on the door, as he couldn't find a doorbell to push. Getting no reply, after a few minutes, he knocked again, then put his head close to the door to ascertain if he could hear someone moving about inside.

The sound of a bolt being drawn back on the door to his left made James jump backwards and land in a puddle. The creaking of the hinge on the door reminded him of an old horror movie, one of those that always seemed to have actor Michael Ripper as the servant with a hunchback opening the door. It seemed that in this road no one oiled their door hinges.

The small obese woman who stood in the doorway, silhouetted from a light somewhere behind her, looked at James with a puzzled expression on her face. He looked at her from head to toe. Her fat legs became fat ankles, which became in turn large, fat feet encased in old, torn, pink fluffy slippers. Her faded purple flowered dress, stained from greasy cooking, was made from some cheap cotton material. Her tired face was wrinkled and rubbery with yellowing skin, her piercing blue eyes that stared at him. A cigarette hanging from the left side of her mouth created a smoke screen around her graying hair.

"Yes?" she said, giving a sneering grin showing her rotting, stained teeth.

"I'm looking for Willie Coates. Does he live here?"

"Yes."

"Is he at home?"

"Yes."

"Can I speak to him?"

"Maybe, maybe not. That depends if he wants to speak to you."

"Can you ask him?"

"Why?"

"Because I think he knows who stole my car."

"What makes you think he might know something?"

"Because I was told."

"Whoever told you is lying. My Willie has been in all night."

"A lady with a yellow umbrella told me. So did his brother Bobby."

"You don't want to believe our Bobby. He never told the truth in his life! Compulsive liar like his father! The old bastard told me I couldn't get pregnant twice and I believed him! Anyway, our Willie knows nothing about your car."

"I think he does. And unless you let me see him, I'll go to the police vehicles down the road and bring an officer back with me and he can question your boys. I'm sure you don't want the police crawling all over your house, now do you?"

She turned without answering and walked into the house, leaving the door open for James to follow her. He closed the door that faced the road behind him. He was in a rough built extension, which had an entrance into the kitchen at the back of the house. He pushed his way past boxes that were piled up to the ceiling and covered all but a very small passageway leading into the kitchen and out into the back garden. The woman had entered the kitchen ahead of him, and he tried to move a little faster to catch up with her. This was hard work, as he kept knocking into the boxes. He caught the corner of one box, which then threatened to bring down all those above it. James stopped and steadied the boxes before continuing on into the kitchen.

At the kitchen door, the smell of rotting food filled the air with a pungent aroma. Pushing the door open, his stomach wrenched at the sight and smell of decaying food. Some of it had obviously been stuck to the plates and dishes for weeks. Cigarette ends had been stuck into the food, and an overflowing garbage bag blocked the door of the grime-covered refrigerator. A cat was scratching at the bag. The feline pulled out a newspaper wrapping with the remains of a fish-and-chip supper and began to eat what was left.

The woman had left the kitchen. James followed her into a large room, which combined the living and dining rooms. It was overfilled with furniture. A single table lamp illuminated the entire room. The woman moved ahead of him with easy grace between the many tables and chairs. He again tried to keep up with her but had to stop to avoid knocking over a table here or into a chair there.

They arrived at a small clearing in the living-room area. A large television stood to the side of a smoldering fireplace. There was a cloth-covered sofa and two chairs facing it. The sofa had once been a light beige color, but was now a grease-stained dark brown. The woman pointed for James to sit down on the sofa as she went to the doorway into the hall. The door itself had been removed.

She called into the darkness beyond. "Willie, you have someone to see you, and you'd better see him or he's going to the police down the road."

She returned and sat down in one of the two chairs facing the television. It was switched on, but there was no sound. James began to wonder why. He looked at the set and noticed that beneath the screen the knobs and dials were missing! The woman looked at James, then at the television, then back again.
"Our Bobby hid the knobs, and now we can't find them, so we have no sound. But it doesn't really matter. There isn't much on the television these days. Mostly American junk with beautiful rich people or British repeats. We can't even find the remote." James said nothing but nodded his head. Even though he was soaking wet, he felt uncomfortable sitting on the sofa and changed his position several times, trying to touch as little as possible.

From the doorway, a young man entered. He was dressed in a black tee shirt, baggy dark blue jeans, and new trainers. His head was shaved and by an unsteady hairdresser. Several scabbed scars were scattered on the blue-white-colored scalp. The corners of his mouth curled up, giving the same sneering look his mother had. Around his neck was a quarter-inch-thick silver chain. Tiny holes in each ear lobe indicated he once had both ears pierced. He entered the room with an arrogant swagger and set his bright, hazel eyes on James as they peered from the deep, black socks of his tired face. "Who wants me, Ma?"

"This young man says unless you tell him were his car is, he's going to the police down the road."

"Why would I know where his car is?"

"Because your daft brother told him you stole it."

"Bobby! I'm goin' to kill you one of these days!"

A strange giggle came from the corner of the room behind the television. James looked hard and could just make out the youth he had met in the alleyway. He was sitting on a high stool as though he were a parrot on a perch. "I never told him."

"None of your lies, our Bobby," said the woman.

Booby giggled again. Willie sat on the arm of the sofa and looked at James, and James looked back at him. The staring game continued for a few minutes until the woman broke it by saying in a fake American accent, "It's high noon at the OK Corral!" She then laughed, and Bobby joined in.

Willie replied, "Yeah, whatever."

"I didn't say you stole my car, but you know who did."

"Where was it stolen from?"

"Outside this house, about two hours ago."

"What was it?"

"A 2000 Honda, black in color with CD player, and there was an orange mobile on the front seat."

"Na, I don't know who took it."

James was looking at him intently. The youth's shifting eyes and the appearance of his forehead ridges told James that he was lying. Willie's left leg began to move up and down as though he were playing a bass drum. His anxiety and nervousness grew. "I think you do know."

"I don't. I told ya! Ma, tell him will ya?"

"Yes you do," said Bobby from behind the television, "and you took the CD player."

"Shut up Bobby, you don't know dick." Bobby giggled and started to whistle a silly little tune.

"I didn't take your CD player."

"But you know who took my car."

"He took the man's CD player."

"Shurr up our Bobby."

"Whose CD player did you take?"

"The man, the one who went into the killing house with the lady," said Bobby.

"You took the CD player from the murderer's car?"

"I don't know if it was the murderer's car because I saw them leave later."

"Did you see what he looked like?"

"Maybe."

"So who took my car?"

Their mother got up and left the room, going into the kitchen. They watched as she made her way though the furniture. James was amazed at her grace of movement around some of the objects. He turned and looked at Willie. "Tell him, tell him," chanted Bobby.

"I think it was my mate Brian Steel. He said something about getting home before it rained. Man, he was stoned out of his head."

"Where does he live?"

"Top of Longbridge Lane, last house second to the last. He is a Hell's Angel sort of, well he lives with them. They use the house as a meeting place and clubhouse."

"Can you take me there?"

"No way."

"Why not? You have a car."

"Err, it's broken."

"No it's not," said Bobby, falling off his stool and yelping like a dog as he hit the carpet. He climbed back on the stool and repeated, "No it's not."

"I could go to the police and tell them what you've just told me."

"Err, no police. Okay I'll take ya, but I ain't going inside. I don't want Bri to know I told ya, let alone took ya to his house."

"Okay, let's go."

Willie stood up and went into the kitchen, James following. As they passed through, Willie shouted to his mother. She had her head stuck in the refrigerator; a cloud of smoke floated out.

"Goin' out, Ma."

"Alright son, be careful."

James stayed close to Willie as he made his way through the stacks of boxes, but instead of going out the front of the house, Willie went into the back garden. The rain was still pouring down, and they both ran to a shed at the bottom of the garden, which gave them a little shelter. Willie opened a gate that led onto an alleyway that ran along the backs of the houses. James left the Coates garden, Willie closed the gate behind them. They ran down the alleyway to the road. A police car passed the end of the alleyway. Seeing it, Willie pulled James back into the alleyway, and they pressed themselves against the wall of one of the houses. Willie may have been slight in build, but he was strong. His arm that held James against the wall was immovable. James tried to push against it to give himself a little more space to breathe.

Once the police car had passed, Willie led the way across the road and up a ramp to another alleyway behind the houses across the road. Prefabricated garages lined each side of the alley. They ran, avoiding the rain-filled potholes, until they reached a garage with a green door on the left side. James watched as Willie unlocked the door and lifted it up. A blue Honda had been parked inside; the rest of the garage was empty. Willie drove the car out of the garage, stopped, and got out of the car. James quickly opened the passenger door and sat on the imitation-leather seat. Willie closed the garage door and locked it. The inside of the car was clean, neat, and uncluttered there was no fancy equipment, not even a CD player.
Willie climbed into the car. "Ya got to lock everything around here this place is full of thieves."
"But the garage is empty."

"Is it?"

James looked back at the garage as Willie drove up the alleyway onto the ramp and carefully inched the car down and onto the road. He turned right and began to hydroplane down the hill. At the cross street, he missed another car coming up the other way by inches. Willie let out a sigh as he regained control of the vehicle.

He drove slowly, hesitating at each crossroad, sometimes indicating left or right before changing his mind. Once they reached Longbridge Lane, James relaxed. Willie didn't instill confidence in his passenger, as his driving was so unpredictable. The journey to the top of the hill seemed to take forever, and Willie sighed every time he put his foot on the brake.

James felt the tension rise as they approached the last few houses on the lane. About fifty yards from the last house, Willie stopped the car and turned off the engine and headlights. "It's the last house second to the last, the one with the motorcycles outside."

"You're going to wait for me, aren't you?"

"Of course," said Willie, fidgeting in his seat, not making eye contact. James got out of the car and began to walk towards the house. He heard Willie's car engine start and smiled to himself. Willie passed him before turning around just ahead. His headlights lit the dark rough continuation of Longbridge Lane. The road looked as if it turned into a farm road. James could just make out a car parked some distance up the road, on a bend. Willie roared off back down Longbridge Lane, honking his horn as he went.

The rain had eased a little, but James still felt very wet and cold as he approached the house. The motorcycles in the front garden were parked neatly on the drive. The garden had a small grass lawn, which was very well kept, along with a bed of roses, some still in bloom.

The porch light above the front door glowed orange, giving the peeling paintwork of the door and walls an eerie look. The stained glass window in the front door had cracked, and many of the intricate pieces were missing or had been replaced with cardboard. In the 1930s, when this house was built, the stained glass window in the front door would have been a selling point. In today's market, if they are still in good condition, they can add extra value to the house. The letterbox slot in the centre of the door was made of imitation brass and had lost its flap. James lifted the fake brass bar knocker attached to the letterbox and knocked loudly on the door.

A little blond-haired seven-year-old girl opened the door. The girls blue eyes dominated her oval face.   She looked tired and had that hungry look some children have. She wore a dirty white tee shirt sporting the slogan "Support your local Hell's Angels. Give them your money." The tee shirt was so big it was more like a dress on her. She wiped her nose on the back of her forearm and then wiped her forearm on the tee shirt.

James smiled at her. She stared back at him without any reaction on her pallid face. "Is Brian in?" he asked. The little girl blinked once or twice, then came forward onto the top step and looked up and down the street.

In the porch light, James noticed bruises on her arms and legs and what had seemed like a necklace were cigarette burn marks around her neck. She went back into the house, closing the door behind her. She was obviously abused, but he knew only too well not to get involved, as the police would blame him or one of his kin rather than look for the real culprit.

A sudden burst of loud heavy-metal music came from inside the house and then went, as someone opened a door inside and then closed it. The blast of music occurred again, and heavy footsteps could be heard thumping down the passageway to the front door. A man about six feet tall forcefully opened the door. His long brown dirty matted hair was in a ponytail, which was slung over his left shoulder and rested on his hairy chest. Someone had been making a braid, but hadn't finished it. His thick motorcycle boots were new and still had a shine. The dark blue, grease-encrusted jeans fitted tightly over his hefty legs. A motorcycle chain belt with a Harley-Davidson buckle was unfastened, and the zip on his jeans was open. He had no shirt on under his leather jacket, and the cigarette in his mouth was unlit. He smelt of beer and stale sweat.

In a gruff, drunken voice, he said, "Yeah, what ya want?"

"Is Brian in?"

"Maybe. Who wants to know?"

"I do."

"And who the fuck are you?"

"I need him to get a car for me."

"Oh! The bastard's probably in the den at the back, round the side. You'll find him there." As the biker finished speaking, he slammed the door shut. Another piece of stained glass fell out and broke at James's feet.

James walked to the side of the house. A light-sensor switched on a lamp, showing him a narrow path that ran along the side of the house. As he followed the path, another light switched on, and he could clearly see an old wooden garage at the back of the house. Above the door was a hand-painted sign that read The Den, and below these words someone had scrawled "Live to love and die."

There was a light on inside. James pushed open the door a little and could see why it was called The Den: the place was full of chairs and tables. At the left side was a small kitchen area with a very large refrigerator and a garbage bin overflowing with beer bottles. The floor was covered with a deep red carpet, which had been used as an ashtray—hundreds of cigarette butts were all over the floor. On the walls were several pictures of naked girls and motorcycles. One picture of a very large-breasted woman had been used a dartboard.

Lying on one of the sofas was a young man in his late teens, his jeans and white shirt covered in grease. He lay unconscious, a beer bottle in his left hand. In his right hand a lit cigarette burning down to the filter. A crash-helmet had partially fallen from his head, exposing cropped hair, with a Mohican stripe plastered back with some kind of hair oil. His face was acne scared. On his chin he had a few strands of hair forming a goatee beard. A light whisper of hair on his upper lip created the early signs of a moustache.

James moved closer to see if the young man was still alive, then turned away quickly at the smell of urine and stale cigarettes. The young man had wet his jeans at the crotch. He suddenly gave a snorting sound and moved his left arm, knocking drug paraphernalia onto the floor from a small table next to the sofa.

James looked around the den before making towards the door, realizing he would get nothing out of this drugged and drunk young man who he assumed was Brian Steel.

"The shit wouldn't share," said a voice from behind James. He turned quickly to see a dyed-blonde-haired woman. She was drunk and staggered into the den. "His best friend Dave, that's my so-called husband, will kill him when Brian wakes up."

Looking at the features of the woman, he guessed that she was the little girl's mother. The similarity was very noticeable. She was in her late twenties, but her extreme lifestyle had taken its toll and now she looked to be in her late fifties. She staggered further into the den, falling over a small stool and landing between two chairs. She pulled herself up and sat down in one of the cushioned seats.

"What ya want the bastard for?"

"I think he stole my car."

"When?"

"Tonight."

"Oh yeah, he probably did. That would be for the parts; good market for cars you know," she said as she rolled onto the floor, laughing. "What make was it?"

"A Honda."

"Nope, we don't have one of them around here, whole or in bits." She laughed again. "You could try up the lane. I think he said he had a crash with a tree tonight!" She stopped talking and fell asleep. James prodded her to wake her up. She didn't, so he shook her a little. She opened her eyes and looked at him. Smiling she touched his face with the back of her hand.

"You want me baby, but what if Dave comes in?"

"No... err, you fell asleep while telling me about a car Brian had crashed."

"Did I? Oh yeah, he crashed one tonight up the lane, said he skidded on the wet road. Bloody drunk more like! Now baby, where were we?" She stood up, took a few steps towards him and tried to grab him. James dodged her and made for the door, running into the man he had seen at the front door. He was just wearing very dirty briefs and still had the unlit cigarette sticking out of his mouth.

"What the fuck's happening?"

The woman suddenly screamed, "He tried to rape me, Dave darling!" Dave turned to hit James, who was already running down the path and out onto the road.

Staggering a few steps, Dave shouted after James, "Leave my fuckin' wife alone! She's my property!" He turned to the woman and grabbed her arm. "Back in the house and finish what we were doing."

James ran hard up the road. At the last lamppost he stopped to catch his breath, looking behind to see if he was being followed. The road was empty. After getting his breathing under control, James looked into the darkness ahead. Somewhere not too far away he could make out the shape of a car. Perhaps it was his car. He began to walk slowly along the unlit road. The pavement had ended, and he found himself walking on the rough road. There was a deep ditch between the road and the hedge of a field. His eyes grew accustomed to the darkness, and he could see that the ditch was full of water.

The noise of the city could still be heard, mixed with the sounds of the countryside. The smell of the rain and sounds of the countryside gave a deep yearning to live on the open road. For him, his grandfather's stories of traveling the open road were romantic if not romanticized. The idea of freedom really appealed to him. Somewhere in the distance a dog barked. He awoke from his short daydream to the reality of being cold and wet. He quickened his pace. Just ahead, at a bend in the road, a car could clearly be seen. He was sure it was a Honda.

A rustle in the hedge made him turn. Although he wasn't scared, he was always aware of danger, but tonight he had been surprised twice by someone creeping up on him. The small animal that had caused the noise had gone. James stopped to listen to the other night sounds. A car could be heard, but he had difficulty working out if it was in front of or behind him. As he approached the turn in the road, a car came speeding around the bend towards him. The driver, seeing James, honked his horn as he drove past. Suddenly another car came from the other way and lit the road ahead. He could clearly see a car sticking out of one of the hedges, up against a tree. He ran towards it, crossing the road and jumping the small ditch into the field.

It was his car. The back seemed all right but looking at the front, he could see it had been completely wrecked. The engine was exposed and obviously badly damaged. The car was a write-off.

He opened the driver's door and saw that the steering column had been broken at the point where the ignition key would be inserted. He sank into the driver's seat, and as he swung his foot into the car, kicked something. He put his hand down on the floor and felt his cell phone. He quickly pressed one of the buttons, it showed he had missed three calls.

He pressed the auto dial for his parents' house. The phone rang and rang until the answering machine picked up. He called his younger brother Paul's mobile. The sound of Paul's voice relaxed him, and he became emotional for a few seconds, unable to speak.
"Hello, who's there? Hello! Is there anyone there? Who's calling?"
"Hi."

"James, is that you?"

"Yes."

"Where are you? We've been trying to contact you for hours."

"My car was stolen and my mobile was in it. But I've just found the car, and the phone was still there."

"How's the car?"

"Write-off."

"Sorry. Dad has been arrested."

"What!"

"That police Inspector came and took Dad off to the station for questioning."

"Is he still there?"

"Yes, but Mom and Donald have gone down to the station. They called Mr. Hoffman. I think he's with Dad now."

"Hoffman's a good lawyer. Paul, can you come and get me?"

"Of course. Where are you?"

"Top of Longbridge Lane, just where it becomes a small country lane. I'll walk back to the streetlight. And please get here quickly, I'm wet and very cold."

"On me way, brother."

James closed his mobile, gathered all his things together, and locked the car. Then he laughed out loud at the futility of his action. He walked back to the last streetlight. He could see the biker house, but there was no movement. The rain began to fall again. James wrapped his coat tighter to him and leant against the lamppost, which suddenly went out.

CHAPTER EIGHT

Gates of Hell

The rain had continued most of the night. After a brief spell of light drizzle, it began to rain hard again. The sound of running water gushing down the drainpipes outside of James's bedroom window was an opus to the natural elements. James lay looking at the ceiling, motionless. His father was, as far as he knew, still being questioned by the police, and this was something he couldn't understand. His father wouldn't hurt a fly, let alone kill someone. Was the inspector so prejudiced that he couldn't see beyond his hatred, or was there another reason, something deeper? James began to wonder if he were to blame for his father's predicament. If he hadn't found that house, they wouldn't have been involved.

He slowly sat up, and putting his bare feet on the wooden floor, felt a cold surge through his body. He had always enjoyed this sensation. When he was seven years old, he would warm his feet in the bed, then put them on the cold linoleum floor of his shared bedroom. He loved the sensation of the cold, but now he found it too much to handle. Standing up, he looked at himself in the full-length mirror on his wardrobe door. His white Marks and Spencer briefs clung to his muscular body. He stretched on tiptoe, trying to touch the ceiling. He felt the need to get back to the gym. He was losing the tone from his body. He wasn't a fitness fanatic, but he had begun to like the way his body looked after a workout at the gym. He was aware that his siblings regarded this as very narcissistic, but he didn't allow their comments to change the way he was. He remembered his grandfather telling him, "If a man didn't have pride in his appearance, then he couldn't have pride in the family." He wasn't sure if it was true, but like so many things his grandfather had said, it stayed in his mind. He showered and dressed.

The phone rang. He looked at it. He didn't want to answer it, and after the fourth ring the answering machine kicked in.

"James, I know you're there! Pick up the phone. It's Anne. I know you're there. James, pick up the goddamn phone! Okay, listen then. The police are still questioning Dad. Mom got hold of Derek Hoffman, and I hope he is with Dad. No doubt the pigs of the police will try to frame Dad." She coughed several times. "Shit! I hate this weather. Anyway, Mom says we are all to keep in touch. Paul says your car's a write-off. Are you okay? Shit! You may be still sleeping, you lazy bum. When you wake up, give us a ring. Bye. Okay... I hate answer machines. Why you can't just pick up the phone when I call, I don't know."

The sound of her putting down the phone and the answering machine stopping made him wish he'd answered it. Now he would have to call her back.

He went into the kitchen, uncertain as to what he should do. He had lived in the place for just a year. His brothers had called it "James's little hovel." But he had transformed it into a home, his home, with a good-sized bedroom and a living room. He had enough space for himself. Everything had its place and he didn't feel cluttered. He had wondered if this was why he didn't get into a relationship. Sharing space with someone else would be difficult after he had been on his own since leaving home. His last girlfriend had spat venomous words at him when they broke up, telling him he was a selfish, arrogant mommy's boy. 'It was always the Pidgley family first,' she had shouted, before running off, never to been seen again.

He made himself some tea and a slice of toast with real butter on it, one of his many weaknesses. This was despite his sister Mary's insistence that he would die young unless he ate whole-wheat bread and no butter. He kept telling her that he would worry about cholesterol when he got old like her! She was three years older than he was and acting like his grandmother.

He took the tea and toast into the living room and switched on the CD player with the remote, but quickly turned it off again. He needed silence, a time to sort out what his thoughts were. "Everything!" he said out loud.

On the coffee table in front of him sat the small Bible he had found in the hiding place at Thirteen Crowhurst Road when Elizabeth Friedman had shown him around the first time. It was hard to believe she was now dead and his father was being questioned about her murder. Opening the Bible, his father's neat handwriting in pencil filled every space that was not printed on. The writing was so small that James found it hard to read. He went to his desk in the corner of the room. The answering machine light was still flashing. He had received two calls according to the display. One call was from Anne, so who was the other one from? He pressed the message button.

"Message one," came from the electronic voice. "James, it's Mom, give me a call." The machine continued, "Press zero to erase," then there was a pause before "Message two." He stopped the messages.

Why had his mother called? His self-imposed guilt of being a neglectful son made him pick up the phone and press the speed dial. The answering machine in his parents' house came on at once. When the message had finished, James hesitated before replying. "Hi Mom. It's me, James, returning your call. Speak to you soon. Love you."

He stared out of the window at the grey and wet day. A miserable day, one that would make anyone feel depressed.

From the desk drawer, he took out a magnifying glass. He had owned it since he was a small boy, when he used to play at being Sherlock

Holmes, solving the crimes of the century. Like who stole his chocolate bar? He never found out, and it still made him tense to think about it. Sitting on the sofa, he sipped some tea then picked up the Bible again and began to read his father's notes:

May 23rd Still can't sit down after the beating, but I didn't bleed this time. Finding it hard to sleep. Watching again, Mr. F at it again with Mrs. G, I'm not sure she really enjoys it, her husband must be on night-shift again at the car factory.

He flicked through a few more pages:

May 28th They have almost finished the road works, I saw them bury something, looked like an old carpet with something inside.

Whatever it was, it wasn't supposed to be there.

James wondered who "them" was. A few pages on he found another entry he could read:

June 1 M.F. has gone missing, I heard dad say she's run off with the insurance man, but he came this morning to collect. A cup was broken and dad blamed me, stood in shed waiting for him for an hour. Broke my wrist with a hammer. Can't sleep, I'm such a bad boy.

At the bottom of the page, to the left of the page number, Matthew had written, "Sorry Daddy." James closed the Bible, opened it again, but stopped. He couldn't read any more. He knew his grandfather abused his father but to read about it made him feel ill. Grandpapa had always treated the grandchildren okay.

James had heard from Grandpa's friends that he had a violent temper when he was really angry.

James changed his thought. So who were Mr. F and Mrs. G? And was Mr. F related to M. F.? Were they connected to each other, and what had been buried in the road, a dead person? The phone rang twice and then stopped. He wondered if it was a wrong number, or someone playing games. He picked up the Bible and went across to the desk, placing it in the bottom drawer. He looked at the caller-ID on the phone. It read, "Number unknown."

The letterbox in the hall opened and closed. This was followed by a knock on the door. James went to the door, opened it, and seeing an envelope, bent down to pick it up. As he grabbed the letter from the floor, he felt a sudden pain on the back of his head, then fell to the floor, losing consciousness.

James awoke in darkness. The smell of car oil and dirt on the rags and the boiler suit his face was buried in made him feel claustrophobic. He could feel the movement of a vehicle suddenly stop. A voice that sounded as if it were coming from the end of a tunnel, was speaking. He wasn't sure if it was speaking to him. "Don't fuck with me or my business, or next time you'll be dead." He once again felt a sudden pain to his head and fell back into unconsciousness.

As he woke, he could feel the trickle of something wet against his face. He was lying on his stomach. The back of his head was still throbbing with pain, and his left arm, which was beneath him, felt numb. It was dark, and he could feel a breeze, as though the wind were blowing and he was outside. He laid for a few more minutes, trying to clear his head of the pain, but something was making it difficult for him to see properly. He was outside and lying on wet grass, still clutching the envelope in his right hand. He started to get up, but immediately felt dizzy and collapsed back onto the wet grass. Gathering his strength he tried to kneel. His eyes began to well up with tears and his vision became even blurrier. He coughed once or twice and found it difficult to breathe. A flowing silk-like ghost passed by him then came a second and a third apparition. White apparitions floated all around him. Using what strength he had, James staggered to his feet. He began to walk slowly into the stream of ghosts, which had become thicker and now completely surrounded and smothered him. One of the ghosts entered his mouth forcing him to cough and stumble again.

He could hear a strange sound a little ways in front of him. It was as if heavy metal doors were opening. A rush of heat hit his body, forcing him to his knees. The ghosts barked at him unintelligibly and then parted to reveal the burning fires of hell. The red-hot coals flared up as he approached. On one side a huge, creature-like dinosaurs was throwing bodies into the flaming coals. He watched as the bodies were tossed from the dinosaur's creature's mouths into the fires. There was a sizzling and a cracking as the bodies hit the fire. The heat overwhelmed him, and he fainted onto the wet grass again.

He could hear voices, and something cold was being placed over his eyes and on his forehead. "Is he okay, Joe?" asked a soft-spoken woman.

"Not sure, luv. What was the silly bugger doing? He could have been killed."

"Is he drunk?"

"Can't smell any booze on his breath. Maybe it's drugs you can't tell these days. Anyway, he is lucky to be alive." James slowly opened his eyes. He focused on the man and then on the woman, who was smiling in a gentle way.

"I think he'll be okay, Joe."

"What happened?" said James. "I was at the Gates of Hell! The fire was so hot, and all these people were being thrown into the flames."

The woman and Joe laughed. James looked at them, but they continued to laugh. "Gates of Hell!" said Joe.

"Yes, white ghosts, and then the Gates of Hell opened, and people were being thrown into the flames."

The woman came closer to James and took his hand. "That was no Gates of Hell, my luv. You stumbled across our Joe and the Agri. You know, the agriculture men from the government, burning the sheep. You know, foot and mouth." James looked at her, completely bewildered, then turned to look at Joe.

"That's right young'un, but what's happened to you? How come you ended up in my field?"

James tried to sit up. His head throbbed, and he remembered being hit in his apartment. "I'm not sure. I remember bending down at home to pick up an envelope off the floor by my front door, and someone hitting me on the head."

The woman leant over him and looked at the back of his head. "Oh yes, you have quite a bump. By the way, what's your name? I'm Irene and this is my husband, Joe. Irene and Joseph Fisher."

"James; James Pidgley."

A knock came at the back door of the farmhouse. Irene and Joe looked at each other. Then Joe went to open it. Standing on the step was a very official-looking man in government issue blue overalls. "Is the young man alright?" he asked.

"Yeah, he's fine. Caught in the heat of the pyre, that's all," replied Joe.

"Do you know the young man?"

"Oh yes, this be James, one of the local lads. He came to see our Trevor."

"Okay then. Just make sure he disinfects before he leaves the farm. I'll say goodnight to you then."

"Right-oh and good night to you, safe journey." Joe closed the door, but stood watching the man walk up the farm drive to his car, which was parked on the roadway.

"Well James, we'd better get you home before those Agri men start asking too many questions. I wonder where our Trevor is? Never around when he's needed, such a lazy bum," said Irene as she crossed the kitchen and opened a door, which led upstairs.

"Trevor! Are you up there, Son?"

"Yeah Ma. What ya want?"

"Get your head out of the dirty pictures on the Internet and get down here! Your dad and I need a little help."

She closed the door and returned to look at James. "I'm worried about that bump on your head. You may have fractured your skull or something."

"Once I get home I'll see the doctor and have it checked out."

"That's a good idea. My brother George got hit on the head, and he went crazy for years."

"Joe, it wasn't the hit on the head that made him crazy. It was the drink."

"True. But it was the head injury that made him drink in the first place."

The door to the stairway opened, and a young man about the same age as James entered the kitchen. Trevor was Irene and Joe's second son, and he worked most of the time with his father on the farm. He was dressed all in black and had dyed his hair black, the natural light brown color showing at the roots. His face had freckles and a suntan most sun worshippers would pay handsomely for. "What ya want, Ma? My turn to do the cooking?"

"Less of your cheek, we need you to take James home."

Trevor came to take a closer look at James. "Who is he, and what's happened to him? Why is he here?'

"He has been to hell and back," said Joe, then burst into laughter. Irene laughed too, and James, looking at them both, joined in. Trevor looked at all three of them, his expression of astonishment making Joe and Irene laugh even louder.

"You lot are mad. What you laughing at?"

James suddenly stopped laughing. "I need the toilet."

"This way, luv," said Irene, helping James to his feet and taking him to a small bathroom off the corridor, which led to the living room of the farmhouse. When James returned to the kitchen, Joe and Trevor were laughing loudly.

"Gates of Hell, that's a good one, our Dad."

"You gonna be all right, young'un?" asked Joe.

"Yes. I think I just need to get home and rest."

"Okay then, our Trevor will take you and Trevor, see that he gets in all right."

"Yeah Ma."

James made his way to the kitchen door. "Thanks for your help."

"Oh, it's nothing," said Joe. "We haven't had such a good laugh since me uncle Rodney got his peepee bitten by our nanny goat."

"Oh Joe, you shouldn't tell that sort of thing. What will James think of our family?"

"Thanks anyway."

As he stepped outside, Irene suddenly screamed, "Wait, I almost forgot, you had this in your hand." She handed him the envelope he was picking up when he was hit on the head. James took it and stuffed it into his pocket. He and Trevor climbed into a pickup truck parked in the farmyard. Trevor started the engine and turned to James.

"Where to?"

"One Twenty-Seven Wadbrooke Road, Bourneville. Do you know where that is?"

"Yeah, I think so, off Linden Road, not far from Cadbury's. I had an aunt who lived in Linden and worked at Cadbury's. She would bring home broken chocolates when I was a kid."

They drove in silence for the first part of the journey, James taking note of where he was and what streets they crossed. Trevor broke the silence. "You like computers?" He didn't wait for a reply, but continued, "I got a PC Pentium Four. Of course, it'll soon be out of date and I'll need to upgrade." James nodded and smiled.

Trevor continued, "It's the Internet I like. I've got friends all over the world. We write to each other, send pictures, not dirty ones! There is this guy I know in America, Micky, that's his name, he sends me pics of these really beautiful girls, says he has dates with them. I'm not sure if that's true. He lives in the desert. What's the place called? Oh yeah, Lancaster, near Los Angeles. He said I could visit. I will one day, when I'm famous."

They turned into one of the main streets from the country lane and continued until they reached Linden Road. Trevor turned left into Wadbrooke Road and began looking at the numbers.

"It's the house next to the school. I live on the first floor at the back." Trevor pulled his truck in front of Number Twelve and jumped out of the truck. He came around to the passenger side of the vehicle and helped James out. They walked slowly up the stairs towards James's apartment. The door of the apartment was open and James feared the worse, but as he entered he could see that nothing had been touched. He sat himself down on the sofa. His wallet and watch were still on the coffee table. He looked around the room.

"You gonna be okay now?"

"Yes, I think so. Thanks for your help."

"Okay then, I'll be off."

"Wait, let me give you something for the petrol."

"Oh, okay." James took a twenty-pound note out of his wallet and gave it to Trevor, who folded it and put it in his back pocket. "You know, you shouldn't go messing in other people's business. The next time they might kill you, so take care."

"Thanks." James was curious as why Trevor had made this comment but he was too tired to ask him. He continued, "you know your way back?"

"Oh yeah. Anyway, I'm gonna go and see me mate. He owes me some money." Trevor left and closed the apartment door behind him. James sank further into the sofa and fell asleep.

The dull daylight had illuminated the living room as James awoke. He felt cold. The phone was ringing, and he picked up the handset automatically. "Yeah?" he said in a sleepy voice.

"James, it's Paul. They've let Dad go."

"Who's let Dad go?"

"James, wake up! The police have been questioning Dad about the murder, remember?"

"Yes, that's good. Where is he?"

"At home. Look, I have to go, just thought I'd let you know."

"Thanks."

Paul hung up. James replaced the handset and stood up carefully. His head was still hurting a little. He made himself some tea, and while waiting for the kettle to boil, he checked the back of his head. The lump felt like it had gone down a little, but he still had a swelling. He sat and drank the tea quickly, washed the cup, and then took a shower. He came out of the bathroom and lay on his bed, looking at the ceiling. This was his place for thinking. Going over the events of the last few days. Something was niggling him something someone had said. He picked up the phone and pressed the speed-dial for his parents' home. His father answered.

"Dad, are you okay?"

"Is that you, James?"

"Yes Dad. Are you okay?"

"I'm fine. The police think I murdered that girl. But they've been blaming us for generations for any crime they can't solve. So what's new? At least they didn't accuse me of stealing your car!"

"Oh, you know about that."

"Your brother Paul spread the news."

"Dad, that's it, the guy who stole my car! Err, Dad, I have to go. I'll call you later, bye." James replaced the handset, looked around the room, then gathered some warm clothes together and dressed. He picked up his wallet and house keys, checked the apartment one more time before leaving, and locked the door behind him.

He left the apartment by the back entrance, going to an old shed in the back garden. Inside, after pushing several boxes and assorted garden tools out of the way, he found his old bike. The tires were a little soft, but everything else seemed okay. He wheeled the bike out into the back garden, and taking the pump off the middle support, he pumped up the tires until they were firm. It had been a long time since he had ridden a bike, but he soon found he had not lost the knack.

As a teenager, while other boys were playing with skateboards, James had become obsessed with his bike. He had ridden it everywhere, to the horror of his parents. Some days during the summer holidays he would ride one hundred, even one hundred fifty miles. He loved the countryside and felt free away from the city that seemed to choke his thoughts. One of his most enjoyable trips was to the Malvern Hills. There he would sit at the top of one of the hills and eat his packed lunch, looking out over the Severn Valley. After one of his uncles introduced him to the music of Sir Edward Elgar. Malvern became a regular adventure, because being there made him understand why Elgar composed the way he did. He liked modern music, as his mother would call it, but there was something about classical, which just got to him.

As he rode along the streets, he realized how bad drivers really were. They acted as though he weren't there, and on several occasions he had to stop abruptly to avoid being hit. He took these opportunities to catch his breath finding himself getting out of breath very quickly. "I must get back to the gym," he thought to himself.

The long ride up Longbridge Lane took its toll, and James had to stop several times before reaching the top. He rode past the house where Brian lived. It was quiet with no sign of life in the place. Only one motorbike was in the driveway.

At the bend in the road where his car had been abandoned he made a U-turn, slowly making his way back towards the bikers' house. On the opposite side of the lane, the last building before the countryside began was a small brick shed, built by the electrical company. James didn't know if it was still in use, but as he pushed his bike behind it, he could hear a humming sound inside. He peered around the corner of the shed and looked at the bikers' house. Although it was about thirty yards away, he had a clear view.

After an hour, nothing seemed to be happening, and James had become bored. He was fed up swatting flies that seemed only to fly around his head. A noise seized his attention peering around the corner of the crumbling brick electrical substation to see a car pull into the driveway of the bikers' house. A young woman jumped out and began screaming at the house.

James sighed and was suddenly startled by the appearance of a young boy by his side. "What ya doin', mister?" James looked at the boy, who was about seven years old. He was dirty-faced with jeans that were at least three sizes too big. The once-white tee shirt was so big that, where it wasn't tucked into the jeans, it looked more like a dress than a tee shirt. "Err, watching. Now go away."

"Give me ten pounds and I will."

"No way!"

"Then I'll go and tell Dave you're watchin' his house."

"Who's Dave, and which house is his?"

"The one you're watchin." The boy came to the corner of the shed and pointed to the bikers' house.

"I'm not watching that house, it's the next one up."

"They're away. You gonna rob it, that will still cost ya ten pounds, mister, or I'll tell the pigs." From somewhere further down the street a woman was calling "Derek, Derek." The small boy jumped.

"That your mother calling, Derek?"

"Yeah. I'll tell her you're peepin' on me sister. She's only fifteen and has big tits."

"Shit, kid, all I got is a pound, now go away." The boy took the money and left. James smiled to himself, because he remembered as a small boy doing the same sort of thing, but he had said the man was molesting him, even though James didn't understand what molesting was at that age. He called it "touch-the-boy game." He made a lot of money doing it, and once while with his mother shopping, he saw one of the men. The man became very embarrassed and dropped his groceries before running away. They picked up the food and took it home, a double benefit from playing pretend "touch-the-boy game".

He peered around the corner again the girl, followed by the young man called Brian, was getting into the car. Brian Steel wore the same clothes James had seen him wearing in the clubhouse garage. James watched as they drove off slowly down the lane. He mounted his bike and began to follow. They weren't going very fast, as the girl was still screaming at Brian, who would then scream back at her. They were so engrossed in their argument they didn't notice James following. They turned right, drove along the road to Daffodil Park, entered it, and parked the car.

James came to a stop and didn't cross the small bridge over the slow-running River Rea that entered the park. It was called a river, but in fact was hardly more than a stream, which had always puzzled James. It ran towards Birmingham City Centre. The river split the park. On his side it was shrubs and trees. The other side was a flat, well-kept grass area with paths zigzagging through it.

He kept close to the railway lines that ran along that side of the park. Beside the river were a number of trees and bushes, which gave him good cover. Wrapping a chain around a tree, he locked the bike to it and moved closer to the edge of the river to spot Brian and the girl. Brian had gotten out of the car. The girl was still screaming at him as she drove away.

Brian walked along the path in the park. He wasn't out for a Sunday stroll. The stride and swagger in his step said he was going somewhere. James watched from behind the bushes and slowly moved with him as Brian walked deep into the park. Brian stopped and turned towards the stream, heading directly towards the bushes James was hiding behind. From the other direction two young men appeared. At first James couldn't make out who they were, but as they came closer to join Brian, he could clearly see

Trevor and Willie. "I knew it," said James under his breath.

The three men shook hands, then hit each other's knuckles before giving a strange little hug. James had only seen something like this on an American television program about Los Angeles gangs. It was a modern-day freemason handshake. From where James was hiding, he couldn't hear what they were saying, but Brian's body language told him that he was not happy about something. He was blaming the other two for what had happened. Willie and Brian got into a very heated argument. Brian then poked Willie in the chest, finally pushing him so hard that he fell to the ground. Trevor stood by and watched, nodding his head every now and then.

Brian became even more agitated and started to wag his index finger at Willie. Then suddenly he stopped and looked at Trevor. Trevor had said something, and both Brian and Willie looked at him, their faces showing surprise. Brian began questioning Trevor, and after a few moments seemed to relax and lose his anger. The three then looked around and came closer together. Brian was giving them some information.

From behind James, there was a loud banging noise. James turned to see what it was, but there seemed nothing near him to cause the noise. When he turned back, he was startled to see all three men walking directly towards him and the riverbank. James immediately jumped into the stream and slid under the eroded bank, so that the overhang of dried mud hid him. As the three men approached, he pushed himself hard against the bank.

"Look man, I heard something."

"Well there ain't anyone here now," retorted Willie.

"Ah fuckin' forget it! I'm not sure this whole thing is worth doing. You guys get one hundred, and if Dave and me are lucky, we get the rest," said Brian. James suddenly heard, and then saw, a thin stream of yellow water enter the stream, just above his head. The smell of urine reached his nostrils. He closed his eyes and hoped none of it would hit him.

"What ya doin', man?" asked Willie.

"Pissin'. What the fuck does it look like? I had a belly full last night, a really good booze up it was."

"Okay, man, Trev and I will move the stuff tonight. I'll nick a van from that rent-a-place. Trev, you be at the back of my house at seven o'clock, and remember to come in the back way. I still got the cops at the front." Said Willie

"Okay. You coming Bri?"

"Na, I've got to deal with that bitch. She says she's pregnant, and if I'm messing around, she'll slice me."

"She found out about Sharon?"

"Yeah, someone told her, and I want to find out who."

"Well it weren't us, was it Willie?" Willie shook his head.

"I'm off. You guys get the job done. Call me on the mobile when it's over." In unison Willie and Trevor said, "Okay." Brian left and began to walk back towards the road. He looked as though he was talking to himself. Willie and Trevor turned their backs on the river and watched him go.

"I'm not sure about him," said Trevor.

"Oh, he's okay, just a jerk trying to be Mr. Big."

"Can we trust him?"

"With your life, as long as you do as he says, but if you shit on him, he'll kill ya!" As they stood talking, the weight of their bodies caused some of the overhang to give way and it began to crumble. Feeling the earth move, they both ran into the park and then laughed as they ran in the other direction to Brian.

Realizing he was about to be buried alive, James quickly climbed out. The overhang collapsed behind him. He was wet and dirty, but he now knew that something was going to happen tonight at seven o'clock, and he would be there to see it. He also had a feeling that what happened to Elizabeth Friedman may have something to do with what they were hiding.

As he unlocked the bike, a train rushed by, and a little way up the track there was a small explosion. Two boys were jumping up and down further along the railway line. They had obviously caused the explosion. James mounted the bike and rode out of the park, hearing another explosion as he went.

CHAPTER NINE

Clever Trevor

James arrived in the alleyway behind Willie's house just after six-thirty. He had been home after his ordeal at the riverbank. Showering then putting on a black sweater over a black tee shirt. The jacket was a very dark brown and his jeans black. He had found a very old black woolen hat and pulled it down to cover his ears. To complete the assemblage, he placed a black scarf around his neck.

The tree was dead and had been for some time. The owner of the adjoining fence had created a three-sided box, so the tree was in the alley, not his garden. James was able to squeeze himself behind the ample trunk into the small space between the tree and the fence.

As he squatted in his hiding place in the alleyway, he kept imagining he could smell Brian's urine in his hair even though he had shampooed it five times. He felt he was in a good hiding place when a man and his dog had passed by and the dog hadn't noticed him. Feeling invisible just a pair of eyes

121

looking out at the world. He watched as people would drive up and down the alleyway to the garages and then disappear into the back gardens of their houses. No one observed him. He was well concealed there, and he still had a very good view of the alleyway, especially Willie's back garden. The weather forecast was for heavy cloud coverage blotting out the moon. James hoped it wouldn't rain again, but welcomed the moonless night. A spider slowly walked down the trunk of the tree towards him. One of the things he had problems with were spiders. He didn't go into a panic, but he always had a fear of being bitten by one and then falling ill. The spider, unaware of this human, continued down the tree trunk. At the bottom, it strolled out into the alleyway under the cars and trucks driving up and down. James sighed with relief, keeping an eye out for any other arachnids.

Trevor's pick-up truck drove by and turned at the garages and parked. James stiffened. At last he was going to find out a part of the puzzle. It may have nothing to do with the murder of Elizabeth, but it would answer a few questions.

Trevor returned on foot and looked both ways before he entered Willie's back garden. James looked at his watch. It was five past seven and no sign of Willie. Trevor came out of the gate and looked up and down the alleyway. He looked at his watch, then dialed a number on his cell phone. He didn't get a reply and closed it, disappearing back into the garden.

A rent-a-truck drove slowly down the alleyway. It passed Willie's gate and parked opposite of where James was hiding. Willie jumped down from the driver's side and began opening the back and letting down the tailgate. He pushed up the door and jumped inside the truck.

Trevor emerged from the back garden and seemed surprised to see the truck. They nodded to each other, and seemingly in answer to a question from Trevor, Willie said, "The first one I nicked had no petrol in it, so I had to go back and nick another one. Ya'd think these places would look after the vehicle, wouldn't ya!"

"D'ya nick from the same place?"

"Yeah!" A laugh. "Anyway, let's get to loading the stuff, the sooner we do it the better." They both entered the garden and propped open the gate. After a few moments, Trevor came out carrying several of the flat boxes James had seen piled up in Willie's house extension. He pushed them into the truck. Willie followed, carrying a few more than Trevor, viciously pushing them into the truck, almost losing one as he did.

Trevor was already returning with another pile of boxes before Willie had re-entered the garden. He pushed them into the truck but then decided to climb in and pack them deeper. Willie emerged again. This time the pile was even higher. A woman was walking her dog past the truck and the dog barked. Willie jumped and almost lost the entire pile. The top one slid off and landed just in front of where James was hiding. Willie didn't seem to notice and returned to get more.

James stooped in his hiding place and tried to stretch his arm to take out what was in the box. He touched the box and felt a plastic bag inside. As soon as he heard Willie and Trevor's footsteps returning, his arm darted back into his hiding place. After they had loaded the boxes and returned for more, James stepped out of his hiding place to grab one of the bags. He quickly slid back into his hiding place as Willie and Trevor appeared, he froze and waited for them to go back into the garden. His heart thumping.

"How many more?" asked Trevor.

"About a hundred."

"Shit! I'm already shagged out."

"Then you shouldn't wank so much!"

"I don't any more."

"You telling me you have someone to do it for ya?"

"No, I just don't do it as much as I did."

They went into the garden, and James continued to pull the plastic bag towards him. Once he had it out of sight, he inspected it. There were several bottles of pills, all had the Crest Pharmacy label on them. James watched as they brought the rest of the boxes out and loaded them into the truck. Willie started to count the boxes. Then he recounted them.

"One box is missing."

"Can't be."

"I'm tellin' ya, there's a box missing."

"I'll look inside," said Trevor, returning into the garden. Willie recounted the boxes. He had to start from the beginning several times as he lost count. Trevor returned. Willie stopped counting and looked at

Trevor, who shook his head and didn't have the missing box in his hands. Willie looked around from his high position standing on the tailgate of the truck. He suddenly spotted it and pointed to it.

"There, must have slid off when I almost dropped them because of that bloody dog barking." James froze, his heart beating so loudly he thought Trevor must have heard it. The box had fallen beneath the shrubbery around the base of the tree. James pushed it a little so it could be seen. Trevor stooped down, picked up the box, and returned it to the truck. He handed it to Willie, who looked inside.

"A bag is missing."

"Well I ain't got it, and there's no one over there where it dropped. I checked."

"Well someone's got it."

"Maybe your Bobby took it."

"Yeah, he could have. I caught him this morning nosing around the boxes. Clipped his ear, nosy bugger." Willie slid the box into the truck and pulled down the door, closing it. He climbed off the tailgate, closed it, and from his right pocket he produced a padlock.

"What's that for?"

"Look man, we don't know what's gonna happen between here and your place. Remember, this world is full of crooks who will steal from the thieves. When I was a kid, my Uncle Tommy told me this story. That was before he went inside for twenty-five years. There was always honor among thieves. Well maybe in his day, but not since Margaret Bloody Thatcher. It's dog-eat-dog now."

"Yeah, you're right."

"See ya at the farm," said Willie, climbing into the truck. Trevor watched as Willie backed the truck up the alleyway and out on the road. He then ran down towards the garages. Moments later he drove up the alleyway in his pick-up truck.

Silence once again filled the alley. James didn't move, but waited quietly and listened and watched. The gate of Willie's back garden opened, and Willie looked up and down the alleyway. He walked towards the garages and then back. His mother appeared at the gate.

"No Mom, no one is here, you must have imagined it."

Mrs. Coates took the cigarette out of her mouth and blew a cloud of smoke into the night air. "Are you sure, Son? I am positive I saw someone come up the alleyway, and they haven't come back yet."

"Yeah Mom, it's one of your television mysteries again. There's no one here. I've got to be going. Trev will be waiting for me."

"Okay Son, be careful."

They went into the garden, closing the gate behind them. It opened again and Bobby Coates stuck his head out. He put one finger to his lips and said, "Shhh!" before closing the gate again. As if he believed in his fantasy mind that someone was watching. Still James didn't move. The woman walking her dog passed by, but no one else came.

James waited for over an hour before moving, then slowly crept out of his hiding place and up the alleyway to the road. He walked down to where he had chained his bike to a lamppost. A man and woman stood by the bike talking. The woman seemed a little agitated. As James approached, the man left and walked up to Crowhurst Road. James bent down and began to unlock the chain.

"So you never got your car back." James looked up and saw it was the woman from the night before, who had the bright yellow umbrella.

"Oh hello, no I didn't."

"Pity! Not much fun riding a bike in this weather. Gonna rain again, so the weather man on the telly said, but you know with him. He never really gets it right."

"It's okay. A little cold, but good exercise."

"They haven't caught the murderer yet, but I heard some Gyppo did it, and it would only be a few days before they arrest him. You can never trust a dirty Gyppo."

The anger grew inside James. All of his life, he had heard comments like this, but he controlled himself, and taking a deep breath, asked "Why?"

"Well, you're too young to know, but they steal things. Even your kids if you're not careful! My friend Polly lost her child, a pretty little girl, and then she told me the police told her a group of Gyppos stole the girl to sell to a rich family for sex."

James found it hard not to laugh and was glad he had controlled himself. He continued to unlock the bike. As he mounted it, he said, "Sorry, I'd better go before the Gyppos steal me!"

"No, they wouldn't steal you love you're too bloody old."

James began to laugh as he freewheeled down the hill. It was cold riding the bike; he really must speak to his brother about getting another car. He rode hard, and after several miles reached Barnt Green Road and the entrance to the road leading to Trevor's farm. He turned into the lane, looking into the darkness and then behind to make sure no other vehicle was coming and he wouldn't be seen.

About fifty yards from the house, he turned into a field and hid his bike. As he came out of the field and was about to walk up the lane to the farmhouse, he saw the stolen rent-a-truck coming out of the farmhouse gate. James darted back into the field and watched for the truck to pass and disappear onto the main road. He waited a few moments to make sure Trevor wasn't following in his pick-up.

He walked up to the farmhouse. As he approached, a dog came up to him. James took a biscuit out of his pocket and gave it to the dog who promptly ran off towards the barn. This was a trick his grandfather had taught him, most dogs love biscuits. After a few years he realized why it was a good idea. On one of his ventures to find a property to buy he had come across a vicious dog. It was a handful of biscuits, which saved him from being attacked.

James peered into the kitchen window. Irene and Joe Fisher were getting ready to go out. She was touching up her make-up in the mirror over the sink, and he was polishing his boots before putting them on. Joe stood up and stamped on the floor. Then he came to the kitchen door and opened it.

"You gonna be long, luv?"

"No, a couple of minutes."

"Okay, I'll go and warm up the car." He left the house, closing the door behind him, and walked over to the barn.

James went to the kitchen door and knocked. Irene opened it, saying "What's wrong, Joe?" Seeing James, she smiled and let him enter the kitchen. "Hello luv, how ya feeling? Your head still painful, is it? Well, I tell ya, it will take time. What can I do for ya?"

"Is Trevor in?"

"Oh yes, upstairs, he just came in. Now he's playing on his damn computer again! Do you know we had to have a second telephone line put in so he can use this Internet thing?"

"Thank you."

She called out to Trevor. There was no reply so she tried again.

"Is it important that you see him?"

"I think so."

"I don't like to leave you but." The sound of a car horn stopped from completing what she was going to say.

"You said you are Trevor's friend?"

"I'm more of an acquaintance, it takes time to become friends."

"That's true, you're not like his usual friends."

"Brian and Willie."

"You know them?"

"Brian has my car."

The honk of a car horn sounded again.

"He's upstairs, door on the left, just go up. Me and his dad are off to the pub. Well, it's talent night, good for a laugh." She picked up her handbag and left the kitchen, closing the door behind her.

James stood there, looking around. He hadn't thought it would be this easy. It was unusual for someone to be so trusting. His mother would never have been. Hearing the car drive out of the farm gate, he crossed the kitchen and opened the door to the stairs. He peered up the stairs there was very little light, but he could just make out a heavy rope handrail on the side. He began to climb the stairs, looking ahead to see if anyone was waiting for him. Stopping after each step, treading carefully, he tried not to make a noise. He wondered if he was running into a trap and Trevor's parents were part of the gang. At the top of the stairs, he peered to the left and saw light under a door. It must be Trevor's room.

James froze as the door opened and Trevor, without looking up, went into the bathroom next to his bedroom, closed the door, and switched on the light. James took this opportunity to move quickly into Trevor's bedroom.

James waited behind the door of Trevor's room. The room was quite large, with a single bed on the middle wall, and by the only window a bookcase, packed tightly with books. To the right behind the door was a computer and what looked like video-editing equipment. It wasn't anything sophisticated, but it looked as if Trevor were making a video. There were also several boxes of tapes on the floor.

The room wasn't dirty, but it needed tidying up. An odd shoe, tee shirt, and underpants lay on the floor. The linoleum flooring needed a good wash. The bed was made, and an old teddy bear with one of its ears missing sat proudly in the middle, against the headboard.

James heard the door to the bathroom open. Then the door to the bedroom opened and Trevor entered. His back was to James as he closed the door and went to his computer. He was editing a video on the computer, and James could see that the location was Thirteen Crowhurst Road.

"So this is your little secret."

Trevor jumped high in his chair. The shock of someone unknown in his room really scared him. He turned and, seeing James, said, "Shit!"

"Your mother let me in and told me to come up and see you."

"She had no right, this is private."

"What sort of movie is it, porno?"

"No way. This is a classic horror movie, but I can't finish it because of the murder."

"So you filmed at Number Thirteen? You broke in, did you?"

"No. Willie let me in."

"You sure?"

"Yeah. Willie has a key to all the houses around him."

"Really? So were you there the night the woman died?"

"Err no, I was with a girl."

James crossed to the bed and sat on the edge. Trevor swiveled the chair around so he could face him. "Listen, Trevor. You can tell me the truth and maybe I'll help you out. Or you can tell the police, and then I think you'll have some problems to deal with, starting with drug dealing. As I own Thirteen Crowhurst Road, you tell me all you know, and maybe I'll let you finish your movie before I do the place up."

"Why didn't you go to the police?"

"We Pidgley's don't go the cops, they hate us and we hate them."

"So you think you're above the law?"

"I never said that, we use the law not the cops."

"What do you need from me?"

"My dad maybe arrested for the murder of the estate agent and you have the answers I need to prove him innocent."

Trevor stared beyond James. He was obviously thinking through what James had said. The lines across his forehead had deepened, and James could almost see Trevor's brain working.

He knew he couldn't let his guard down this was the most dangerous time. Was Trevor a threat to him, would he run and tell the others. Trevor's mother had not really questioned him about why he was there and just told him to go upstairs. It could be a trap, any moment they could rush in and drag him off to the field again. It was hard to read Trevor's the body language or even his facial expression. Trevor just stared at the wall behind James.

They sat in silence for several minutes. "You want a cuppa?" Trevor suddenly asked. He rose from the chair and, not waiting for an answer, left the bedroom and went downstairs to the kitchen. A little light on the telephone next to the computer came on. James carefully picked up the phone and, placing a hand over the mouthpiece, listened.

"Willie, its me, Trevor. You'd betta not come over tonight again. I gonna go down to the pub with me mom and dad, okay?"

"Nothing wrong, is there?" said Willie.

"No man, nothing wrong. They just keep nagging me about spending some time with them."

"Okay, I'll see ya Tuesday to load the stuff up for Bri. What day is it today?"

"Willie it's Saturday."

"Oh yeah, See ya then"

"Yeah, see ya."

The phone went dead. James put the handset carefully back onto the cradle. James crossed to the bed again and sat down. On the floor by the bed was a script: *Bloodbath Two* by Trevor Turner Jones. He picked it up and was beginning to read. The story is simple but compelled him to continue to read. He was no expert of scripts but he could image the scene he was reading and the dialogue seemed believable. Trevor entered the bedroom carrying two mugs of tea. "Willie was supposed to come over later tonight, but I just called him on his cell phone and told him not to. If I tell you what I know, can I finish my movie?"

"If you tell me everything you know, yes. Is this the script for it?"

"Yeah, *Bloodbath Two*."

"It's quite good."

"I don't think it's my best, but it has a good story. I want to use it to get me self into film school."

"If the video is as good as the little bit of the script I just read, you should get in. What do I know? I don't know one end of a camera from the other!"

"It's not difficult once you start, I learnt a lot from books."

"Tell me everything that happened the night the woman got murdered."

Trevor sipped at his tea, looking directly at James. He gave a little giggle. He had clearly been shaken by the appearance of James. James looked back at him, holding the mug in both hands, waiting for it to cool. He wasn't sure if he should drink it or not.

"It's not poisoned! You can have mine if you're not sure."

"It's okay, but it's hot."

"I like it hot. Anyway, Willie, the mate I just called, and a friend called Brian and I had some business to take care of early that evening." He stopped and took another sip of tea. "Afterwards, I went to Number Thirteen and finished cleaning up the living room for the final scenes in the house. At nine o'clock, I went to pick up Cheryl Dobson. She's the girl in the movie. I knew her from school, and she always said she wanted to be an actress. So I convinced her to be in the movie in exchange for a copy she could use as a show reel. She's got a nice figure and dresses really good."

He took another sip, and this time put the mug down next to the computer. "She's not a bad little actress. I think she needs some training, but she listens and does as you tell her."

"So what happened next?" said James, smelling the tea, then taking a sip. It tasted just like tea. James relaxed.

"It took me about thirty minutes to go and pick her up. She had too much makeup on, so I made her take some of it off. Then we drove back to Number Thirteen and we went in by the back door. Cheryl walked into the living room from the kitchen." Trevor took another sip, staring straight ahead of him.

"Cheryl turned and asked me, 'Who's the woman lying on the floor?' 'I thought I was the only woman in this movie'. Cheryl had gone pale and seem to be shaking, I think out of anger." I said, 'What woman?' and went and took a look. There was a woman there all right. I touched her. She felt warm, but she wasn't breathing. I told Cheryl the woman was dead. She sort of screamed and fainted. I carried her to the car. Cheryl, that is and drove her home."

Trevor had maintained eye contact with James as he told the story. His manner showed panic as he recollected that night. "I have nightmare about it. I just want to finish the film is that being cold uncaring. She was dead I didn't kill her, I'm sorry but I have to go on. Do you know what I mean?"

"Did you call the police?"

"No. When I got back and took another look at her, someone had made the living room look more like a film set. There was fuller's earth. Its like dust they use it in films. I don't think it's legal now. Someone had put it all over the carpet. I don't know where it came from. I didn't want to get my footprints in it."

"You mean after you and Cheryl left, someone had changed the place?"

"Yeah. They must have been in the house when Cheryl and I were there, really creepy like." They both took a sip of tea. "Shit, they could have killed us!"

"Who knew you were filming inside the house?"

"Willie. And maybe Brian, but I didn't tell him."

"I see," said James, drinking more tea. They stared at each other for a moment, then Trevor picked up a video tape and placed it in the machine. He began to run the tape. It was the living room of Number Thirteen.

"This is how I set the room up." Heavy black curtains hung in front of the windows to keep out the light. Cobwebs hung from the ceiling. A white chalk cross was marked on the carpet.

"See, no dust on the carpet, but when I went back it was all over the place, covered everything. And the cross I had chalked on the floor had gone." The video continued, showing the whole of the room. At one side, an array of candles, some of them lit. "The candles weren't there," blurted Trevor.

"But you could see the body?"

"Yeah."

"So where was the light coming from? The hallway?"

"Yes, the light by the front door." They continued to look at the video. James finished his tea and put the mug on a side table. Trevor watched the video intently, making notes in a small notebook. The tape came to an end, and the screen went blank. Trevor ejected it and placed it on a shelf with other tapes so the label was visible.

"You want more tea? I do."

"Yes, I think so. It may help me think."

"That's what my mom says, tea solves everything."

Trevor led the way downstairs and into the kitchen, each of them carrying his own mug. In the kitchen, Trevor filled the kettle and placed it on the old Aga oven. James went to the sink and washed the mugs.

"The business you and Willie had to take care of, was that the prescription drugs?" Trevor shot round from the Aga and looked at James, the color drained from his face. "I know that you, Willie, and Brian stole prescription drugs from Crest Pharmacy and stored them at Willie's before bringing them here tonight."

"Shit! We originally stored them in the back garden shed of Number Thirteen, but that woman kept coming around, so we had to move them."

"The estate agent you mean, Elizabeth, she kept going to the house?"

"No, not her. I think her name is Miss Marsh. She lives a few doors up she's a really nosy old bag."

"I don't think I've met her."

"Bobby Coates said you spoke to her the night Brian stole your car."

"The woman with the yellow umbrella! Saw her tonight talking to some man."

Trevor took the mugs and put a teabag in each one. "Actually, it was Brian and Dave Lilly who stole the drugs."

"Why did you get involved? For the hundred pounds, or to use the drugs yourself?"

"I don't take drugs, it's a mug's game. How do you know so much?" The kettle whistled and Trevor poured the hot water onto the teabags. He put the kettle back on the Aga, then turned and faced James. "Why do you care what happens to me?"

"Because I think you're a good guy with bad friends, and the need of money to feed your passion got you carried away. But really I need your help to solve the murder."

"They're bad aren't? My mother keeps telling me they are rubbish."

"She is a nice lady."

"Why are you really helping me?"

James ignored the question, "Trevor, tell me about Brian."

"Oh him! Shit, man, he and his best mate Dave are bad news, I suppose, a couple of real nutters."

"So tell me about them.""Dave is married and has a kid. He's been in jail a couple of times for selling drugs. He is dangerous. If he felt you were going to mess in his business, he could kill you as soon as look at you. I think Brian would as well. He smokes pot and takes other things all the time, then gets really angry."

"Would Brian really kill?'

"He says he has already, but I'm not sure. He went to Borstal for derailing a train when he was a kid. But that was a long time ago." Trevor added milk to the mugs, dunked the teabags a few times, and removed them.

"Stop," said James. "Let's go and have a pint. I need some fresh air."

"Mom and Dad are at the Old Bull on Barnt Green Road. We could go and join them. I told Willie I was, and if we go, I'm not lying, am I?"

"That's true."

"I've told too many lies lately, especially to my parents. I made a mistake because I needed money. Mom always said money was the root of all evil."

Trevor ran up the stairs shouting behind out, " I'm going to turned off my computer and pick up my trainers."

James looked at the telephone expecting the light to go on it didn't. This had been too easy, was Trevor playing for time. Had he some how given Willie a message when he called him. He would still have to be cautious and not trust Trevor.

Coming down the stairs Trevor felt in his pocket. "I ain't got any money."

"That's okay, I have enough for the both of us, and we'll be able to buy your parents a round. I think I owe them for saving me from the Gates of Hell." James switched off the kitchen light and closed the door as they left the house.

"Are you going to lock it?"

"No, we don't have to around here. Where's your car?"

"Brian stole it."

"Oh yeah. How did you get here?"

"On my bike."

"We can put it in the back of the pick-up and take it with us."

"It's just along the lane in a field."

They climbed into Trevor's pick-up and drove out of the farm gate. As they drove down the lane, James shouted, "Stop," hopped out of the pickup, and disappeared into a field, returning with his bike a few moments later. He carefully placed it onto the flatbed of the truck and climbed back in. Trevor revved the engine, let out the clutch, and they sped down the lane.

At first they didn't notice the black car parked in a little lay-by at the end of the lane. After they had turned onto the main road, the black car began to follow them, the driver keeping a safe distance. Trevor kept looking in his rear-view and then side mirror.

"What's wrong?"

"That black BMW. I'm sure it came out of our lane."

James turned slowly so he could look in the side mirror. "Are you sure?"

"No."

"You're just being paranoid." They turned into the car park of the Old Bull and parked the truck at the back of the place. As James climbed out, his cell phone rang.

"Hello?"

"James?"

"Yes."

"It's me, Anne."

"Hi! What's the problem?"

"I've been kidnapped."

"Sure and dad is a member of the Royal family."

"No listen…"

"Anne stop lying."

"I'm not. Two men jumped me. They told me to tell you to stop messing in their business or they'll kill me."

"What? Is this a joke?" James stood by the truck as he spoke to Anne. Trevor decided to go around the corner to find his parents.

"It's not," said Anne.

Before she could continue, James heard her give a little scream, and a man spoke into the phone. "I fuckin' told ya we're keepin' her until we get rid of our stuff, so back off, Gyppo boy. If you go to the cops we will kill her, got it."

The phone went dead.

James ran around to the front of the public house, almost bumping into Trevor and Willie, who were arguing. James stopped and looked at them. Their shouting had brought several people out of the pub.

James grabbed Willie and pushed him up against the wall. "Where's my sister?"

"I don't know."

"Well, your friends do. And they said they would kill her."

"What friends?"

"Brian and Dave."

Trevor was looking at Willie. "Tell him, man."

"I don't know. I called them after you called me to tell them he was with you and I thought you split on us."

"They're a couple of nutters. They'll kill her, you, and me, Willie. Do you know how much those drugs are really worth? It was on the news, 500,000 pounds, and they were doing us a favor giving us a hundred each! We're the mugs, and I want no more part of it." Willie looked at Trevor, then at James. Panic came over his face.

"She can't be far from their house."

"Why d'ya say that?" said Trevor.

"Because before I told them about you, Brian had called me and told me he was at home, but they were going out to get a little bit of security and I was to keep him informed."

"What about the drugs?"

"They'd be gone sometime tonight. That's why we put them in the barn next to the road. It was so they could get them when they wanted, and we wouldn't hear them."

"Err, I think I should go," said Willie, who then ran to the stolen BMW. James and Trevor watched him leave the car park.

"I'd better find my sister."

"How?"

"Not sure but I think I'll need some help."

"What can I do?"

"You'll help me?"

"Yes. I don't need you as an enemy. You found out what was going on, the drugs and all. You got too much information and I don't know how. I wanted to get out of this; if my dad found out he would beat the shit out me. Oh yeah he comes across a mild, kind man but really he can be very hard. Especially where the police are concerned. I will need your help when he finds out. Where do you think we should start?"

"I'm not sure, but I wonder how they knew about my sister?"

"That's easy, after you asked Willie who stole your car he told Dave, who spoke to his supplier, who has ways of finding out about you and your family."

"Who's his supplier?"

"I don't know their name, but I think they may be Scottish. Mac something."

"I'll call home and inform the family, maybe they've heard something." James called his parents' home.

"Hi Dad."

"No, it's Paul. Is that you, James?"

"Yes. Is Dad there?"

"No, he's been arrested proper for the murder of that woman."

"What!"

"That cop thinks he did it."

"He didn't."

"I know that."

"Where's Mom?"

"At the police station."

"I see. Listen, Anne's been kidnapped."

"Right, who told you?"

"She did."

"Figures. She is playing one of her games, trying to take the attention from Dad, as usual! Look, Eileen just arrived. Got to go. Get to the house as soon as you can."

The phone clicked. James looked at Trevor, who gave a weak smile.

"I think we're on our own.".

CHAPTER TEN

Missing

Trevor drove the truck past the bikers' house, made a quick U-turn, and parked on the opposite side of the road at the top of Longbridge Lane. James' bike rattled in the flat bed of the truck. They sat in silence looking at the house, which was in complete darkness.

"I think I've been bloody stupid," said Trevor.

"Nothing that can't be fixed."

"All I wanted to do was finish my film. I didn't see the wood for the trees as my granddad would say. I could still go to jail."

"We all make mistakes when it comes to friends."

"So why are you helping me? You are going to help me?"

"Good question."

"I'm a loser."

"If you say so."

"So what's the answer?"

"Trevor I don't trust you, not yet anyway. I need to find out who murdered Elizabeth Friedman and I think you may have some of the answers."

"I didn't do it."

"I know that, but I think you may have information."

"Like what?"

"I have yet to find out."

The roar of a motorcycle coming up the hill made Trevor and James slide down in their seats. The rider drove his Norton bike into the front garden and parked on the grass. Climbing off the bike, he lost his balance, staggering and almost falling to the ground several times before regaining control. He took off his crash helmet and placed it on the handlebars. He reeled up the steps that led to the front door, trying to light a cigarette as he went, without any success. He pushed open the front door with his foot as he was still trying to light his cigarette.

James and Trevor quietly slid out of the truck and moved towards the house, looking around as they crept into the front garden. The biker could be clearly seen inside, opening and closing doors, the unlit cigarette still hanging from his mouth. He was calling some indecipherable words as he peered into each room.

Trevor began to climb the steps towards the front door when James's mysterious sixth sense made him grab hold of Trevor. Trevor turned and looked at James, and seeing the panic on his face, started to walk down the steps. James grabbed hold of his arm and began to run, pulling Trevor with him. Behind them the biker opened the kitchen door and stopped to light the cigarette. Once back on the road, Trevor and James ran and hid behind a parked car.

The explosion seemed more like one used on a film set rather than a real blast. The front of the house on the ground floor blew out into the garden and the street. Bricks and mortar began to rain down onto the pavement and the car James and Trevor were hiding behind. The heat from the blast could be felt. Trevor slowly raised his head to get a better look James pulled him down again as more debris crashed to the earth.

Car alarms began to shriek, lights in houses up and down the road switched on, and doors opened as neighbors came out of their homes to see what had just happened. James took his mobile out of his pocket and started to dial 9-9-9 for emergency services. Just as he was pressing the second nine, the phone rang. "Hello?" "Bang bang, you're dead!" said Brian, laughing as he disconnected the call.

"Who was it?" asked Trevor.

"Brian I think. They know we are here." James looked around to see if he could see where Brian was hiding. The electrical substation he had hidden behind looked like the most obvious place. He couldn't see if any one was behind it.

A man from a house across the street approached James and Trevor. "Are you both okay? This reminds me of the war. We had a bomb hit our house. My Auntie Doris was killed."

"Yeah, we're okay, but I don't know about the biker who went inside the house," said Trevor, standing up.

"Oh, it's one of those bikers, is it? Well good riddance, I say!" The man turned and went back to his house, totally unconcerned at what had just happened as soon as he learned it had to do with the bikers.

Trevor helped James up, and they looked at the devastation that was left. The front of the house had been blown out, and the second floor was caved in. The garage clubhouse at the back of the house, where James had first met Brian, was engulfed in flames. In the distance, the sound of a fire engine could be heard.

"Let's get away from here before someone asks why we're here," said James, looking around at the houses on either side of the road. A shadowy figure slid behind the electrical substation, as James looked at it. He wasn't sure if he had seen someone but realized they need to get away.

Trevor and James moved slowly back towards the truck, trying not to bring attention to themselves. It was a little dusty but hadn't suffered any real damage from the blast. As they sat and watched the onlookers gather, Trevor gave a shudder.

"Shit, man, Bloody hell. That could have been us inside that house."

"Yes, so now we know what we are up against. Let's go to your place and think out what we should do next."

Driving down Longbridge Lane, they were passed on the other side of the road by five fire engines, two ambulances, and several police cars. They sat in silence on the journey to the farmhouse.

James mulled over the thought of what could have been if they had entered the house. As they entered the gate to the farm, Trevor slowed down and stopped twenty feet from the house.

"Strange all the lights are on," said Trevor. He cautiously approached the house, James following behind. Inside the kitchen, nothing seemed to have been touched, including two meals on the table. It was as though someone had just vanished at the beginning of their meal.

Trevor rushed for the stairs, jumping them three at a time, and ran into his parents' bedroom. Nothing had been moved. He checked his mother's jewelry box, but all her cheap jewelry was still there. The expensive ones were kept in a safe in the cellar. He ran to his own bedroom, checked all his equipment, and then his secret hiding place. Nothing was missing.

James looked around the kitchen and then wandered into the sitting room, which was very tidy and clean. It looked as if it was never used, and this was something he understood. He went into the dining room. The elegant furniture seemed out of place. He looked at the small side table. Knowing a little about furniture, he thought it could be a Chippendale. After checking underneath, James was surprised to find that it was. This was obviously furniture that had been handed on, and Trevor's mother had really taken care of it.

The next door he entered revealed a sophisticated and high-tech farm office. James looked around and saw that the gun cabinet was open, but there were no guns inside. James immediately ran up to the second floor. Trevor appeared out of his bedroom. "It looks like they took all the guns, the gun cabinet is empty. But nothing else has been touched."

"The guns are kept in the cellar, and as no one can ever find the door to the cellar, we don't worry about them."

"Did you find your parents?"

"No."

"Then they are missing, because no one leaves a meal and the place open like this."

"They could be out on the farm. If an emergency happens, we all leave whatever we are doing and run to help."

"Then we should look around for them."

Back in the kitchen, Trevor seemed very nervous and a little scared. He walked up and down the kitchen. "You don't think they were taken, do you?"

"I'm not sure. I really don't know to what extent Brian and Dave would go. That's not true, they would do anything to protect themselves."

"Mom and dad could be tied up somewhere or even dead. Oh shit, this is all my fault."

"Trevor, we don't know if anything has happened, so let's go and find out."

"Dave once said if any of us ratted on them, he would kill our families first and then us."

"Talk, just talk. Now, you know the farm, so where should we start?"

"Err, the barn."

The barn was a large brick building with heavy wooden doors. Trevor put his ear to the big doors. He shook his head and then slid them open. Inside were pens holding cows, who looked up as they entered but then went back to eating hay.

"You look in the pens and I'll check out the loft and the back part." James watched as Trevor climbed the ladder with incredible agility and then disappeared. He went to the first pen and looked inside. A cow looked back and then came towards him. James moved on to the next pen. It was obvious that Trevor's parents were not here. The third one was empty, and as he looked into the fourth, he could see that it was a larger pen with a back part that was difficult to see into from where he was standing. He climbed the pen gate, walked to the back part, and looked inside. It was dark, but after letting his eyes adjust, James was able to see a cow with a runny nose.

He began to make his way out of the pen, but two of the cows came towards him and began to push him with their heads. He backed up as a third cow joined in the ambush, it too began to push at James. The third cow became very aggressive, and as James stepped backwards, his foot became stuck in months' of cow dung and straw. He fell to the ground, and the three cows came close and towered over him. Every time he tried to get up, one of the cows would push him down. He had visions of *Animal Farm,* and expected to see a pig giving orders any moment.

The sound of a whack to the rump of one of the cows made it move. The other two followed and went back into the enclosed part of the pen. Trevor was standing in the light and, looking at James started to laugh. Standing up, James said, "Talk about *Animal Farm;* those three are real terrorists!" And then he too broke into laughter. He had lost one of his shoes, and tried to look for it in the dung and hay.

"Wow, you stink."

"Tell me about it. I haven't smelt like this since I fell into a sewer ditch near Redditch when I was a kid."

"Nothing up in the loft or out the back. If it is Dave and Brian, then we should check to see if the drugs are still here."

"I've lost my shoe."

Standing next to the roadway was a smaller barn. Its main door was padlocked. Trevor unlocked the padlock and swung open the door. The place was empty, and the side door on to the lane was open and had been pulled off its hinges.

James's mobile rang. As he took it out of his pocket, he wiped some of the cow muck off it. "Still working then," said Trevor.

"Hello?" said James.

"And the cupboard was bare!" It was Brian's voice. He laughed again, and just before he hung up he made a grunting sound.

"They're watching us. Right now someone is out here in the fields."

Trevor looked out. "They could be anywhere, there are so many hiding places."

"We need to change that and become the watchers ourselves."

"I wonder where Mom and Dad are. Their vehicles are in the driveway, they can't be far."

"Do you have pigs?"

"Yeah, three of them in the old sty. Why?"

"Let's look there."

Trevor ran out of the small barn, and James had trouble keeping up with him, his shoeless foot treading on the rough earth of the farmyard. The sty was on the other side of the farm. After they had passed the house and begun to run up the left side, a light suddenly came on, lighting a brick-built pigsty. Trevor climbed over the wall into it. The covered part of the sty had a door, and sticking out of the door were two legs. James opened the sty gate, and once inside he could clearly see Irene and Joe. Both had been hog-tied and were lying face down on the wet, muddy floor of the sty. One of the pigs was lying next to Irene as though it were trying to keep her warm.

Trevor untied his mother's ropes James undid Joe's. Once Joe had stood up and seemed okay, James went to give Trevor help with Irene. She stood still for a moment, and wiping the mud from her face, gave them both a smile. "I though we were goners." She took Trevor in her arms and gave him a hug and kiss on both his cheeks. James smiled, and then he too was hugged and kissed by Irene.

"I'm not sure if anyone is still around," said James.

"Let's get back to the house, I have my guns just in case they are," said Joe.

They slowly walked back to the farmhouse, James and Trevor looking around expecting Dave or

Brian to jump out at anytime. Trevor was helping his mother, who had to stop several times to shake her right leg. "I think it fell asleep, and the circulation has only just began to come back. Give us your arm, Trevor, before I slip on me backside."

Trevor put his arm around her and helped her as they crossed the farmyard. Joe was walking with James. They looked as though they had been in a mud fight. The silence between them was uneasy. They both tried to open a conversation, but failed, and walked behind Irene and Trevor, heads towards the ground.

Inside the kitchen, the extent of their appearance could be seen. Irene and Joe were covered in the mud and slurry from the pigsty. James was covered from his waist down, and one of his shoes was missing. Trevor seemed to have escaped. All he had was a little mud on the bottom of his jeans. Joe looked from one to the other then began to chuckle. Irene with her infectious laugh joined in, quickly followed by Trevor. James looked at all them they looked back at him, and this made them laugh even more. Finally, James joined in too.

"I think we need a cup of tea and a good cleanup, then a little chat," said Joe. Irene put the kettle on the Aga and laid out four mugs on the kitchen table, clearing away the uneaten meal. Trevor looked at his father and then lowered his head.

"So, Trevor, what's this all about?" Trevor kept his head down and didn't answer.

"Your mother and I have been subject to being tied up and almost murdered in our own home. I think we deserve an explanation."

Trevor raised his head and looked at his parents. "Dad, I..." he faltered, looking at James with a "pleading for help" expression on his face.

"Come on, Son, you've always been able to talk to your dad. What's the problem now?"

James felt the embarrassment and spoke first. "Mr. Fisher."

"Oh please, call me Joe. It's not like you're a stranger now."

"Joe, your son was conned into helping two very dangerous men. I don't believe Trevor really knew what he was letting himself into, and the two guys are very persuasive."

"Is that true, Son?"

Trevor lifted his head and looked his father in the face. He gave a weak "Yeah," and then lowered his head again.

"Your son became an unwilling helper in a gang who stole prescription drugs. They were hiding them in the barn by the road and came tonight to move them to some other hiding place, having found out that Trevor had become my ally."

"Really?" said Irene, pouring hot water into the teapot.

"I think Trevor has learnt a hard lesson, that money must be earned honestly to be worth anything."

"So true," said Joe.

"Being creative, Trevor's mind sometimes tricks him into thinking he's in a film rather than real life."

"Now, that's true. I remember when he was a small boy he would always dress up as this person or that character. You remember, don't you, Joe?"

Joe ignored the question and asked James, "So what are you going to do now? And why were we tied up and half killed?"

"Because they were trying to scare me and Trevor and using you to get to us, so I wouldn't try to find my sister."

"Your sister?"

"Oh yes. They kidnapped my sister in the hope I'll keep my mouth shut."

"About what?"

"Well, about the drugs for a start, and secondly about the murder of a woman."

"What murder? What woman?"

"The one up by the car factory. You know, Mom, that woman who was found in the empty house," said Trevor, finding his voice and becoming alive again.

"Oh, but they've arrested someone for that," said Irene.

"Yes, my father."

"Oh," said Irene, her mouth staying open for a few moments.

"But he didn't do it, did he?" asked Joe.

"No. Just a prejudiced policeman with a blind on."

"What are you gonna do?"

"First we have to find Brian and Dave, then get his sister back, and finally prove they did the murder," said Trevor, looking at James and giving a weak, puppy-dog smile.

"They always seem to be one step ahead of us. We know they are following us somehow."

"Some one is, it could be Willie or one of the others they have conned into helping them."

"You need to trap whoever is following you and find out who he is reporting to," said Joe.

"It could be a girl, Joe, you don't know these days. Not like in our days, we all knew who the wrong 'uns were."

"Who might that be, Mom?"

"Well, it was always the kids from Birmingham who came here during the summer looking for work. Right bad lot they were."

"Oh, I thought you were gonna say the Gypsies."

"Never," said Joe. "They may have been painted as the thieves, but all the ones I knew were the salt of the earth, never stole from me."

"Well, it looks like you boys need a plan and a place to use as headquarters, so if it's okay with Joe, you can use here."

"It's okay with me. I was just wondering how you were going to find Brian and the other guy, can't remember his name."

"Dave," said Trevor. James looked at Trevor, and they both spoke simultaneously: "Willie!"

"Who's Willie?" asked Irene.

"You remember, Mom, the thin guy who couldn't stop talking."

"Oh him! He's involved in this as well?"

"Yeah, it was him who got me involved by saying I could make some quick money to finish my…" Trevor didn't finish what he was saying and lowered his head again.

"Seemed like a nice kid. As you said, he talked a lot. Anyway, you drink your teas. I'm gonna go and get cleaned up. Trevor, you next, then James. You'll need some clothes, James. I know, you could borrow some of our Neil's. I think you're about the same size." James looked at Trevor questioningly.

"Neil's my older brother, he lives in Rubery with his girlfriend but keeps most of his clothes and things here."

Irene left the kitchen. All three watched her leave, and once the door was closed, Joe looked directly at Trevor. "So what did you get out of this, for helping these crooks?"

"Money, Dad, so I could finish my film."

"Oh, not that film stuff again!"

"It's quite good, well, the bit I've seen. The script is very readable," said James.

"Really? You mean he is not wasting his time?"

"I don't think so but I'm no expert. All he's missing is money and maybe a little morality."

Joe laughed.

"Look Dad, I did a stupid thing. I didn't realize they were as crazy as they are, but I have a chance to put it right, if James will let me." Joe and Trevor turned and looked at James, who was pouring himself another cup of tea. He turned and saw them looking at him.

"What?"

"Well, can our Trevor help you?"

"I don't think I can do this on my own, so any help he can give will always be appreciated. And, as I said before, he can finish his film in the house once this mess is sorted out."

"So boys, what's the plan?"

"I think we have to find Willie he is the key to this. But first we must lose whoever is following us."

"Good start. And I think I know how you can get rid of the stalker," said Joe. Irene entered the kitchen from upstairs in a clean dress, her hair wrapped in a white towel like a turban.

"Trevor, your turn, and then you, James. I've left Neil's things out on the landing by the bathroom. Are you boys hungry?"

"Oh yes, I'm staving," said Trevor. James nodded his head.

"When you've finished cleaning up, I'll have bacon and eggs for us all."

"And I'll call our Neil, I think we need his help," said Joe.

Trevor and James left and went upstairs. At the top, Trevor put his hand out to stop James. "There's something I need to show you." He entered his bedroom, put on the light, and pointed to the wall above his bed. Someone had spray-painted a message on the wall: 'Squeal any more and you die with the pigs.'

"I don't want Mom to see this."

"Do you have a flag or a large sheet to cover the wall?" Trevor opened a drawer, which was built into the base of his bed, and took out a large camouflage-colored sheet. He then took a box of thumbtacks from a drawer next to the computer.

"Everything has a place."

"'And everything in its place,' my grandmother used to say."

"I'll put the sheet up. You go and get cleaned up and changed."

Trevor handed James the thumbtacks, and picking up some clothes, went to the bathroom. James carefully took off his shoes, socks, and his jeans and climbed onto the bed. He hung the sheet as though he were hanging some expensive curtains. When he had finished, he stood back and looked to see if he had covered the graffiti. After a little tug here and there, he climbed off the bed.

Replacing his jeans, he found a wooden box and placed it in the centre of the room. Sitting down there, he had a good view of the whole room. To the quick glance it looked a bit messy, but as James looked closely, he realized that there was order in the apparent chaos. Most of the books on the bookcase behind the door were to do with film and were in author order. Books on how to make a film, write a film script, even one on how to raise money to get your script made. The bottom shelf was full of scripts. The top one read "by Trevor Fisher." James leaned over and picked it up. The title of the script was *Fast Food Horror*, and he began to read it.

Trevor returned with a blue towel wrapped around him. James looked up as he entered the bedroom. "This is really good," said James, showing Trevor what he was reading.

"It's okay, but the ending's a little weak. It needs a rewrite and some characterization changes. Your turn now, I haven't used all the hot water, only most of it."

James put the script back, and picking up the clothes Irene had left for him, went to the bathroom. Once locked inside, he gave a long sigh and looked in the mirror above the sink. Emptying the pockets of his jeans, he placed his mobile, wallet, and keys on a small low chair. Taking off his jeans and shirt, he could see that the farm muck had gone through to his underpants. He discarded them and placed them in his jeans pocket.

The bathroom was of quite a modern design, with a bath and shower. He sat on the edge of the bath and dialed his parents' number on the mobile. It rang and rang, and after a few minutes, James hung up. He turned on the shower, the water came out as a light spray with no real pressure behind it. Once he had dried himself, he put on Neil's clothes. To his surprise they fit quite well. He gathered his dirty things and went back to Trevor's room.

"I've been thinking," said Trevor. "Whoever is following us is in touch with Brian and Dave. If we capture him, maybe we can get their phone number."

"Don't you have it?"

"No. Willie did all the calling, but I don't think he called their mobiles."

"It's a good idea, we have to start somewhere."

"Let's get some grub, I'm staving."

162 | EDWARD ARNO

As they entered the kitchen, the beautiful
smell of eggs and bacon made them feel even hungrier.
The table was laid, and Irene and Joe were already
seated. After they had eaten, Trevor rose from the
table and kissed his mother on the cheek. "Thanks
Mom."

"Yes, thank you, Irene."

"You're welcome. Oh James, you need some shoes."
She ran out of the kitchen into the hallway, returning
with a pair of sneakers. "I hope these fit. Our Neil
never wore them. Silly bugger said they weren't
fashionable enough or something like that."

James tried them on. "They fit fine."

"Then Cinderella, you shall go to the ball," said Joe.
Leave your other clothes and I'll wash them for you."

"No, you don't have to do that."

"Just leave them, lad, no good arguing with her!" said
Joe.

"Well thank you, Irene."

"Okay lads so the plan is to find this Willie kid? What
if he is the one who is following you?

"It's unlikely, he was never really committed."

"Sounds like he should have been."

"He was your friend, anyway you'd better get going.
And be careful," said Joe. James wrote his cell phone
number on a piece of paper and gave it to Joe. "I'll go
up to the loft window. I can see the whole of the lane
from there, and if I take my night sight, I should be
able to see if anyone is following you. Then I'll call
James on his cell phone."

"Get a car plate number if you can, Dad."

"Okay."

Irene gave them both a hug and kiss. Joe shook James's hand and punched his son on the arm.

Climbing into the truck, Trevor asked James, "They gonna be safe?"

"I think so."

As they drove down the lane, they tried to act normal but looked carefully into each field as they passed. They turned into the main road and headed for Crowhurst Road, Trevor constantly checking his mirrors. James's mobile rang. "Hello Joe, half a moment I need a pen."

Trevor handed him one from the dashboard and a small notebook from the door pocket. "Okay Joe, I'm ready. XPZ 571 Z, a black Ford, windows blacked out. Thanks. Call us if you need anything."

"It's about four cars behind us. I think it has one person in it. Shall we box him in?"

"No, I don't want to give Brian and Dave any clue that we know we are being followed. Just drive as though nothing's happened and stick to the plan."

"Okay. Can I ask you something?"

"Yes, anything."

"Who were you calling when you were in the bathroom?"

James smiled, remembering the creek of the floorboards outside the bathroom while he was sitting on the edge of the bath. "You were listening, I called my parents, but no one answered."

"Oh I, err, was just wondering."

"Still don't trust me?"

"I do its just... You stuck up for me with my parents. It's kind of strange, someone doing that for me."

"Why?"

"Because all the people I know, friends like, would stab you in the back, lie to save themselves before helping you."

"Then they're not real friends, are they?"

"I suppose not." They drove in silence for a few miles, Trevor checking behind to see if the black Ford was still following. "Thanks."

"What for?"

"For understanding, being a friend."

"As the Americans say, you're welcome."

Trevor smiled and began to relax. As they drove up Thurleston Road, he passed the entrance to Crowhurst and entered the alleyway that ran behind Willie's house. He didn't stop at the back of the house, but continued up the alleyway and past the garages to the brick wall at the other end. As they both climbed out of the truck, they could see a truck in the far corner. A truck that looked the same as Trevor's. The headlights quickly flashed. Trevor and James both smiled then made their way to the gate of Willie's house. As they looked up the alley, the black Ford was parked on the street opposite the entrance to the alleyway.

Entering the gate, they went through the overgrown garden to the covered walkway, which was now empty of boxes. Trevor knocked on the kitchen door, and after a few minutes Mrs. Coates opened it and showed them into the living room. Bobby was once again in his corner, perched on the stool.

"Willie's not here," said Mrs. Coates.

"Do you know where he has gone?" asked Trevor.

"Nope. Sodded off last night, and I haven't seen him since. Bobby you know where your brother is?"

"Nope. Sodded off, he did."

"Where?" asked James.

"In a hiding place only I know."

"Which hiding place?"

"Can't tell you because you don't have the password."

"Which password, Bobby?"

"The right one."

Trevor put his finger to his lips to stop James from asking questions. James nodded. "Is it a rude password, Bobby?" asked Trevor.

"Yeah."

"But it's not a dirty word, is it?"

"Nope."

"Is it tits?"

"Nope."

"Then it must be pussy."

"Yeah, that's right."

"So where is Willie hiding?"

"By the water."

"Upper or Lower Bittell?"

"Nope."

"Why do you want to know where my Willie is?"

"Willie and I got mixed up with Brian Steel and now he is mad at us." Said Trevor.

"I never liked that Steel lad. Bobby, tell the gentleman what he bloody wants to know, will ya!"

"Hopwood."

"Thanks Bobby."

"Do I get a pressie?"

"Yes you get a present, once we have found Willie."

"Better be quick because others are looking for him."

"Who?"

"Bazza and Dazza."

"Brian and Dave," whispered Trevor to James.

"Well, we had better be going if we are going to find Willie tonight. Thanks for your help, Mrs. Coates, and you, Bobby."

"Find the silly bugger and tell him to come home, his brother misses him." James nodded and shook Mrs. Coates's small plump hand.

Once they were in the covered walkway by the kitchen door, Trevor gave a deep sigh. "I'm going to move the truck around the front. You wait here and let me in when I knock on the door."

James stood by the locked door, which led onto the street. After what seemed like several hours, but only a few minutes in reality, the back garden door opened and a man about James's height and build entered, followed by a small woman. Both were in their early twenties. She was dressed in clothes that would not have looked out of place on a hot summer day. Goose bumps had appeared on her arms from the cold.

"Hello," said James.

"I'm Neil, Trevor's brother, and this is Michelle. Trev's putting his truck around the front, hopefully your stalker will follow."

"It all seems a bit odd to me," said Michelle.

"Think of it as one of Trevor's films. Remember."

"Yeah, I remember."

"Michelle, you stay here. I'm gonna see if the stalker took the bait." Neil left by the back door, and James gave Michelle a very weak smile.

"It's getting cold, my Mom reckons we're gonna have snow soon. Be nice for Christmas, won't it? I like that song."

"Which song?" asked James.

"You know... Err, 'I'm Wishing for a White Christmas.' Is it wishing? No, it's dreaming. Yeah, that's it: 'I'm Dreaming of a White Christmas.'"

"Err, yes, nice song."

Neil came back, a smile on his face. "It worked."

"Hey Neil, love, this bloke agrees with my Mom and thinks it's gonna snow." James just shrugged his shoulders. A knock came at the door leading to the road, and Michelle made a little squeal. James opened it and Trevor entered.

"You guys met?" Asked Trevor. James and Neil nodded.

"Okay, let's get into position. Wait about five minutes, and then you and Michelle leave. Make some noise so whoever is following us knows it's not us. James and I will sneak out the back garden to your truck parked in the alleyway. Hopefully he'll go down the alleyway once he realizes it's not us leaving via the front of the house and check to we if we are there. Then when he has lost us, he'll go to where Brian and Dave are," said Trevor.

"Let's hope so. Take care, Little Brother, and call if you need help. Be careful with my truck."

Trevor and Neil high-fived, James shook Neil's hand, and went into the back garden. Trevor stopped James from opening the garden gate, "I'll check no one is in the alley." He then opened the gate slowly, looking out into the alleyway. The woman with the yellow umbrella was there, walking away from them. Once she reached the road and had turned onto it, James and Trevor entered the alleyway and moved towards their car.

They drove down the alleyway with the headlights off, turning right at the top to go down the hill. Then Trevor suddenly stopped and made a U-turn, climbing back up the hill and parking under a street lamp, which wasn't working. They had just gotten into position when Trevor's truck sped out of Crowhurst Road and turned left, going down the other side of the hill. Trevor and James sank into the seats as the black Ford that had been following them came speeding out of the road. It suddenly stopped before turning into the alleyway behind the Coats house.

"Right so far," said Trevor.

The Ford re-emerged and turned out of the alleyway to follow the direction of Trevor's truck. James and Trevor followed at a safe distance. At each turn they held back long enough so as not to be seen.

Finally, the Ford pulled up outside a row of terraced houses.

The stalker ran into one of them. Trevor parked, looked up the road and pointed. Trevor's truck was parking a little way up the street.

"Neil must have been waiting and followed us." Said James.

"I told him to, my brother will stay close, just in case we need him and he can have his truck back."

"Why did he bring Michelle?"

"She sticks to him like glue, he doesn't seem to notice. A real pain she is."

The stalker appeared out of the house and was standing on the step talking to someone on his mobile. Trevor and James got out of the truck and hid behind a privet hedge before making their way up the garden path of the house next to the stalker. The stalker had sat down on the step and had his head bowed. The mobile was on the ground next to him. James picked up the mobile and placed it in his own pocket.

"Well, well, Philip Lewis," said Trevor.

"Hey man, is that you, Trev?"

"So why are you following us, Phil?"

"I'm not."

"Really! Well, we've just followed you, after you thought you'd lost us."

"Err, they said if I followed you and told them what you're doing, they'd give me some stuff."

"Stuff? You a druggie, Phil?"

"Yeah."

"But you were the brightest kid in our class! You went to university."

"Hey man, it doesn't always work out. I dropped out when I met this girl. She got me into it. But I can give it up when I want to."

"What did they tell you to do once you told them you had lost us?"

"Told me to get lost!"

"So you didn't get the stuff?"

"Oh, I got it, they left it in the house for me."

"You know where they are?"

"No. They just call me when they want me to do something."

"What about Willie Coates you know where he is?"

"They're looking for him," said Phil, continuing, "They think he is by Hopwood, but I've looked and he ain't there."

"So what happens now?"

"I get a blow and some sleep." Phil rose and opened the front door. As he stepped inside, he turned and said, "Don't tell them you saw me. I think they are at Brian's mother's house." He closed the door.

Trevor and James met up with Neil at the entrance to Phil's house.

"Any luck? Are Brian or Dave here?" asked Neil.

"Plenty. But I'm not sure what's the best thing to do next."

"I'll call home and see if Paul, my brother, can find out where Brian's mother lives. What's her last name?" asked James.

"Steel, I think," said Trevor.

"Okay guys, if you need anything else, just call. I'm going over to see Mom and Dad."

"Thanks Neil."

Neil drove by in his truck as James used his mobile to call Paul at home, but there was still no answer. Trevor called his parents. "Hi Dad, it worked. Yeah, we're gonna try and find Willie. We believe he knows where James's sister is. Okay, thanks." He closed the phone and gave it to James.

"They haven't called, I wonder why?" said Trevor.

"Did you and Willie ever have a place you always played in as kids?"

"Yes, 'the Grove.' We even built a tree house there."

"Let's go there we'll need a flashlight."

"I think I've got one in the truck."

"Let's go."

CHAPTER ELEVEN

The Max House

The orange glow of the lights of Birmingham illuminated the night sky, masking many of the stars. James and Trevor walked at a steady pace about twenty yards from where they had parked the truck.

Trevor had nervously checked the truck before leaving it, so that upon their return he could see if anyone had tampered with it. James had also done his own inspection, but not just of the truck. He had scouted the area around it, both convincing themselves that they were not paranoid. They walked in single file because the barley crop in the field grew very close to the hedge. The flashlight Trevor was carrying dimmed as the batteries lost power. "I should have stopped and bought better batteries."

"We'll manage," said James, trying to be positive and release the tension, which was building.

The Grove was a forty-foot-square piece of public land that had been used as a play area for generations of children and teenagers. It was stuck in the middle of three fields, much to the annoyance of the farmer.

Something moved in the thick-growing crop. Trevor stopped suddenly, and James walked into him. Trevor put his finger to his lips and pointed to a kit fox just ahead of them. The fox stopped, its ears erect, and then ran into the dense crop.

As they came level with a gate into the next field, two strong flashlights shone in their faces. "What ya doin' in my field?" said a deep voice with a Birmingham accent.

"Looking for my brother," replied James.

"Where?"

"In the Grove, of course. He's gone missing."

"When?"

"Tonight."

"I see."

"Mr. Bartlett?" said Trevor.

"Who's askin'?"

"It's me, Trevor Fisher."

"Well why didn't you say? This your friend that's lost his brother?"

"Yes, James."

"Is that all the light you boys got?"

"Yeah, the bloomin' batteries are dying."

"Here, borrow this big one, we've got two more in the bag." Mr. Bartlett's son Ronny passed Trevor a very powerful flashlight before disappearing back into the darkness.

"Thanks, Mr. Bartlett. What are you doing?"

"Trying to catch some kids who keep runnin' 'round here. You know sometimes they are naked. I can't have them runnin' through the crop, they'll ruin it."

"Well, if we see them up at the Grove, we'll give you a shout."

"Okay then, Trevor, now you take care. And I hope you find your brother, Jamie."

"James."

"Right Jamie."

As they passed, Mr. Bartlett remarked, "Odd that his parents call one son James and the other Jamie!"

They continued along the edge of the field, the new flashlights clearly showing them the narrow pathway. As they came close to the Grove, Trevor turned the light off. They stood still, their eyes growing accustomed to the darkness, and listened to the noise emanating from the Grove. Slowly they moved closer. At a broken gate, which led into the Grove, they could see the campfire of whoever was hiding out there. Tall dark trees grew close together on the triangular land, except for the small path and open oasis where the campfire was. The rest of the Grove was covered with bushes and shrubs. Climbing over the broken gate into the Grove, they could see several men and women sitting around the fire.

A young man in his early teens ran from behind some bushes, wearing only his underpants. A young girl, looking no older than sixteen in her bra and panties, screamed and ran after him. Seeing Trevor, she stopped.

"Hi ya, Trev, come to join the party?"

"Err, sort of."

"Cool." She began to run after the young man, who had come back to find out why she was not following him.

"Sarah, have you seen Willie Coates tonight?"

"He was here when we arrived, but as soon as some of the boys built the fire, he ran off. Right scared he was."

"Which way did he run?"

"Not sure."

"Thanks anyway."

"You not staying? I thought we could have a little fun like."

"No, we gotta find Willie."

"See ya then." She ran off into the Grove.

"He has flown the coop." Said James.

"Looks like it. So what's next?"

"Dave and Brian, I think—time to catch the rats. Who was the girl, Trevor?"

"Sarah. I went to school with her sister. She's the daughter of Bartlett, only thirteen, but you wouldn't think so to look at her."

"Right. I thought she was at least sixteen."

"Just like her sister. One big tease."

"You going to tell Mr. Bartlett?"

"Oh yes. She caused me so much trouble last year, I think it's pay-back time."

"What did she do?"

"Told the cops I was making pornographic movies."

"What happened?"

"They took all my tapes, and then when they found nothing, returned them. That's why Dad is funny about the film stuff."

"I see. Why did she do it?"

"She wanted to be in one of them with her boyfriend, and I said I didn't need her. She got real angry and told the cops out of spite."

The path seemed narrower on the return journey, James feeling the heads of the barley against his right hand. Farmer Bartlett appeared as they approached the gate into the next field. "Find your brother then, Jamie?"

"No, they said he'd run off when they arrived."

"Oh, there are people up there?"

"Yeah," said Trevor, "Your daughter Sarah is one of them."

"What, our Sarah? She be at home."

"No, she's there. We spoke to her. She was in the bushes messing about with some bloke in his underpants."

"Mike, Adam, and Ronny, get your things. We are going to rescue your sister from some pervert. I'm not having anyone touch my little girl. Thanks, Trevor."

"You're welcome, Mr. Bartlett." Mr. Bartlett and the three boys hurried up the path, the light from their flashlights illuminating half the field.

"I forgot to give back the flashlight."

"You can give it to him later," said James, thinking the may need it when they searched for his sister, wherever she was being kept.

Trevor and James continued down the path towards the road and the truck. As they approached the road, James stopped Trevor and they circled carefully around to see if anyone was waiting for them or was hiding nearby. Trevor, using the flashlight, checked the truck. All seemed clear as they climbed in. Once settled, Trevor looked around to see if there was any movement.

James's cell phone rang, "Yeah. Paul I need an address for Mrs. Steel. Local I think."

During the pause while Paul looked up the address, James tapped the pen on the dashboard. "Yes, that sounds like her, I'll tell you about it later." He closed the cell phone.

Trevor started the truck. "Where to?"

"Mrs. Steel's."

Arriving on the street, it took them a few minutes to find somewhere to park, which gave them the chance to observe the house without drawing too much attention to themselves. Trevor turned off the engine. The sound of an ambulance could be heard getting closer and closer. It turned the corner and stopped outside of Mrs. Steel's house. The door of the house opened and a slightly hysterical woman rushed out, screaming at them to hurry.

James and Trevor watched from the truck as neighbors emerged to see what had happened. The paramedics wheeled a stretcher up to the house and then took it inside. A young man with his arm around a younger girl leaned against Trevor's truck, but soon moved, because it was still hot from the drive. James joined a group of women who had gathered at the gate that led up to the house. Others gathered around the ambulance.

The paramedics wheeled the stretcher out of the house. A woman in her late sixties was lying on it. She was pale and very thin strands of her grey hair lay across her face. A blanket covered most of her frail body, making it difficult to see where she was hurt.

"It's Mrs. Steel," said a woman dressed in her nightgown and bathrobe, and wearing her husband's work boots. The throng watched in silence as the stretcher was wheeled down the path, behind it the hysterical woman, now being calmed by a paramedic carrying a small bag. The woman who'd announced it was Mrs. Steel pushed forward. "What's happened, Sylvia?"

"Our Brian stabbed Mom."

"Where is he?"

"Ran off, didn't he, with one of his mates to hide, but they'll catch the coward."

The paramedic loaded Sylvia's mother into the ambulance, helped Sylvia climb in, and then drove off, sirens blaring. James walked back to the truck. Trevor was standing on the pavement talking to an old man. "Sylvia, that's his sister, said Brian tried to kill his mother and her. I reckon the police will be after him now. He always was a bad lot ever since he was a kid. Should have been locked up years ago, if you ask me." Said the old man. He then slowly walked back to his house.

"So what really happened?"

"Like the old man said, Brian stabbed his mother; I don't know why. But now he is on the run."

"That's gonna make our life even more difficult." They climbed into the truck. "What now?"

"I suppose we should go back to the farm." Philip Lewis's mobile rang inside James's pocket.

"Shit, I forgot I had this," he said as he took it out of his pocket. "Should I answer it?"

Trevor took the phone from James and pressed the talk button. He spoke in a very low soft, drug-slurred voice. "Yeah, yeah, yeah, maybe at his dad's farm, yeah, okay man, the Max House, yeah got it." He handed the phone to James and pointed to the number still showing. James noted the number and then closed the mobile.

"What's happened?"

"They thought I was Phil. Wankers! I told them that we maybe at my Dad's place. They told me to watch, and if there was a problem, to go to the Max House."

"What's the Max House?"

"I don't know, but Phil must. Let's walk down to his place and ask him."

Phil's house was about one hundred yards down the road. They looked around as they made their way, making sure no one was looking or following. The door to Phil's home was still open. Trevor knocked, and after getting no answer, he went into the house. "Phil? Phil, are you here, man?"

The house was a mess, with clothes and garbage and weeks of unopened letters on the floor. They entered the living room. Phil was lying on the floor, a syringe sticking out of his left arm. James called 9-9-9 from Phil's mobile. "Ambulance, drug overdose."

Trevor had knelt down and lifted Phil's head. He searched for a pulse in the neck. "He is still breathing. Phil, Phil, it's me, Trevor."

Phil opened his eyes, trying to focus on whoever was talking. "Hey man, good stuff!"

"Yeah Phil, it looks it! Phil, where's the Max House?"

Phil fell back into a coma. Trevor laid his head on the floor and straddled him, gently slapping his face. "Phil! Wake up, Phil!" Once again Phil opened his eyes and looked at Trevor. "Phil, where is the Max House?"

"Nugguggger hursst."

"What?"

Phil sank back into a coma, and after a few slaps, Trevor gave up. He looked at James, hopeless. "That's it. We won't get any more out of him. Let's go before the cops and medics arrive."

Not wanting to go down the path from Phil's house, they crossed into the next-door garden, passing the front window. A family sat watching television, completely unaware that anyone was so close to their home. They continued along the path, which ran under the windows of the houses, before walking down to the road. The sound of the emergency vehicle's sirens became louder, and then the ambulance itself appeared, racing down the road. Trevor and James sat in the truck, watching the paramedics run into the house.

"What now?"

"I'll call Neil he used to hang around with Brian when they were younger. If anyone knows where Max's house is, he will." Trevor dialed the number, it rang and rang. The impatience on Trevor's face became very clear before finally someone answered.

"Hi, Big Brother. Things are going okay, but we need to ask you something. Do you know where Max lives?" He listened intently. "They said Max's house, Max House, something like that."

James stared out of the window and watched as the paramedics placed Phil into the ambulance. The neighbors had reappeared to enjoy the true-life drama unfolding in their street.

"Oh, thanks. Yeah, we'll call if we need help." He closed the phone and sat silently as the ambulance drove down the road. "It's not Max's house: it's the Max House, an old place on Nuthurst Road. It was a sort of half-way detention centre for kids. It has been closed for about ten years, and now it's the home to many a druggie."

As they turned onto Nuthurst Road, James became very apprehensive. "This could get very nasty."

"And it's getting darker."

"That's because it's going to rain."

"I know. But after what they did to Mom and Dad, it's war, and we are gonna win." He pulled the truck onto the side of the road and switched off the lights. They sat looking out into the stillness.

"How do we know they are here?"

"Look, there's Brian's car. And I think that blue one is Dave's. What do we do now? Set a trap?"

"I'm going to look around." James left the truck, keeping to the tall privet hedge as he moved from one house to the other. A covered passageway ran from the front to the back between two houses. It was unlit, and James ran down into the darkness, hoping his eyes would become accustomed to it. The back alleyway behind the houses, which ran the length of the street, was also unlit. James pressed himself against the brick wall of the house, looking to see if anyone was there. Not seeing anyone, he crept into the alley, and keeping to the wall, slowly walked towards the Max House. The garden was surrounded by a high wooden fence, which had fallen into disrepair. He squeezed through an opening and stood surveying the garden.

To his surprise, Brian was there, urinating against a post. James wondered if he had ever heard of toilets! His nostrils filled with the smell, but he dismissed it as being psychological, since he wasn't close enough to smell it. Brian was standing at the entrance to an underground bunker. The wooden door to it was open, and beneath that was a heavy iron grill designed to swing over and keep unwanted visitors from entering when no one was using it. Brian finished urinating and entered the bunker.

James furtively moved deeper into the garden, amazed at how big it was. He then made his way to the house. It was a big Victorian, which had been converted into a half-way house for teenagers. He looked into the various rooms on the ground floor.

Although the windows had been boarded up at some time, most had been ripped off and the windowpanes broken. Most of the rooms were empty, except for an odd garment left by some squatter. On the right side of the house, one window had been re-boarded. The board didn't quite cover the window, so it was possible for James to see inside. The boxes containing the prescription drugs that had been stored at Willie's, with their distinct markings, could clearly be seen pushed up against the window. "So this is where they had moved the drugs," thought James. Hearing a noise from somewhere in the back garden, James made his way back to Trevor's truck.

"You were gone a long time."

"Sorry. Brian was in the garden pissing."

"Figures."

"They are using some sort of World War II bunker, and they've stored the drugs inside the main house.

"Really? I wonder why they didn't put the drugs in the bunker."

"Right, that is strange."

"So what's next, James? We storm the battlements?"

"No. We have to get them out of the bunker so we can see if Anne is down there."

"So we need a diversion, and for them only one thing will work, if someone is stealing their drugs." Trevor dialed a number on his mobile. "Pig, is that you? Want some stuff?" James looked at Trevor, who grinned. "Max House."

"Right-hand side from the road," said James.

"Right-hand side from the road, on the ground floor..."

"Only window boarded up."

"Pig, it's the only window with a board on it. And you had better be quick, there's a ton of the stuff! Okay man." Trevor immediately dialed another number and repeated what he had told Pig. He did this several times, and became conscious that James was looking at him intently. "Problem?"

"No. It's just that you know so many people who are into drugs."

"How do you think I paid for all that equipment in my bedroom, farming?" They both laughed.

"Now we have to sit and wait. But not here, the cops check the streets around here. Let's move around the back into the alley so we can see the bunker."

"We'd better be very quiet." Trevor nodded and moved the truck into the back alley, making as little noise as possible. They could see the house and the entrance to the bunker from where they were parked.

"Don't tell me Mom and Dad how I paid for the equipment, will you? I don't want to upset them."

"I won't. We have all done things we wouldn't want our parents to know. And if this works out, I can put some work your way."

"Not weddings! Please, no weddings! I did a friend's and it was a nightmare. And they didn't appreciate it. I had multi cameras, and lights as well."

"Don't worry, it's not weddings. I need empty properties filmed."

"Why?"

"So my brothers don't have to look at properties I think we should buy. I can show them the video, and they can decide from that."

"Great! I might even find some new locations." Suddenly a figure dressed from head to toe in black ran past the truck. He stopped and peered into the garden of the Max House before running up the alleyway between the two houses and disappearing.

"Just like the white rabbit in *Alice in Wonderland*."

"More like a black ferret! Who was it?"

"I think it was Jazza. If it was him, then he's lost a lot of weight." They watched as another figure dressed in black, with a yellow-swoosh trademark on the clothes and shoes, appeared by the side of the house, then disappeared.

"Get ready, it's about to happen." Said Trevor. "They'll attack from all angles. I'll go and look in the bunker. Here's the key to the truck. When we get out, you hide somewhere in the garden so you can see what's happening. Once you've locked the truck, if you need to send me a warning, hit the alarm button on the key chain and scream, 'Police!' or something like that."

Trevor handed James the keys, then leaned back and stretched his left arm behind the passenger seat, producing a thick pole. "Protection. You don't know these guys. I do. And remember, if you think I'm in danger, hit the alarm button."

"Trevor, be careful."

Trevor nodded. They both quietly left the truck. James locked it and turned to Trevor, but he had already disappeared. James moved quickly into the back garden, hiding behind some bushes. He had a good view of both the house and the bunker. There was a ripping sound of wood being wrenched off a window, then of glass breaking. Out of nowhere, dark-clad figures ran from the right side of the house and then off in all directions, carrying the boxes and bags of drugs.

Dave was the first out of the bunker. "I fuckin' heard something." One of the thieves ran past him carrying a box of drugs. Dave screamed down into the bunker, "Brian, get up here they're pinching our junk!" Dave chased after the young man. Brian came out the bunker, and seeing Dave chasing the man, he started to run after Dave. Then he noticed another person carrying a box of drugs and began to chase after him.

Trevor went to the entrance of the bunker and descended into it. James became tense, his finger poised above the alarm button. He was so nervous he had to move his finger away from the button, as he almost set the alarm off several times.

Suddenly, Dave returned and was about to enter the bunker when a girl carrying two boxes of drugs ran across the back of the house. He gave chase, tripping on one of the boxes the girl had dropped, and fell to the ground. He staggered to his feet and continued to chase her.

James heard a noise behind him and froze, turning slowly to see who it was. A young man was climbing the fence, having left his bike leaning against Trevor's truck. The young man crossed towards the bunker and was about to enter it when Brian came around the side of the house carrying several boxes of drugs. Seeing the cyclist, he shouted, "Hey you!" The cyclist ran from the bunker towards the left side of the house. Brian dropped the boxes and ran after him.

James looked at his watch Trevor had been gone a long time. He fingered the keys, maybe he should press the alarm. He tried to stand up, as his legs were getting a little cramped from stooping for so long. A hand was suddenly placed gently on his shoulder. He didn't move, but turned slowly to see who was behind him. Trevor stood grinning at him and motioned that they should go to the truck. At the fence they stood still. The cyclist had returned and was removing his bike. Once he had gone, they moved quickly into the truck.

They sat in silence watching Brian and Dave, out of breath, gathering up the drugs that had been dropped by the many druggies. Dave pointed at the house and then at the bunker. Brian understood and started to carry the boxes of drugs down into the bunker. He was saying something to Dave, who ignored him and leaned against the back of the house, watching him.

"Your sister's not there. They've got a nifty setup, though. They could live for weeks down there."

"I wonder where they have her."

"I think they killed the estate agent."

"Why?"

"They have her handbag, and there are pictures of her lying on the floor, like she was when I found her, some with set-dressing and others without. Also, they had your sister's purse. Here." Trevor unzipped his jacket and gave Anne's purse to James. James opened it, her credit cards and bits and pieces were still there, but no money.

"It was like that when I found it."

James gave Trevor a disapproving look. "She never carried money. That's why we all call her 'Princess': because she thinks she's royalty, or at least like the Queen!"

James had only met Dave briefly, and now watched him leaning against the house. Like Brian, he was still wearing the clothes he had on at the biker house. He was a lot fatter than James remembered, and his hair had been shaved or burnt off. It was hard to see from where James sat, but it looked sort of fuzzy, the way hair goes when it's burnt or singed. They sat in silence, watching Brian move the boxes from the house into the bunker. He was getting more and more angry with Dave for not helping him. Trevor lowered the window so that they could hear what Brian was saying.

"Shit, man, help me, will ya?" Dave didn't say a word. Brian threw a box down the stairs of the bunker. "If ya not gonna do it, nor am I."

Dave stood up and looked at Brian. "Someone told them. The only person who knew about us and this place was Phil. I'm gonna kill him when I see him." Dave picked up a box Brian had dropped earlier and took it down into the bunker. Brian immediately went to the house and continued to move the boxes.

Soon, all the boxes had been moved from the house into the bunker. Brian and Dave sat at the top of the bunker talking, but it was hard for James and Trevor to hear what they were saying.

"You got Phil's phone?" James took it out of his pocket and handed it to Trevor, who turned it off.

Dave was on his mobile, pacing up and down. He tried a number several times before exploding. "Fuck, fuck, fuck, the bastard turned his phone off! I'll kill him when I see him. We'd better check the area. You do the front, and I'll check the back alley. Look into the cars to make sure no one is watchin' us."

Trevor and James slid out of the truck and climbed through a hole in the fence into the garden. They watched as Dave entered the alleyway and began checking the cars. Trevor tapped James on the shoulder and motioned towards the house. Keeping in the darkness of the bushes and trees, they moved closer to the house. Running across the small open space between the cover of the bushes and the house, they entered the house, climbing to the second floor. Looking from a front-room window onto the street, they watched as Brian checked the street and the cars. He tried the door on one car, and when it opened, he searched for something to steal.

Trevor moved to the back of the house. From there he could see Dave checking the cars and gates in the alleyway. Dave was a little more careful in his inspection. He double-checked one car to see if anyone one was inside, as the windows were tinted black.

James joined Trevor in the room. "Does Dave know your truck?"

"No, I don't think he has ever seen me in it."

Satisfied that no one was in the alleyway, Dave made his way back to the bunker. Brian was already there, sitting on the edge. The window in the upstairs room was broken, so James and Trevor, peering down into the garden, could clearly hear them talking below.

"Anything?"

"Na. Couple of cars open, but no one around. And you?"

"Nothing." Dave tried calling someone on his cell phone again. "Shit, still has his phone off!" Dave began to pace up and down again. This irritated Brian, who took a bottle of pills out of his pocket and swallowed a few. Dave stopped in front of him and held out his hand. Brian poured two pills into his hand, but Dave snatched at the bottle and emptied a few more before popping them into his mouth as though they were sweets. He took a small bottle of alcohol out of his pocket and drank some. Brian held out his hand, which Dave ignored, and when Brian made a grunting noise, Dave said, "Get ya own."

Trevor and James froze in their positions as they heard the noise of someone trying to enter the house below. Trevor watched as Dave stopped pacing and looked at the house. He had heard the noise too and ran to the house and pulled someone out into the garden. "Gotcha!"

It was a young man, about eighteen years old, wearing very baggy clothes with flower patches sewn on them. Dave punched the young man in the face he staggered back. Raising his arms in defense as Dave punched him again, the young man fell to the ground. Brian came over and kicked the young man in the stomach. They both laughed as the young man dragged himself to his feet, only to fall down again. Brian aimed a kick at the boy's stomach as though he were preparing for the winning try at a rugby match. The blow hit the youth squarely in the centre of his stomach. Whatever was in his stomach spewed out, just missing Brian's feet.

"Shit!" said Brian, jumping backwards out of the way. He bounced off Dave and fell to the ground. The young man took this opportunity to stagger to his feet and tried to leave. Dave aimed a kick at his backside, but he missed and landed flat on his back. Brian, still on the ground, began to laugh. Dave joined in. The young man staggered around the front of the house and escaped.

Trevor and James repositioned themselves by the window so that they could look down on the two men. "I wish they would go into the bunker," whispered James. Trevor nodded.

Dave got up and helped Brian to his feet, both still laughing. Brian ran down into the bunker and reappeared with a couple of beers. He handed one to Dave, who began to pace up and down again. "Call Phil again," said Brian. "I feel like beating the shit out of him."

Dave tried the number. "Nothin'."

"The batteries okay?"

"No, on the blink."

Brian took out several phones from his pocket and handed one to Dave. "Try this one." Dave tried again.

"He's got it off. I fuckin' told ya we shouldn't have given him that shit. He'll be out of his head." They sat down on the edge of the bunker, drinking the beers. The sound of a police siren brought them back to life. They checked around quickly before going down into the bunker.

Trevor and James watched. This was the moment they had been waiting for. Brian came out again, and facing the house, he urinated. Trevor turned away and mouthed to James, "Not again." James laughed silently. When Brian had finished, he ran down the stairs of the bunker, reappearing to close the heavy wooden door.

Trevor and James made their way down to the ground floor. They scanned the garden. The bunker door was still closed. The light which shone through the door crack went out. They moved quickly, and one on each side, they swung the iron grid over and into place pushing the locking bolt over. James sat on it so it couldn't be opened.

"We need something to lock it."

"Sit on it I have something in the truck." Said Trevor who ran to the truck.

He can back panting and produced a nut, bolt and spanner. He put the bolt through the hole a padlock would normally be placed and screwed the nut, locking the iron grid. James tried to open the iron grid, the nut and bolt made it impossible for Dave and Brian to get out.

They went back to the truck. Trevor opened Phil's cell phone. "Just in case they call. I don't want them calling someone else."

"Good thinking. Is there only one way out of the bunker?"

"Yeah, don't worry. Now we have to find your sister."

"Any idea?"

"No, but let's call the farm. And you call your parents, just in case she's turned up."

James called his parents' home, but it was still the answering machine.

Trevor was talking to his mother. "Okay Mom, speak to you soon, and don't worry." He closed the phone. "Nothing else has happened."

Phil's mobile rang. Trevor opened it and held it in such a way that both he and James could hear what was being said. "I've gotta take a piss and the fuckin' door won't open. The iron grid is over. Are you sure you didn't close it, ya moron? Phil, is that you, ya wanker?" It was Dave.

"Hey man," said Trevor in a druggie voice.

"Someone has closed the iron grid, and we're locked in the bunker. Phil, two things I need ya to do. Let us out of the bunker, but first go to the old substation. You know, the one by the school on Longbridge Lane. Untie the rope hanging by the door, and you'll find a lot of shit and money in an old bag. Bring it to me. You got that, Phil?" Trevor didn't answer.

"Phil, man, you got that?" shouted Dave into the mobile.

"Yeah, man."

"Good. When you've done that, get over to the Max House and let us out."

"Yeah, man."

"Yeah, bye," said Dave. He didn't switch the phone off, so Trevor and James continued to listen. "Once he's killed gyppo's sister, he'll try and get the drugs. If the floor gives way in the substation, he's dead. Shit! Then he can't get us out! I'll call again and tell him to get over here and let us out first."

"Why don't ya fuckin' call someone else?"

"Because I don't want to. We don't want too many people knowing we're here. Someone will talk and the pigs will come and then it's goodnight for us."

Trevor closed the phone, it rang immediately. He opened it. "Yeah?"

"Phil, come over to the Max House first and let us out."

"Yeah, man." Trevor closed the phone and switched it off. "Let's go and save your sister. By the way, is she pretty?"

"I don't know, she's my sister, and most of us think she's a right bitch."

"Sounds like my type of girl!"

They looked at each other and laughed

CHAPTER TWELVE

Finding Anne

The electrical substation had been built in the 1930s and was made to look like a house. The privet hedge around the front garden was overgrown and completely out of control. The garden gate now consisted of one vertical and two horizontal planks of wood hinged at the top. As James touched it, the gate collapsed noisily.

"Shush! We don't want to wake the neighbors."

"Sorry, but the owner doesn't keep his property up to the regulation standards!"

Trevor pushed past James into the garden. After the very wet summer, the ground was covered with lush green weeds and the occasional flower whose seed had flown into the garden and taken root. Standing in front of the imitation front door was a large metal sign. The lettering had faded and only read "Priv el p o."

"Let's find the way in. From what Dave said, the entrance is at the back, and it could be booby trapped."

"Yeah, we need to find another way in. It does look like a house-front from the outside."

"I know, clever. If the entrance is around the back, I reckon that's where we will find a window or something to climb inside."

The back of the substation had not been made to look like the front, and two metal doors with a chain and padlock on them were the only visible means of entry. A six-foot-high brick wall ran around the very small garden. Trevor shone Mr. Bartlett's flashlight on the back of the substation. There was an old tree, and one of its branches touched one of the real windows on the second floor.

"There, that branch. If we climb onto the wall, we should be able to crawl along it and reach the window."

Phil's mobile rang in Trevor's pocket. He took it out and opened it. "Yeah man, I'm here at the house. But hey! The doors are locked. What, climb the tree? I see the window. No man I can't see a window. What climb in and untie the rope? Okay man." Trevor listened. "What, you want me to come to the Max House first? But man, I'm here. I'll get the stuff, man I need the stuff and then I'll come right over. See ya man." Trevor closed the phone.

"Aren't you going to switch it off?"

"Not yet. We may need their help."

"So what's happening?"

"Dave wants me to go over the Max House and let him out."

"We're not going."

"No. I'll string him along about being inside the substation."

"If you think he will buy it."

"I know how they think, and if they were going to call someone else, they would have by now. They are scared someone will steal their drugs. You saw what happened when someone tried to."

Trevor climbed the tree, and once on the branch, quickly made his way to the building, suddenly disappearing. James wondered where he had gone. A moment of doubt entered his mind. Was this a trap?

Then, Trevor's head appeared as though hanging in the air. "You coming or what?"

James climbed the wall and then onto the branch. He hated heights, so he climbed along the branch very slowly, taking deep breaths and not looking down. Just under the eaves was a metal door about three feet high and two feet wide. When the place was built it had been a window then converted to a metal door. James climbed through the opening, a cautious feeling still hovering inside his head. Trevor was waiting for him, a big childlike smile on his face.

"Clever idea, that, you can't see it from the ground outside." Trevor shone the torch around the building. It was just a shell, which had housed an electrical substation at one time. They were standing on a gangway that ran all around the building, with large wooden beams running from the back to the front. Trevor shone the light on the floor of the building. It had collapsed into the basement, which was filled with water. Slowly, he searched for the rope Phil was told to untie. Just by the two metal doors, at the foot of a metal ladder that ran from the floor to the roof, there was indeed a rope. Trevor shone the light onto it and followed it up to the beams running across the roof. There was James's sister, Anne, with a brown cloth hood over her head.

She was standing on a wooden platform held in place by ropes. These ropes were connected to the main rope, which was in turn tied to the wall by the entrance. A wooden pole was connected to this and fixed to the metal entrance doors in such a way that, if you were to open the doors, the platform holding Anne would collapse and fall into the basement. Trevor walked around the catwalk to the wooden beam holding Anne. He shone the light up and looked at the ropes and the way they were tied.

"Oh shit!"

"What?"

"They've got a noose around her neck. If we let the platform down, she will be hanged."

"Anne, can you hear me?" shouted James. She didn't reply. A sudden thump made them both freeze and listen. Someone was outside trying to hit the metal doors. James retreated to the entrance on the gangway and looked out into the garden. He quickly returned to Trevor.

"A couple of druggies trying to get in."

"Let's move, then." Trevor carefully put his arm around the beam and lifted his weight off the gangway. Seconds later, there was a splashing sound from below. James shone the torch onto the opposite wall, where the wooden beam was fixed. The bricks and mortar had begun to crumble. The building was beginning disintegrate after years of neglect. Another enormous thud was heard from outside as the druggies tried to batter the door open.

"I'm gonna risk it. We have to." Trevor climbed onto the beam and edged himself along, the bricks and mortar meanwhile continuing to break up. He stopped every so often, hoping it would stabilize. Below, the druggies again attacked the door. Each time it jolted the platform on which Anne was standing as the ropes holding it in place loosened. Suddenly, the platform dropped a foot and Anne gave a little squeal.

Trevor continued edging himself along to where Anne was, stopping to make sure the platform was not moving. He finally arrived at a point just above her. She had fallen about eighteen inches. He leaned over and tried to undo the rope tied around the beam that held the platform. It was tight and very well tied. He leaned over and managed to get hold of the rope around Anne's neck. But just as he began to untie it, the druggies hit the door again and the platform fell a few more inches. James, watching from the gangway, began to jump from one foot to the other, becoming more anxious each time the druggies hit the door. Trevor leaned over and untied the rope around Anne's neck. Taking the rope, he tied it around her middle, but then he changed his mind and put it under her arms, squeezing through on each side, as her hands had been tied behind her back. Just as he was finishing, the druggies broke open the door and the platform began to drop even more, then suddenly gave way and fell crashing into the water below.

Anne dropped until the rope around her pulled her to a stop. She screamed out.

The druggies gave one hefty heave on the metal doors and they flew open. One druggie came in with the doors and fell into the water. "Hey man, it's a swimming pool!" he shouted.

"Bugger me, man," said the other druggie, who was peering into the substation. He began to take his clothes off, and once down to his boxer shorts, he jumped into the water.

Moonlight from outside now streamed into the place, and James could clearly see the predicament Anne and Trevor were in. Trevor pulled himself up on the beam and began to pull Anne up. The bricks and mortar continued to crumble. The beam fell and hit the top of the metal gangway. Trevor had to let the rope go, and Anne fell once again. James jumped up and down even more. Trevor once again started to pull Anne back up, stopping several times to catch his breath.

Below, the druggies were having fun in the filthy water. It was like watching children at a public swimming pool. The one who had fallen in had climbed onto the only remaining floor, removed all his clothes, and was preparing to dive into the water. James watched as he dived gracefully in. After a few seconds he didn't appear, but the other druggie didn't notice and continued to mess around in the water.

James went back to watching Trevor, who had finally succeeded in pulling Anne up. As soon as he could get a grip on her, he dragged her onto the beam. She lay there on her stomach, with his hand carefully placed on her back. Softly he whispered to her, "Keep still, I'll untie you in a moment, once I've caught my breath."

"Mappppa maaarrra," said Anne through the gag. James watched, feeling helpless. This stranger had just saved his sister. She may be the bitch of the family, but family she was. He felt inadequate.

Trevor began to untie Anne's hands. "Once your hands are free, don't move, just lie still." Anne did as she was asked. Trevor carefully helped her put a leg over the beam and straddle it. Her hands grabbed at the beam.

"Before I remove the hood from your head, I think you should know we are about thirty feet above a basement filled with water on a wooden beam. Do you understand?" Anne nodded her head. Trevor removed the hood from Anne. She looked at him and then saw James standing on the gangway, but to her he was just a dark figure.

Trevor took the tape off her mouth, peeling it carefully. "What took you so long, I've been stuck there for hours, who the hell are you?"

"I'm your knight in shining amour!"

"Oh, very funny. Who's that over there, my fairy godmother?"

"That's your brother."

"Which one?"

"James. But enough questions, my sweet damsel. I think we should get off this beam as quickly as possible."

"I think you need some help. I'm not your sweet damsel. I'm an independent woman who could kick your arse." Trevor smiled and made his way to the gangway. James helped him off the beam. Anne inched her way in a very unladylike straddle along the beam. When she reached the gangway, both James and Trevor helped her off. She gave James a punch. "Next time get here quicker. Who's your demented friend?"

"Anne, meet Trevor; Trevor, meet my sister Anne."

"A pleasure to meet you," said Trevor, blushing a vivid red.

"Under the circumstances, likewise. How did you know I was here?"

"It's a very long story, but I think we should get home first." Below, the body of the druggie that had dived into the water surfaced. The other druggie ignored it at first, but soon realized there was something wrong and went into a panic, splashing and beginning to scream and yell unintelligibly.

"Who's that?"

"We're not sure, but I think we should leave them to their little game." James took Anne's hand and led her towards the small open door. Trevor passed them and climbed through first, then helped Anne. James looked down and watched as the druggie dragged the body of his friend out of the water. The unconscious man had a very large cut to his head from hitting something hidden below the water.

James put one foot outside on the branch, the moment he did so, the beam Anne had been tied to gave way and fell crashing into the water taking most of the gangway with it. Standing on the branch he took a deep breath. He would only be happy when he had both feet on the ground. As he climbed down from the wall, Anne and Trevor watched the two druggies. The one was trying to give the other the kiss of life but kept passing out.

On their way back to the truck, Anne suddenly went weak at the knees, and both men had to help her. Trevor phoned the police on Phil's phone; "There's been an accident at the old substation in Longbridge Lane. I think someone may be dead." He switched off the phone and sank into the seat.

"Was he really dead?"

"I think so. It was hard to tell without checking."

"You need to get me home. I stink," said Anne.

"You okay to drive, Trevor?"

"Yeah. If I put what has just happened in one of my films, people wouldn't believe it was real!"

"Stop the chatter and get me home. You sound like a couple of lovers."

"Anne, shut up."

"Listen, Brother, you and your friend may have helped me get off the beam, but I was the one in danger, not you. I was the one who was going to get killed, and now I need a bath and some fresh clothes. So if you would put your small-talk on hold, I would be grateful."

Trevor turned and looked at Anne. "When James told me you were a real bitch and no one in the family liked you, I didn't believe him. You are not only a bitch, but ungrateful, possibly selfish as well. So if you want me to take you home, I suggest you shut that big mouth of yours, or I will stop the truck and throw you out."

They drove to James's parents' house in silence. Anne sat rigid in the seat, staring ahead, only moving when they arrived. Trevor turned off the engine. Paul opened the door, looking worried, and ran to the truck. "What's happened?"

"It's a long story. Put the kettle on and make some tea, and get a blanket for Anne."

"Why, what's happened to her? Another one of her dramas?"

Anne sank into a chair in the kitchen as Paul filled the kettle.

"Where's Mom?"

"She's over at Donnie's. Said she was going to stay the night."

"May be a good thing. I'd rather she didn't see this just now."

"So what happened?"

"Anne was kidnapped and held hostage, and we stupidly rescued her," said Trevor.

"Who by? I'm Paul, by the way. Thought you were joking, James, when you called earlier. Sorry."

"Well, it was true."

"So who kidnapped her?"

"Trevor, my name is Trevor…"

"Nice to meet you, Trevor."

"… and she was kidnapped by some real jerks."

"I think the same guys who murdered Elizabeth Friedman." Said James.

"And that's the next thing we have to prove. Brian and Dave killed her."

"Right, Trevor, but it's late, and I think we should go to my place. Clean up and sleep before we go back." Said James.

"Sounds good to me, but can I finish me tea first?"

"I still don't understand," said Paul.

"Paul, once this thing is over, I will explain everything, but for now could you look after Anne for us?"

"Okay. I never get any of the fun jobs!"

"That's because you're the baby," said Anne.

"How is Dad?"

"Still at the police station."

"I'd better call my parents to make sure they are okay." Trevor moved into the scullery to make his call.

"James, who is he?"

"A good friend who's suffered a lot."

"My knight in shining armour," said Anne.

"I think you should put Anne to bed. She seems delirious."

"No I'm not. At last I found a real man."

Trevor returned. "They are okay. I told them I was staying with you, and that we had rescued Anne."

"Thank God they haven't had any other problems. We'd better go."

Anne stood up, turned to Trevor, and gave him a kiss on the lips. She held him for a few seconds, until Paul coughed. "Thank you, Trevor, I hope to see you again, very soon."

"Err, me too," said Trevor, blushing.

"Let's go. This is like a bad movie!"

James and Trevor left the house. Trevor was embarrassed by what had just happened.

"What was all that about?"

"I think my sister may have found her match, and just fallen in love."

"With whom?"

"You."

"Me, why? I thought she hated me."

"Not any more. I think your outburst in the truck has turned her."

"Bloody hell."

They drove the rest of the journey in silence.

Arriving at James's apartment, Trevor seemed very tired, but James was still running on adrenaline and could have gone on for several more hours. He knew some sleep would refresh them and get them ready for the next step. He opened the door to the apartment gingerly, expecting something or someone to jump out. He let Trevor pass and enter the living room while he examined the bedroom, kneeling down to look under the bed. Nothing was there. Then he checked the bathroom that too was clear.

When he returned to the living room, Trevor had taken off his shoes and was lying on the sofa, asleep. James smiled. Trevor looked so innocent.

James took a blanket from the chest near the front door and draped it over Trevor. Switching off the living room light, he entered the kitchen. He fancied a cup of tea, but didn't feel like making it. He grabbed a glass from the cupboard and filled it with ice-cold water from the refrigerator.

Entering the bedroom, he debated whether to close the bedroom door. In the end he didn't close it, but left it ajar. Taking off his clothes, he unconsciously put on a pair of pajamas and sat on the edge of the bed, his elbows resting on his knees and his head resting in his cupped hands. He gave a long deep sigh. It wasn't over yet, and he wasn't looking forward to the next day. Somehow they had to get Brian and Dave to confess on tape that they had murdered Elizabeth. He lay back on the bed, switching off the bedside light, with his thoughts on how they were going to get that confession. Falling into a deep sleep.

The early light of another gray day spilled into the bedroom as James awoke. He wasn't sure where he was at first, but soon his thoughts cleared and he remembered everything. He went to the window and opened the curtains. It had rained again during the night. He gathered some fresh clothes and took a shower, washing himself several times as though he was trying to rid himself of the dreadful events that had taken place. Refreshed, he went into the living room to wake Trevor. The sofa was empty, and the blanket lay neatly folded. James looked around. There was no note or any sign to say where Trevor had gone.

James picked up the phone and started dialing the farmhouse number but then paused before entering the last digit. He switched off the phone and replaced it in the cradle. Trevor had gone, and it was up to him, James Pidgley, to finish the job. He didn't relish the thought. Making himself a pot of tea, he sat in the kitchen waiting for it to brew. If his mother would have seen him doing this, she would have made fun of him: "A watched pot never brews!" she would say.

A bell rang, and James picked up the phone. "Hello?" Then he realized it was the doorbell, and laughed at his mistake. He opened the door a little and peered out to see who was there. Trevor stood on the doormat with a big grin on his face. He had a pile of clothes in one hand and a big carrier bag in the other. James opened the door wide. "I thought you'd given up!"

"No way, man! I just went home to get some fresh clothes, and Mom cooked up some breakfast. If you don't mind, I'll take a shower here. Yours is so much better than the one at home."

"Sure, that's fine. How do you know mine is better?"

"I tried it this morning, ours just trickles." Trevor handed him the carrier bag and went into the bathroom. James noticed he didn't lock the door. Trust between them had begun.

In the kitchen, James opened the brown bag Irene Fisher had sent. Inside was scrambled eggs, bacon, and sausage, with a pile of French toast. He placed the food into the oven to keep warm, and after laying the table and pouring himself another cup of tea, James sat and made a list of things he felt they should do. Once Trevor had showered and they had eaten breakfast, James produced his list. "I've been thinking."

"A dangerous thing, that."

"What?"

"Thinking. You never know where it will lead you."

"Trevor, be serious! We need a plan on how to get them to confess."

"Do you have a tape recorder, a hand-held one?"

"Yes, it's a Sony."

"The make is immaterial, as long as it works and we have plenty of tape and batteries."

"We should pack some food and water or tea."

"I put Phil's mobile on charge this morning before I went home. I think we may need it."

"I never thought of that."

"Well, that's it, you're the beauty, I'm the brains!" They both laughed. "Mom said we will need a jacket or coat. It rained last night, pouring down it was. The farmyard is water logged, and there is supposed to be more today."

"What else?"

"We need a back-up plan, and I've talked to our Neil. He said he would be over if we need him. According to him he thinks we should make them sweat a little. Dave hates not to be in control, and will say anything if he thinks it will get him what he wants."

"How does the bunker get fresh air?"

"There's a flue that comes up in the bushes. It's painted brown, so most people don't see it. We could smoke a confession out of them."

"True. But wouldn't that bring others who saw the smoke? We need something a little more subtle."

"Right. By the way, I heard on the radio the druggie died. The police are calling it an accident."

"I wonder if Brian and Dave have a radio? I feel bad about that guy dying."

"Why? He was a stupid druggie. He got what he paid for. That's life. Or in his case, death."

They looked at each other, then away and back at each other. James broke the silence; "I wish I knew how we were going to get them to confess."

"Hey man, Phil here," said Trevor in his most spaced-out voice.

James laughed. "Do you think it will work?"

"Leave it to me. I'll do all the talking."

"Let's hope it does. All we have to do is get them to confess, call the cops, and give them the tape."

"Make a copy first."

"Very good idea. Mind you, the police have enough to keep them busy, with all the drugs in the bunker."

"You collect what we need, and I'll wash up."

James began to collect the things together, the tape recorder and tapes first. By the time he had gathered everything, Trevor had finished washing up the dishes and cleaning up the kitchen. "You have a nice place. I've often thought about a place of my own. The trouble is, it costs so much."

"That depends. When this is over, we will talk about it, if you like."

"Hey, that's right. Your family has places to rent, don't they? But then there's Mom and Dad. I think they need me."

"Let's get going."

They piled into the truck, and as they were backing out, James suddenly shouted, "Stop! I've forgotten something." He jumped out of the truck and ran past the street entrance to the apartment, but continued up the side of the building towards the back, returning moments later with a box. He placed it into the back of the truck and climbed into the front.

It was still quite early, so there wasn't much traffic going in their direction. "I wasn't being nasty about the kid dying. But when you've seen as much drugs as I have, you realize that people have the choice to take them and suffer the consequences or go straight."

"Trevor, I understand. I think it's such as waste of life, that's all."

"Well, if he wasn't killed by drugs, he would probably end up in jail."

"Another waste." They reached the Max House.

"I'll circle around to see if anything has changed." Brian and Dave's cars were still parked in the same places, and the front of the Max House looked the same. Trevor drove slowly into the alleyway at the back. He parked the truck and they looked about, seeing if anything had changed or seemed wrong.

"Looks the same to me, but I'll just check to be safe. You prepare the tape recorder." Trevor left the truck. James watched him walk up the alleyway, checking on all the cars and the entrances to the other homes. He disappeared into the alleyway between the two houses. Moment's later, James saw him looking around the Max House. He carefully approached the bunker and then returned to the truck.

"Everything looks okay. I think they are still in the bunker."

"Let's hope so."

Trevor took out Phil's mobile and opened it. "We just have to wait for them to call, let's hope they aren't too long."

It had begun to rain lightly. Trevor pulled the hood of his jacket up. "Good job I brought this." James took a woolen hat out of his pocket and pulled it on his head, covering his ears. They had only been waiting for about ten minutes when the phone rang. Trevor let it ring several times before he answered it. "Yeah," he said in Phil voice.

"Where the fuck are ya, man?" asked Dave.

"I'm here, man. Where are you?"

"In the fuckin' bunker."

"Right man."

"So where are you, for crying out loud?"

"I'm at my house."

"Really! Well, we're stuck in the bunker in the back of the Max House, so come over here and open the iron grid and let us out, ya moron."

"Okay man, but I need to do some stuff first." Trevor closed the phone. "It'll take about fifteen minutes to walk from Phil's house, so we'll give them at least thirty-five. No need to rush."

"At least we know they're still in the bunker."

"I told you there was only one way out." The light rain became heavy, and the gentle pitter-patter on the roof of the truck became louder and heavier, like the drums of a military parade.

"Down!" shouted Trevor. They both slid down in the truck as a police car drove down the alleyway, checking the area. It stopped a few yards up and an officer got out. He climbed through the fence of the Max House and ran towards the house, disappearing through one of the open doors.

Trevor turned off Phil's mobile and peered over the steering wheel at the police car. "Can you see him?"

"He went into the Max House."

"What for?"

"I don't know, but let's hope he isn't long." They could hear the squawking of the police radio, and still the policeman didn't reappear.

"Shit. I don't think I can take much more of this."

Trevor again peered over the steering wheel. "Patience, my friend. After last night, nothing will ever scare me again."

"Thanks for saving my sister."

"She's cute."

"No, she's not! She a real bitch, as you well know."

"Well, I think I like her. She's got determination a woman with spirit."

"You need your head examined."

"Shush, he's coming out with a woman and they're kissing, dirty bugger!" The policeman kissed the woman and watched her go around the front of the building. Then he returned to the police car, not looking at the bunker as he passed it. He sat in his patrol car for a moment, speaking on the car radio, before driving off.

"He won't be around again. He's had what he wanted from this area."

"Yeah, well, let's hope you're right."

"I usually am."

"Modest, too."

"Of course. If I don't blow my own trumpet, who will?"

"Anne."

"No, she will have forgotten me by tomorrow."

"Trevor, I told you she is an argumentative, stubborn, selfish bitch."

"Maybe now, but when I've finished with her…"

"If you get a chance. Okay, are you ready for this? The rain has eased up a little, so we should go now."

James carried the small black bag holding the tape recorder and other equipment. They climbed through the fence and crossed the garden. As they approached the bunker, Trevor opened Phil's mobile. James went to the hinge side of the iron grid so he couldn't be seen. Trevor had moved to the other side, but didn't get too close. James took out the tape recorder and fixed the microphone to it. He then passed the microphone to Trevor, who fixed it so it hung from the grid above where he thought Brian or Dave would speak to him.

Phil's mobile rang and made Trevor jump. He dropped it into the long wet grass and took a few seconds to find it. "Shit, it's wet." He walked towards the house, cleaning off the moisture. The phone continued to ring.

CHAPTER THIRTEEN

Get A Crowbar

Trevor let the phone ring several more times before he answered it.

"Yeah?" he said, in the 'Phil' voice.

"Where the fuck are ya, man?" screamed Dave.

"Here at the Max House. Where are you?"

"Down in the bunker. I gonna kill that moron when I get hold of him."

"Why are ya gonna kill me, man? What have I done?"

"Phil, open the iron grid on the bunker, will ya? Shit, he really is thick."

Trevor switched off the mobile, stood up, and walked around the bunker until he came to the lock side again. The door of the bunker opened about half an inch as it pushed against the iron grid.

"Phil, pull the iron grid open so we can get out," said Brian, who had squeezed his fingers through the tiny gap.

"I can't."

"Why the fuck not."

"It's got a sort of lock on it."

"What?" screamed Dave. "He said it's got a lock on it."

"Who put the lock on?"

"I don't know."

"Ask him, you moron."

"Phil, who put the lock on?"

"I dunno. Someone, I suppose."

"He said someone put a lock on it."

"I heard him. Shit, you're as bad as him! Tell him to unlock it."

"Hey Phil, unlock it."

"I can't."

"Why not?"

"I don't know how too."

"Do you know how to undo it."

"Shit, I'm working with two of the dumbest morons in the world! Who put the lock on it?"

"Phil, did you put the lock on it?"

"No."

"Then who did?"

"There was a copper here when I arrived, that's why it took me so long. Maybe he put it on."

"Shit! Phil, you're gonna have to go to my car and get a crowbar out of the boot. You got that?" said Dave

"Yeah, which is your car?"

"It's the blue one, remember? The one you threw up in."

"Oh yeah, that one. Where are the keys?"

"It's open. I never lock it. Who's gonna steal an old wreck?"

"Terry Butcher—he'll pinch anything."

"Phil, just get the crowbar."

"Okay man, I'll be back. Now don't you go anywhere."

Trevor indicated to James to follow, and they moved to the side of the house, out of earshot. "You stay and listen to what they are saying, I'll get the crowbar." James returned to his listening post. He had difficulty with the headset and removed his woolen hat, put the headset on, and replaced the hat.

"Look, when the moron returns and opens the grid, we'll drag him down here and beat the shit out of him."

"Ya don't think he put the lock on, do ya?"

"Brian, get real! The guy is too out of his head to know what he's doing."

Trevor returned, carrying a crowbar. He stood next to James and put on the second headset to listen to what they were saying.

"Did he say if he killed the Gyppo's sister or not?"

"He must have killed her. That's why I was trying to listen to the radio although the reception down here was useless. The radio report said someone had died in an electrical substation last night, but I can't remember who they said it was."

Trevor moved to the other side of the bunker door, bent down, and knocked on it. "Hey man, which is your car again?"

"Oh bollocks! It's the blue Toyota. It's parked outside the house next door."

"Right man, I'm going. What am I getting again?"

Together, Dave and Brian screamed, "A crowbar!"

"Oh yeah, bye then." Trevor returned to James, replacing the headset.

"He really is stupid. Why do I have to have such morons as partners?" A car alarm went off in the street. "What!" said Dave, who then hit the door with his fist. "If he brings the cops here, I'll kill him in front of them."

Trevor returned to the other side of the grid, carrying the crowbar. "Got it, man. I went to the wrong car."

"We know. Hey, Phil, did ya kill a girl?"

"What girl?"

"The one at the substation."

Trevor looked at James, who put a finger to his lips.

"Did he kill her?"

"He didn't say."

"Phil, it's me, Dave. Did a girl die at the substation last night?"

"Yeah."

"Did you kill her?"

"Sorta."

"What ya mean, 'sorta'?"

Trevor looked at James, who nodded and mouthed, 'Go for it'. "Well, when I broke open the door, she sorta somehow got hung."

"Really?" said Dave in a sarcastic tone.

"Yeah man, it was real bad. I didn't mean to do it."

"But you murdered her."

"I didn't mean to, man. You won't tell the cops, will ya?"

"But ya did, and now the cops are looking for ya, and they're gonna getcha."

"Shit! I betta go and hide."

"'I betta go and hide,'" mimicked Dave in a whining voice.

"What am I gonna do?" said Trevor in the Phil voice.

"Open the grid first and let us out, and maybe we can help ya."

"But you told me to go and kill the girl."

"We didn't tell ya to kill her, we told ya to let her out."

"No, you told me to kill her."

"Oh, Phil. That was the drugs talking."

"Man!"

"Phil, just please open the iron gird and let us out, and we gonna help ya."

"How do I know that? Ya said ya gonna kill me, and now ya saying I murdered the girl, when I know ya told me to."

"Phil, don't worry. Ya one of us, we're gonna help you."

"I don't know…"

"Phil, it's Dave. Now you are my oldest and best friend. We've known each other almost all our lives. Right, man?"

"Yeah."

"I thought I was ya best friend!"

"Brian, shut the fuck up! I'm trying to be diplomatic and get the moron to open the grid."

"When you get us out, Phil, I'll give you all the drugs you ever need, and Brian will give you an alibi, so ya don't have to worry about a thing. Now open the friggin' grid."

"But you said you were gonna kill me, Dave, and you keep calling me a moron, and I'm not, man. I finished school. Had a job once, too."

"'I had a job once,'" mimicked Dave. "Phil, you had a job in a greengrocers until the owner found you making out with a melon."

"I was bored."

"Fuckin' perverted, more like. Now open the bloody grid."

It began to rain. James placed some plastic he'd brought over the microphone and another piece over the tape recorder. He pulled the collar of his coat up high to protect himself from the rain. Trevor started to hit the grid with the crowbar.

"What ya doin' now?" shouted Dave, with frustration in his voice.

"I'm gonna have to think this thing out. You lied to me before, Dave, and I ended up in prison for you."

"That's history, Phil. We all have a new life now, and once you get us out of here, I'll make sure we will always look after you as though you are family. How's that sound, Phil?"

"It's starting to piss down. I'm gonna get out of the rain and think."

"Phil, Phil, there's a new coat in my car boot. You can use that. Shit, it's locked! Dave, move and I'll pass him the keys."

"Why is ya car locked?"

"Too many thieves around, and I have all that stuff in it."

The bunker door strained against the iron grid as Brian pushed the keys out. Trevor took them and then stood on the edge of the wooden door through the iron grid, trapping Brian's fingers. Brian gave out a scream.

"Okay man, I'll get the coat, but I'm still gonna have to think this thing out." Trevor walked to James's side of the grid and indicated that he would go to the car and see what was inside it. James continued to listen to Brian and Dave.

Trevor found Brian's red car and unlocked the passenger door. It smelt of cigarettes and stale beer. On the dashboard was a piece of paper, which Trevor placed in the plastic bag if found on the floor of the car. He closed the door and went to the boot. He had a little difficulty opening it, but inside was an Aladdin's cave full of new clothes, some with the shop tag still on them, and underneath tapes, records, video cameras, and other electronic goods. He found a small black notebook with a zip around it. Trevor placed it in the bag, along with a video camera and some tapes. At the side, he found three umbrellas, still with the store electronic tags on them. He heard a man cough behind him. He quickly closed the trunk and locked it. The man passed with his head down, holding a newspaper over it to try and keep dry. The newspaper had begun to sag from the rain.

James was surprised to see Trevor return with umbrellas. Trevor handed him two and the plastic bag before returning to the other side of the grid. James made a small tent out of the umbrellas and began to look at the things in the plastic bag. The paper from the dashboard was a drawing of the substation, with notes on the way Anne had been tied up and how the noose around her neck worked. James shuddered as he looked at it. The notebook seemed new, and after unzipping it, James was surprised at the amount of information written in it. Phone numbers of drug contacts and dates when shipments were due, along with many other crimes Dave and Brian were obviously involved in.

Trevor and James both jumped as Brian hit the bunker door and shouted. "Phil, Phil, are you there?"

Trevor hit the iron grid. "Yeah man, I'm here, and I don't feel too good. It's raining a lot."

"Did ya get the coat?"

"Na, but I found an umbrella."

"Good, now open the grid, will ya, Phil?"

James suddenly waved to catch Trevor's attention. Trevor crossed to the other side of the grid to see what James was so excited about. It was a description of some of the things Dave and Brian had done and of how they were going to make Phil take the blame.

Trevor read the next few pages, closed the notebook using his finger as a bookmark, and returned to the other side of the grid. "Hey man, I found this notebook."

"What notebook?" screamed Dave.

"It was in Brian's car, and it says here that you were gonna blame all the shit you guys have done on me."

"What's he talking about?"

"It's me notebook, so I don't forget things when you've told me to do something. You know, like a diary."

"You moron. You wrote everything down?"

"Yeah. It's nothing, Phil, it's nothing. Man, don't worry about it."

"Don't worry about it! The moron up there now knows what we've been doing because you wrote it down and gave it to him, you stupid fuckin' idiot."

"I didn't give it to him. He found it in the car."

"It's as good as giving it to him."

"It says here that ya robbed some old lady in Edenhurst Road and ya left my watch there, the one I gave ya to hold for the drugs until I could get the money together."

"No, no, Phil. Oh shit!"

"Phil, this is Dave. I knew nothing about this. And once I get out of here, I'm gonna kill this moron. Then you and I are gonna do everything together. So Phil, get the lock off and let me out."

Trevor had continued to read the notebook. "Oh man, you bastards were gonna stitch me up again. I should just let you rot down there."

"No, Phil. Look man, we're sorry, but that's how things are. But from now on you and me are partners, right?"

"Yeah, right, and pigs fly!"

"No, really, Phil, come on open the grid."

"I need some stuff and time to think."

Trevor joined James, who had motioned him over to the house. They sat under the small porch by one of the doors. James produced some cake, biscuits, and bottled water, and they sat in silence, eating.

"Where did this food come from?"

"I put in the box from my house."

"Listen to this. They say they killed Elizabeth and were going to make Phil take the blame. They really are dumb, putting all this in writing."

"Just like the guys in Los Angeles who took a video of themselves shooting paint balls at people and left it around for the cops to find! In the old days, according to my Dad, they would just boast about their exploits. Today they film them, and some even put them on the Internet. Now that's dumb."

"Okay, what's next? They're becoming desperate, but not enough to confess."

"I think it's time for the water torture."

"What's that?"

"I'll be back." James left the garden and went to the truck, taking the box he had placed on the flat bed. He returned and set it down next to Trevor, who opened the lid.

"Brilliant." Inside the box was a hosepipe, curled up like a snake.

"We'll connect the hose to the standing pipe over there, put the other end down the air pipe, and just let the water—slowly, at first—run down into the bunker."

"It'll take several hours to fill the bunker, but I think Dave is ready to snap, so we might not have to wait that long." James connected the hosepipe to the standing pipe and tested it. The water gushed out. "Not too much at first," said Trevor.

Creeping over to where the air pipe came out of the ground, James had difficulty finding it, as the vent really looked like a small tree trunk. He carefully and silently pushed the end of the hose down the vent, then signaled to Trevor, who turned on the water. They returned to their position above the bunker entrance. Trevor hit the iron grid with the crowbar. Brian was at the door listening for him.

"Ya back, Phil?"

"Yeah, man, I needed some stuff to get my head straight."

"Right just open the grid and I'll make sure you get what ya want, and I won't let Dave hurt ya, Phil." Before Trevor could answer, he heard Dave calling to Brian from somewhere inside the bunker. "Dave's calling me, Phil. You stay there and I'll be right back."

James moved quickly over to the air vent and put his ear to it. He could just hear Dave: "There's fuckin' water pouring in here, man. If we don't get out of here, were gonna drown. Now get that moron to open the grid."

"What shall I say?"

"Just tell him anything and get him to open the grid before I kill you."

"Okay man, calm down."

Brian returned to the door of the bunker. "Phil, are ya there man?"

Trevor giggled as James whispered in his ear what Dave had said. "Yeah," he answered.

"Phil, listen man, what's the problem? Why won't you open the grid for us?"

"I'll open it, but I need to know what's going on."

"Nothing's going on, man. Dave and me have got locked down here, that's all."

"Why?"

"Why what?"

"Why did you get locked down there?"

"Oh man, someone locked the grid, and we need you to open it."

"Yeah, but what about the other stuff?"

"What other stuff?"

"Ya know. The things ya did and ya gonna blame me for."

James went over to the standpipe and slowly increased the water flow. "Phil, it must be pissing it down out there."

"Yeah, I'm getting wet, and the garden's already flooded, man. I've got to go home for me tea and get some dry clothes."

"No, no, Phil. Let us out first, and we'll drive you home."

"It's okay man, I can walk. I'm already wet."

"What's wrong now?" asked Dave.

"He's going home for his tea."

"What! Just tell that fuckin' moron that if he doesn't open the grid now, I'll kill him when I do get out."

"Hey Phil, just open the grid."

"No, not until Dave stops saying he's gonna kill me. I'm going for me tea."

"Shit, man, you and your mouth! I was getting to him until you started saying ya gonna kill him."

"Well maybe I should kill both of you. We really fucked up this one."

Trevor rose and walked over to the porch. The rain had increased a little, and he was getting very wet and cold. "Okay, we'll turn the water up and give them about half an hour. Then we'll go back for the kill, so to speak."

James turned the water up. Trevor sat and read some more of the notebook. "It says here they killed Elizabeth and set me up, but something went wrong. I wonder what that could be?"

"Willie was there."

"Yes. And that's why he has gone into hiding. I reckon he is scared out of his wits."

"We need to find him."

"You remember about a month ago, there was a petrol station attendant who was mugged?"

"Vaguely."

"They did it. We must give this to the police."

"Only if it doesn't incriminate you and the others."

"Brian calls us by our street names—well, the ones he invented."

"What was yours?"

"Farmboy."

"And Willie's?"

"The Locksmith or Lockie."

"What about Dave's."

"Are you ready for this? Mr. Big!"

"Is there anywhere in the book that gives the real names? And Brian's street name?"

"Yes, here at the back."

"Take that page out." Trevor ripped the page out and handed it to James, who folded it and put it in his back pocket. "What was Brian's street name?"

"Slick."

"Figures."

Trevor returned to the notebook. "There's a piece about you here."

"Me? What's it say? And do I have a street name?"

"Yep, you're the Gyppo. Sorry about that."

"Hey, don't worry about it, I've been called worse! So what's it say?"

"That you went to Dave's house about your car and made a pass at Dave's wife."

"Half true. Brian had stolen it! And I met Dave's wife in the clubhouse."

"I wonder where she is, and the kid. You don't think they…?"

"No. She's probably gone to her mother's or something. Well, let's hope so."

"How long has it been?"

Trevor looked at his watch. "Fifteen minutes. Doesn't time go slow when you're having fun? Where's your watch?"

"At home. I forgot it."

"It says here," said Trevor, pointing to a page, "They sell the drugs to virtually everyone in the district. It gives names and phone numbers, including cell. Wow, I know her. I went to school with her. She was hot." They sat in silence and looked out at the rain, which had become quite heavy. Someone entered the garden by the alleyway.

James stood up. A young boy approached he nodded to Trevor, but eyed James suspiciously. "You got anything, man?" Without looking at the boy, Trevor replied, "Later." The boy nodded and left the same way.

"How old was he?"

"About ten. Listen, I've seen eight-year-olds hooked on speed, and their parents don't notice. Brian, Dave and others start pushing when they're young, then they've got them for life—however short that will be."

"If we only get them put away for the drugs, we'll save a lot of lives."

"Don't kid yourself. Once Brian and Dave have gone, another ten dealers will step in and take their place."

A smartly dressed woman in her thirties came around the corner of the house. She smiled at James but approached Trevor, who was still sitting on the floor. Before she had chance to speak, Trevor said, "Later." The woman continued walking and disappeared around the front of the house.

Trevor looked at his watch, "Two thirty-five we need to move. The kids from the infant school will be out soon, and everyone will come by here looking for some stuff." Trevor and James repositioned themselves by the bunker. James changed the tape in the recorder and checked the batteries. Trevor hit the grid.

"Phil, is that you?" asked Dave in a very desperate voice.

"Yeah, man it's pissing down out here."

"Look ,man, I'm sorry for what we did to ya, but I promise we'll put it right if you get us out of here. The water's already a foot deep."

"Okay, I'm gonna let you out. But first, it said in the book you killed that woman."

"What woman? No, we didn't kill any woman."

"But in the book it says ya did."

"Brian, get the fuck over here and talk to this moron. He's been reading that book of yours."

"Hey Phil, how ya doing?"

"Okay, man. It's a bit wet."

"Down here too so what's the problem?"

"In the book, ya said you killed a woman, and Farmboy was to take the blame."

"I didn't kill her Dave did."

"What the fuck are you telling him?"

"The truth, man. If we don't, he ain't gonna let us out, and we're gonna drown."

"Shit man, ya gonna get us hung."

"They don't hang anymore. Phil, listen, let us out and I'll tell you the whole story."

"Tell me first. Then I've got something on you."

"That's fair. So let me begin at the beginning."

"Fuck man, this is not children's hour!" shouted Dave.

Brian ignored the comment and continued,

"As you know, we stored the drugs at Number

Thirteen Crowhurst Road. Willie said it would be safe there. That was until the Gyppo started poking around."

"Right. So where does the woman come into it?"

"She was the one selling the house to the Gyppo. Dave, me, and Willie had gone over to the house to see if the drugs were still okay and work out when we were gonna move them. When she came in and caught me in the kitchen, I told her I was looking for a place to sleep for the night. She said she was going to call the cops."

"Right, so who murdered her?"

"Dave did. He came up behind her in the kitchen and hit her over the head. We cleaned the drugs out and moved them over to Willie's place. His mom weren't half angry about it. Then we left the house and her lying on the kitchen floor."

"Where's Willie now?"

"I don't know, man. But, knowing him, he went to the Gyppo and Farmboy. But if we gonna go down, we are gonna sink both Willie and Farmboy."

"What ya gonna do to them?"

"I don't know, but Dave has something hidden in a bag somewhere."

"What about me?"

"Shit, Phil, I keep telling ya let us out and we'll look after ya."

"Okay, I'll get the crowbar."

"He's gonna let us out. I told ya tell him the truth, and he'll do anything I ask."

James and Trevor removed the microphone and tape recorder. They stood under the porch and replayed a little of the tape: "And hit her over the head. We cleaned…"

"Okay we must gather everything up and put it in the truck, then call the cops before any kids arrive and let them out."

James turned the water off and rolled up the hosepipe, collected the umbrellas, and together with Trevor, took them back to the truck.

"You call. I've never snitched," said Trevor, handing James Phil's mobile.

James dialled 9–9-9. "Hello. If you go to Nuthurst Road at the corner of Longbridge Lane, used to be the Max House, you'll find a couple of drug dealers with all their drugs locked in the old World War II bunker in the back garden. You'll need a spanner. Yeah, my name is Brian Steel. I'd be quick, before someone lets them out."

James closed the phone and switched it off.

"Okay, let's move from here and find a place we can watch what happens. I think if we climb that ridge, we should be able to see what's going on." Trevor and James drove up the small lane to the top of the ridge. It was just possible to see the back garden and the bunker from there, but the rain had made it a little dull, so the view was not as clear as they would have liked. Trevor produced a pair of binoculars from under his seat.

"Bird watching."

"What type of bird?"

"Feathered. I'm no peeping Tom."

They watched several people entering the garden but leaving when they found no one around. It took the police ten minutes to get to the scene. A single car drove up, and the policeman who had met his girlfriend at the Max House entered the garden and made his way straight to the bunker. He tried to pull it open, then spoke into his communicator.

"What's happening?" asked Trevor. James handed him the binoculars. They could just hear the sirens of a fire engine as it raced to the scene. More police cars arrived, followed by a group of onlookers.

"Just in time, the kids are out." Trevor handed the binoculars back to James. He looked at the young kids as they gathered at the Max House.

When the fire brigade arrived, they brought heavy cutters and removed the nut and bolt. Brian and Dave emerged from the bunker and were handcuffed by the police. A fireman in waterproof waders entered the bunker, returning a few moments later carrying a box of drugs. The crowd of onlookers surged forward. The police moved them back and sealed the area.

"Phase one over. Now what?"

"Back to the farm for some of Mom's cooking. We can make copies of this tap. We'll give the cops a copy of the whole thing and a copy of just the special highlights."

"We also need to copy the notebook."

"No problem. Dad's got a copier in the farm office. We may look like country bumpkins, but in fact we're really high-tech."

When they arrived at the farmhouse, Irene Fisher was so pleased to see them. "Come in, boys. I bet you're hungry."

"Starving, Mom."

"Settle down and I'll get some tea for you. Steak and kidney pie okay?"

"Perfect," said James.

Trevor smiled. "Let's do the copies while Mom prepares the food."

In Trevor's bedroom, the cover James had hung to hide the graffiti had been removed, and the wall had been painted white again. James looked at the wall. "Me dad," said Trevor. "I told him when I called. He said he'd look after it once me mom was out."

Trevor placed the tape into a dual machine, rewound it, and then made a copy at high speed, repeating the process for the second tape. He then opened the computer and played the second tape again. Once it had been played, he put the originals in the drawer under the computer.

"We'll lock them in me dad's safe, but I don't want to get them mixed up." He then played the tape through the computer, hitting a key each time an important part came up. Once he had done this, he placed a new cassette tape in the recorder and typed something in the computer. The Record light lit up on the machine. James looked on with amazement.

"I'm only copying the bits we want. I audio-edited it. That's how I got into films. I used to copy stuff from the Internet, and then edit and bootleg it to friends."

"Clever stuff."

"You have a computer?"

"Yes, but I think I'm a little behind on the technology."

"Okay, we can let this do its thing. Now to copy the book. We're going to have to do that manually, I think."

In the kitchen Irene was busy preparing the meal.

"Is Dad in the office?"

"No, he's out with the cows."

"I want to photocopy something is that okay?"

"Sure, but be careful you know how he is about his office. Tea in about ten minutes."

"Smells good," said James.

In the farm office, James placed the first page of the notebook on the glass of the copier and began the slow process of copying it. As each page came out, Trevor picked it up and read it. "We should turn this into a film."

"Maybe you can when this is over."

"You can be my producer."

"What will it cost me?"

"Not a lot." They both laughed. It took about twenty minutes to copy the notebook, and they were just finishing the last page when Joe Fisher entered the office. He gave Trevor a look of *You shouldn't be here*, but on seeing James, he relaxed and smiled.

"Hi boys."

"Sorry Dad, we needed to copy something, and Mom said it would be okay."

"That's fine. James seems to know what he is doing."

"Nice office, Joe."

"It's okay. You need it these days, with all the reps and Agri officials who keep coming around. I think we saved the rest of the herd. And it looks like we didn't have foot and mouth in the first place. Killed all those cows and sheep for nothing, bloody shame."

James looked at the man, he was like his own father, a hard-working man who seemed to get knocked down at every turn.

"You'll be compensated for the loss?"

"Oh yes, handsomely, but it's not the same."

At that moment, Irene called from the kitchen. "Tea's ready. Trevor, call your Dad."

Trevor replied. "What shall I call him?" Father and son both laughed. The three of them entered the kitchen and ate the feast Irene had prepared.

After the meal, James began to clear away the dishes. "Shall I wash?"

"No, love, I have a dishwasher now and if that broke, Joe would do the dishes, wouldn't you, my love?" Joe gave her a look, and they both began to laugh.

"Mom, Dad, we have to deliver this package, so if you'll excuse us."

"Thank you for a really nice meal."

"James, you are welcome here any time."

Trevor and James left the farmhouse and got into the truck. James sat with the large envelope balanced precariously on his knees. He had written on the cover, Re: Elizabeth Friedman murder, a confession by Brian Steel and Dave Lilly.

"Let's hope this works."

"It better, or we will have to start all over again."

Turning into the main road, Trevor's cell phone rang. "Hello Dad. Right, thanks." He hung up. "Dad said no one was following us."

"Thank God."

As they approached the Longbridge police station on Bristol Road, both James and Trevor became a little hesitant.

"Okay, you can take it in," said Trevor as they pulled up outside the police station.

"Err, okay, if you insist." James got out of the truck and went up the steps. He hesitated, and then seeing a police car parked behind Trevor's truck with the window open, he quickly turned and ran down the steps, dropped the package on the driver's seat, and raced back to Trevor's truck.

"You hate them as much as I do."

"Maybe more. They cause more problems for my people than the ordinary man on the street will ever know." They watched as a policeman came out of the station and went to the car. He picked up the package and ran back into the station.

Trevor and James shook hands.

CHAPTER FOURTEEN

Conspiracy

Trevor pulled up outside the Pidgley house. He and James sat in silence looking out into the street at all the cars parked tightly together. James knew most of them, they were his brothers' and sisters'. He wondered if any of his siblings knew what had happened over the last few days.

"You come from a big family?"

James turned to face Trevor, who was as white as a sheet. "Yes, there are ten of us."

"Wow! Your Dad was busy."

"Yeah, but not just Dad, Mom as well," laughed James. "Trevor, I wanted you here because you helped, and I think it's important they all understand that."

"Will Anne be here?"

"Yes, Anne will be. And you'll see what she is really like."

"A sweet, determined, beautiful woman."

"You're sick! I think I need to take you to see a shrink."

"Okay, let's go and face the Pidgley firing squad."

"Oh, we won't shoot you. Well, not at first."

Climbing out of the truck, Trevor looked up at the house with its three floors and a basement. "Big house."

"With ten kids, it had to be. And when we were all here, it always felt overcrowded." James rang the doorbell.

"You don't have a key?"

"Yes, but this is my parents' home and I respect their space, as they do mine. Except when we had our Sunday lunch ritual, but that's gone now."

"Wow, the whole family for lunch."

Elizabeth opened the door. She gave a big grin when she saw James and gave him a kiss and a hug. "This must be Trevor."

Trevor blushed bright scarlet and held out his hand to shake. She ignored the hand and flung her arms around him, hugging him tightly. "Wow!" said Trevor, once Elizabeth had released him.

"Everyone's in the dining room. Mom's made a buffet. Donny's not here yet." James led the way into the dining room. As he opened the door, all those assembled turned. His mother crossed the room and gave him a quick kiss on his cheek. Then whispering in his ear, "Thank you."

Elizabeth followed and announced, "Everyone, this is Anne's hero, Trevor." Spontaneous applause broke out, and Trevor went even redder.

James went to his father and gave him a hug. Matthew didn't release the hug, but held his son for several minutes. Anne made her way to Trevor, and as she came close, she pulled him towards her and gave him a hug. Her siblings all cheered. "Wow!" was again all that Trevor could say.

"Now eat, everyone," said Sarah as she led Trevor to the food, placing herself between him and Anne.

Paul passed a plate to Trevor. "You won't like my sister. She can be a real bitch."

"Only to you, Little Brother," replied Anne, trying to squeeze herself next to Trevor.

Matthew indicated to James to follow him into the front room. They sat as they had when James had told his father he wanted to buy Thirteen Crowhurst Road.

"James, thank you, without you and..."

"Trevor."

"I should know that by now, Anne doesn't stop saying, 'Trevor this or Trevor that!'"

"He's a good guy."

"He must be for Anne to go on and on. You not only saved your sister from... I don't want to think about it... but you managed to get me released too."

"Dad, I only did what you taught me. Family first."

"But still, thank you, and Trevor. So do you think he'll ask Anne for a date?"

"If he gets the chance. But I think Little Miss Bossy Boots will ask him first!"

Jane popped her head around the door. "Oh there you are, James. You'd better come and help your friend before Anne embarrasses him even more."

"Right," said James.

Anne was recounting yet again how Trevor had rescued her from certain death. Trevor sat listening but kept interrupting her, telling her not to keep adding to the story.

When Anne had finished, Peter, who had sat silently through it, turned to James.

"Well, James, what's the real story?"

"Anne's got it almost right. One thing she did forget. I was there!" Everyone laughed.

"Did she mention how horrible she was to Trevor when he risked his life to rescue her?"

"That was before I realized he was a powerful force to be reckoned with."

"You mean before he told you to shut that big mouth of yours or he would throw you out of his truck." Anne didn't reply, giving James a scathing look.

"Good one," said Paul, shaking Trevor's hand. The dining room door opened and Donald entered, carrying the early evening papers.

"Is there something in them about what happened?" asked Paul. Donald handed him a copy, and Paul searched for the relevant item.

"Here it is. 'Today police arrested two men, Brian Steel, aged twenty-two, and David Lilly, aged thirty-one, for the murder of the estate agent, Elizabeth Friedman. A police spokesman said they had confessed on tape to stabbing Mrs. Friedman and placing her body in the living room of Thirteen Crowhurst Road, where it was found last Tuesday, May sixteenth. They will be brought before a magistrate tomorrow morning, and a trial date will be fixed.'"

"Doesn't mention anything about the drugs or the bunker," said Trevor.

"Sorry, I left that bit out. It said there would be other charges for drug dealing and theft."

"That doesn't matter they have been caught for the murder of that woman, and hopefully they will be convicted," said Donald.

James took the paper from Paul and read the article himself. Something was puzzling him, and he read and reread the news item. Suddenly he put the paper down and announced, "Trevor, they didn't kill her."

Silence fell over the room. "Why do you say that?" asked Anne.

"Because they didn't stab her," said James.

"That's right. They said they just hit her on the head and left her in the kitchen," said Trevor.

"Well, maybe the paper got it wrong," said Peter.

"Yes, that's it. The paper missed out most of the story and got the facts wrong. They are doing that all the time," said Anne. Everyone started to talk again as though that were the answer. Trevor and James stayed silent and moved to a corner of the room.

"It's not what they said. We know it's not," said Trevor.

"Right. And I'm not going to be responsible for putting anybody away for a crime they didn't commit."

So what are we going to do?"

"Not sure yet. But let's not spoil the party." They joined the rest of the family. Family members gradually started to leave, and James and Trevor took the chance to leave.

"Thank you for inviting me," said Trevor to Matthew and Sarah.

"Don't be silly you were the guest of honor."

"Wow! Thanks."

"Oh Trevor, say hello to your father from me," said Matthew. "I used to play with him when I was a little boy."

"Okay, but I thought you were…"

"Romany, Travellers, dirty Gyppos."

"I didn't mean that."

"I know you didn't. I met your father when we came to this part of the country. Your grandfather would let us stay on their land. Even gave the elders work."

"I remember him talking about the Gypsies. It was the people from Birmingham he didn't like."

"Oh yes, they were a rough lot gave us Romani a bad name."

"I'll make sure I tell Dad, he won't half be chuffed."

James sat in the truck, waiting for Trevor to say good-bye to Anne. As they parted, Anne gave him a kiss on the lips and then ran into the house. Trevor climbed into the truck, his face red.

James smiled. "Who asked whom for a date?"

"I didn't have a chance."

"I won!"

"What?"

"I told my Dad that she would ask you, because you wouldn't have a chance to ask her."

"She is a little bossy."

"That's Anne!"

"But she is cute."

"No comment." They both laughed.

"Can we go to the farm? I need to say something to my parents, and I need to say it in person."

"Sure, it'll give me time to think this over."

They pulled into the farmyard. Trevor turned off the engine and sat looking at the farmhouse. James had already gotten out of the truck when he realized that Trevor was still in it. He slowly walked to the house and waited for Trevor to join him. They entered the kitchen, where Joe and Irene Fisher were sitting at the table.

"Hi Mom. Hi Dad."

"Hello," said Irene. "We weren't expecting you."

"I know, but I needed to come and see you both."

"Well, that was nice."

"I wanted to say thank you."

"For what, son?"

"For everything, Dad. When I saw James's family, I realized how good you both are and how lucky I've been."

"We just did our best, Son."

"I know, Mom, but you did more than that. I almost got myself into a great deal of trouble. Thanks to James, I think it's going to be okay, but the main thing is you both stood by me and helped me." Trevor gave his mother, then his father, a hug. James had crossed the kitchen and filled the kettle to make some tea.

"Oh, what a good idea, James."

"Hope you don't mind."

"Mind? Why should we mind? You're almost part of the family."

"Well, I might be."

Trevor gave James a quick look, and Irene caught the look. "Meaning what?" she said.

Before James could answer, Joe said, "I think our son may have a date."

"Who with?"

"My sister Anne, Trevor is her hero."

"Oh, that's nice." Trevor blushed as his father punched him on the arm.

"James and I don't think Brian and Dave killed that woman," said Trevor, trying to change the subject.

"Why?"

"Well, they think they murdered her, but in their confession they say they hit her, and the police say she was stabbed."

"Then who did it?"

"We're not sure, but we're going to find out."

"But they were crooks?"

"Oh yes, and they should be in the slammer, but not for murder."

"Sad for the family, that."

"Mom, Dad, there but for the grace of God go I."

"True, son, and James found the Gates of Hell just in time." They all laughed.

"Oh yeah. Dad, James's father says hi. Apparently he played with you when you were kids."

"Really? I don't remember."

"My family are Romani, Gypsies. Dad and Mom traveled, but none of us kids have."

"That's it. I knew that I knew your name! Your father's Matt, 'Matt the Brat,' the only kid who could outdo me in naming all the plants and trees. He was good with animals as well. He had an uncle who would sit on one of our gates and sing Gypsy songs to the cows. My Dad said the cows always gave more milk when he did that."

"Uncle Harold still sings, usually in the pub these days."

"So what's your sister like?" asked Irene.

"That's it!' said James. "Brian has a sister called …?"

"Sylvia," said Trevor, sighing with relief that James had not answered his mother's question.

"We'll see if we can get her to ask Brian if he or Dave stabbed the woman and put the body in the living room."

"Okay, we'll go after some tea."

They all sat around the kitchen table drinking tea. Irene produced a fruitcake. "So our Trevor, what's this young lady of yours like?"

Trevor groaned. He thought he had escaped that line of questioning.

"Mom, she's not my young lady, well not yet anyway. She's James's sister and I think she's very pretty, but you should ask him. On second thought, maybe not!" James and Trevor laughed, to the bewilderment of Joe and Irene. They left the farmhouse, Trevor trying to brush off his mother's suggestion that Anne should come for Sunday tea.

As they parked outside of Brian Steel's mother's house, the man who had spoken to them when they had been there before passed the truck and waved as though he knew them.

"So why didn't you say something about your sister?" James grinned. "Nothing to say, really, Brother-in-Law." Trevor punched him on the arm.

They knocked on the Steel's front door. A small blond woman opened it. Her eyes were red from crying, and she was very pale. "Sorry to bother you, Sylvia, but we need to talk to you about Brian."

She recognized Trevor, and seeing a neighbor open her door, said, "you'd better come in. I don't want the neighbors knowing all my business."

They entered the house and were shown into the unused front room. It smelt damp, and a thin film of dust lay on the furniture surfaces.

"My mother's still in hospital. Brian stabbed her, you know."

"We know. How is she doing?"

"Oh, she'll recover. But the latest news hasn't helped. I've tried to keep it from her, but someone gave her a paper."

"That's why we're here. We don't believe your brother and his friend murdered that woman."

"Well, they confessed."

"I know, but something doesn't quite add up. We need you to ask Brian some questions so we can prove they didn't kill her."

"I'm not going to ask him anything. He can rot in hell for all I care, after what he put my mother through."

"But Sylvia."

"No, I don't want to know. And if you know what's good for you, you'll do the same."

"You won't reconsider?"

"No. Now if you don't mind, I need to go to the hospital."

As they left the house, James asked her, "Does your mother need anything?"

"No, she's got all she wants, but thanks for asking, and I'm sorry I can't help you."

They sat in the truck. The sky had turned grey again, with some heavy black clouds gathering over the Lickey Hills. "Now what?"

"If Mohammed won't come to the mountain, then we'll have to go to him!"

"You mean, go and see Brian?"

"Yes."

"In prison?"

"Yes."

"But what if he won't see us?"

"That's a chance we'll have to take. If we tell his lawyer that we might be able to help, he'll tell Brian to see us."

"Okay, if you think it'll work. Tomorrow then."

The alarm clock rang at seven o'clock, and James found he couldn't get into the bathroom. Trevor had beaten him to it. The sofa bed had already been converted back to a sofa and the bedclothes neatly folded. Trevor entered the living room a smile on his face and a towel around his waist.

"Breakfast in ten minutes."

James showered, his thoughts on what questions he should ask Brian. If they got to see him, that is. He was impressed with Trevor's cooking, and after they had eaten, Trevor took control of the situation.

"I'll wash up, you phone the lawyer."

"Okay. I wonder what his lawyer's name is?"

"It's in the paper, Frankenstein and Son, or something like that."

James looked in the paper. He scanned through the article and made several grunting sounds when he came to the name. "Frank Warsaw."

"Yeah, that was it."

"Frankenstein! You've been watching too much television."

James phoned the number, and although it was only ten minutes past eight o'clock, Frank Warsaw was in his office and answered the phone. "Mr. Warsaw, I believe you represent Brian Steel."

"Yes, I do. May I ask who is calling?"

"My name is James Pidgley. I believe your client did not murder Elizabeth Friedman."

"Why do you say that?"

"I have reason to believe that someone else did. If I could see Brian and ask him some questions, then I might be able to prove it."

"It's up to my client who he sees."

"I know, but if you tell him it's in his best interests..."

"I'll certainly mention you called, Mr. Pidgley, but as I said, it really is up to my client who he sees. But if you have any material evidence, I would be very interested to hear it."

"Okay. Where is he being held?"

"Winson Green Prison. Visiting times today are two o'clock to four o'clock, and his prison number is 7291584. He is in 'P' wing."

"Thank you, Mr. Warsaw."

Trevor came out of the kitchen. "What's he say?"

"He was a little suspicious. Well, of course he would be. But we might be able to see Brian if he's prepared to see us."

"What time?"

"Visiting hours start at two o'clock."

"What can we do until then?"

"Let's go and see if Number Thirteen is still a crime scene. If not, I want to take a closer look at the place. Something Brian said makes me think we missed something."

"Okay. I'm ready."

They turned into Crowhurst Road just after nine o'clock. The police serious-crime mobile unit had gone. Trevor parked right outside the house. The blue and white tape had been removed and so had the crime scene notice on the front door. James put the key into the lock and opened the door. Black dust from the search for fingerprints was still visible on all the doors. They went first into the living room. The heavy black drapes had been removed from the window, and daylight illuminated the room. The footprints in the fuller's earth made it look as if a herd of elephants had been in the room. White chalk-marks indicated where the corpse had lain, but the rest of the set dressing had disappeared. Trevor walked into the kitchen.

"Hey James, take a look at this." James joined him. The kitchen looked much the same as it had when Elizabeth had shown him around.

"See how the centre of the floor looks like it's been washed? That's how it was when I came back that night, and I also remember it was sticky. Here," continued Trevor, pointing to some footprints. "Those are mine."

"So someone did clean up the place. I wonder why the police didn't see this. Maybe they did."

"You don't think we are making a mountain out of a mole hill, do you?"

"No, something's not right. Something I've seen in that room. But whatever it was, it's not there now."

"When did you see it?"

"I'm just not sure."

"Let's look upstairs."

James led the way and, at the top of the stairs, hesitated before entering the master bedroom at the front. He looked out of the window. "Trevor, who's this woman?"

Trevor looked out of the window at the woman below. She was dressed in a red coat and was walking past the house as though she were going to turn right down one of the arms of the cul-de-sac. "I don't know her name, but she lives a few houses up on this side of the road. Why?"

"Because I keep seeing her, and I think she has something to do with this, but I just don't know what."

"Well, it's not surprising you keep seeing her here. She lives up the road."

"I'm seeing conspiracy everywhere."

"As long as you don't tell me the government did it."

"They may have, along with aliens from the planet Zorcum." Trevor looked at James, who burst out laughing at the suggestion.

"So where were the drugs stored?"

"I'll show you." Trevor led James into the back bedroom and went to the window. "See that door, just at the end of the outhouse? That's a small storeroom. We put the stuff in there so we didn't have to come into the house."

"Okay, so what were Dave and Brian doing in the house? And where was Dave when Elizabeth found Brian in the kitchen?"

"Well, I don't know."

"Unless they had something else to hide."

"Like what?"

James went out onto the landing and opened the cupboard to the water tank, lifting the plank where he had found his father's Bible. There was nothing there.

"Maybe up there," said Trevor, pointing to a trap door in the ceiling. Trevor cupped his hands as James put his foot in them. Lifting himself up, opened the trap door, then pulled himself into the loft.

"I think I need a flashlight, it's dark up here."

"I'll get one," said Trevor as he disappeared down the stairs.

James's eyes started to become accustomed to the darkness. There was something a little way in front of him, but he wasn't sure what. Trevor returned and threw the large flashlight up to him. Switching it on, James scanned the loft. He was about to jump down when he shone the light on two small bumps in the loft insulation. He picked at the insulation and revealed a small dark blue suitcase, and behind it a black rucksack. He lowered them to Trevor and jumped down onto the landing.

"Where did you find them?"

"Under the loft insulation."

"Why didn't the police find them?"

"I almost missed them myself. They were right under my nose, just inside the loft." Trevor stared at them. He looked tense, as though he were scared of what was inside them. James opened the suitcase to find it was filled with money.

"Wow!" said Trevor.

"Wow' it is!"

"How much do you think there is?"

"Whatever it is, half's for you and half's for me."

"Really?"

"Yes. I'm not giving this to the police. It's my house and therefore my money, right?"

"Right."

He opened the rucksack. It contained more money and two videotapes. James put the money from the suitcase into the rucksack and then threw the suitcase back up into the loft. Trevor again cupped his hands, and James precariously closed the trap door.

As they left the house, James locked the door, checking several times to make sure he had locked it properly. The woman whom they had seen in the red coat was walking past again, but this time wearing a yellow coat and hat. She smiled at them and said, "Hello."

They both replied, "Hello."

Once she was out of hearing, James whispered to Trevor, "The lady with the yellow umbrella. And she keeps changing her clothes." Trevor looked at him, puzzled by this remark.

"Let's take the money to my place and then go to Winson Green Prison."

"Can we count it, before we go?"

"Sure I want to know too."

They sat in the living room of James's apartment, the money in neat piles on the coffee table. "Eleven thousand, seven hundred and thirty-two pounds. A nice little sum!"

"What are we going to do with it now?"

"Half for you and half for me."

"You're serious about that?"

"As I said, if we hand this over to the police, it will only get lost in some bureaucratic money maze. We're going to solve the murder, aren't we?"

"Yes."

"Well, this is our fee!"

"Right. So that's... err... 5,862 pounds each. Wow! I can make twenty big-budget films with that.

"Or get your own place."

"Yeah. So what are we going to do with it now?"

"I'll put it in the safe, and when this is all over, you can have your share."

Trevor's face had an expression of doubt.

"Don't you trust me?"

There was a long pause before Trevor replied, "Yeah."

"Obviously not."

"I do. I do trust you. It's just that everyone else has always screwed me over."

"And you think I'll do that to you?"

"No, but it's hard to get used to someone being nice to me. Sorry."

"Don't be sorry. It's always good to be a little cautious. I even had my doubts about you, but I was proved wrong."

"When?"

"At the bunker. It doesn't matter now, but sometimes you just have to believe."

"You're right. You could have shopped me to the police at any time."

"I suppose I could, yes."

James stood up and took the money into the bedroom. When he returned, Trevor was watching one of the videos. "What is it?"

"It's porn, amateur type. That's Dave there. I haven't seen the girl's face yet, but the way she's moving, I'd say she's drugged out of her head." They continued to watch. Brian was the cameraman and kept appearing in shot, telling Dave what to do. Dave had removed the girl's clothes, and the camera panned over her body and up to her face.

"Mary Lewis! She's only thirteen years old. She's just a kid for God's sake! He must have raped her. The bastard's going to pay. I want to hand this over to the police. It's the one thing I really hate. If you can't get sex without forcing someone, then you shouldn't have it."

"Let's look at the other tape."

Trevor changed tapes. He turned the sound up as a title appeared on the screen, *Coronation Souvenir*. It was a copy of an old eight-millimeter film of the 1952 Crowhurst Road party for the Queen's Coronation, which someone had converted to video.

James leaned forward. A little four-year-old boy was standing behind the other children who were playing a game. "That's my Dad. I know it is. I've got pictures of me looking just like that."

A little girl, a few years older than the boy, came and stood next to him. "Who that is I don't know. I don't think it's one of his sisters." The film changed and showed a long table with the children of the road sitting around it, eating. The little boy who had been behind the other children earlier was now at the end of the table, sitting alone. A young man turned and smiled at the camera.

"That could be Willie."

"Most likely his father. They've lived in the road since it was built," said Trevor, who suddenly moved forward and paused the tape.

"Look at that man and woman."

"What about them? They're just kissing."

"Yeah, but it's wrong somehow."

"Why?"

"It's as if they shouldn't be."

"Trevor, I told you. You're seeing conspiracy everywhere!" James pressed play, and the film continued. The children had some more games after they'd finished eating. This was followed by a big sit-down meal for the adults. Several people took to the stage and sang or told a few jokes. The man and woman were seen again talking. Another man joined them. He seemed a little upset, but later he was seen dancing with the woman. The film stopped, but the video continued and another film began. This showed the building of the road and preparations being made for the party. The trench in which the woman's body had been found could clearly be seen. It was wider than James had expected, and a man was looking into it.

"Who's that?"

"I'm not sure, but my Dad might know."

The film then showed Number Thirteen. Someone had put graffiti on the door and windows: 'Gyppo's live here! Lock up your kids before they steal them.'

"Shit! They had taggers even in those days. I'm sorry, but at least you don't have the same problem your Dad or his father had."

"No, but the prejudice is still there if they find out. I remember my Dad telling me about this graffiti problem. It went on for years, and they never found out who did it."

"My grandfather used to let you use the bottom field, because he felt you got a bad press. Of course that was good for him at harvest time, because he got cheap labor."

"That's probably how your Dad and mine met, or at least they played together. You know, Trevor, there's something in that film. We are seeing it, but we don't know what we're seeing."

"Why did Brian and Dave have it?"

"Good question. We'll ask Brian if we see him."

"Yeah," said Trevor, in a very doubtful voice.

"Let's go then and bring that second video. I want to show my father after we've been to the jail." As Trevor opened the door, an envelope fell to the floor. James gave an "Ah" sound as Trevor bent down and picked it up.

"What?"

"Just a little déjà vu."

"What?"

"I have been here before."

"Oh! It's for you." The envelope read, in very childlike handwriting, "Mister James."

"I wonder when it was delivered?" James opened it. A white sheet of paper had two words on it. 'Free Willie.' James turned the paper over, but there was nothing on the back.

"Looks like an advert for a film!"

"You don't think it's something to do with our Willie?"

"You think Willie's being held captive or got himself locked in somewhere?"

"And we've got to get him out. Who do you think sent it?"

"The handwriting looks like a child's, or an adult with little or no education."

"His mother or brother?"

"Maybe. I think we need to visit those two again. She could probably tell us more about the Coronation Party."

"If she remembers."

"Some things we never forget. They're buried in our memory, and they can be triggered to resurface."

"There's hope for me yet, then. Two years ago I hid one hundred pounds, and I can't remember where I put it!"

"You'll be eighty years old and reading a book you haven't picked up for years, and a hundred pounds will fall out. You will not know why it was there, and you'll spend the next twenty years trying to remember!"

"Thanks for that. I can really imagine it."

"Okay, let's go."

"Err, I need the toilet."

"Well hurry up."

Trevor dashed into the bathroom. James inspected the envelope. He could just see an impression of something written on it. Carefully holding it up to the light and twisting it around until the light caught just the right angle, he was able to read it. 'Mrs. Helen Coates,' plus part of her address, 'Crowhurst Road.'

When Trevor emerged from the bathroom, James showed him. "This was sent from either Willie's mother or Bobby. I can read her name from something else she wrote. Look, it left an impression."

"Shall we go and see her?"

"No, it's time we went to the prison. You don't want to go, do you?"

"No. I just don't like the place, like the dentist."

"Scared they may keep you in and not let you out, eh?"

"Yeah." This made James laughed. So did Trevor. Then they saw Trevor's truck in the driveway.

Someone had written "Free Willie" in the grime on the wing. Somebody was definitely trying to tell them something important. But there was no time to pursue that now.

They drove out onto the main road. "Where's the prison?"

"Winson Green. It's next to the hospital. Drive towards town, and I'll tell you when to turn."

"Meaning you don't really know!"

"I have a pretty good idea. If not, we can always ask a policeman." They both laughed.

"That film is haunting me. What is the something that we've missed?"

"If we knew where they found it and why that person had it, then maybe we would have some answers."

"A lot of maybes. Let's hope Brian will talk."

They drove to the prison, completely unaware that an unmarked police car was following them.

CHAPTER FIFTEEN

The Inside Man

"I think we're being followed," said Trevor. James didn't turn around.

"What's the color and make of car?"

"Dark blue. Can't see the make, but looks like a Ford."

James slid down in the seat and looked into the side mirror. He could just see the dark blue car about two vehicles behind. Suddenly Trevor put his foot down hard on the accelerator, and the truck sped through a yellow light just as it turned red. The dark blue car followed him. A police motorcyclist Trevor had spotted at the junction gave chase and pulled the dark blue car over. Trevor took this opportunity to turn off the main road and continue their journey to Winson Green along the side streets. When they found the prison, they took care to park on a side road. Although an old prison, modernization had given the place a look of being from the 1960s *Doctor Who* TV series. The two blue domed towers at the entrance and giant sliding doors painted in a bright blue stood out against the brown brickwork. The windows high above with their white metal crosshatched grills gave an Arab architecture flavor. "A bit more modern than I thought it would be," said James. "Looks like a French public toilet to me. I remember seeing them when I went to Calais on a one-day school trip."

"Brian Steel must feel at home then, living in a toilet."

"What happens now?"

"Trevor, my friend, I do not know, but let us go and find out." Outside the prison, a line of women and a few men stretched along from a sign that read Visitors' Line.

"Let's join this line."

As they walked down to the end of the line, James noticed that some of the women were carrying very small babies. Most of them looked as if they really didn't care about their appearance and wore clothes that made then look fatter and very poor. One woman stood out. She was dressed in an imitation leopard-skin coat and black, very high-heeled shoes. She wore a lot of gold jewelry and was smoking a cigarette in a very long holder. Her nails were painted in a leopard-skin pattern. She looked at James and smiled softly. Just the corners of her mouth turned up. He smiled back and was about to speak to her when Trevor drew his attention away. He had become very anxious and couldn't keep still. They were still a long way from the front of the line, and Trevor became more and more fidgety. "What's the problem?"

"Nothing."

"Then why can't you stand still?"

"It's just I hate this place."

"You're scared, aren't you?"

"Okay, what if I am! I told you before." He started to move about, swinging his arms and jumping up and down. He bumped into the woman who was standing in front of them. She turned and gave him a scowl.

"I'm sorry," said James. "He doesn't like this place."

"None of us do, love, and with having to book every visit in advance, it gets really annoying when they still keep you waiting for hours. Its not like I haven't got work to do!"

"You have to book a visit?"

"Oh yes, seven days in advance."

"Trevor, your wish has come true."

James dragged Trevor out of the line. But for some reason, Trevor decided to drag his feet, which caused James to bump into a young man dressed in a suit and carrying a small attaché case. "Sorry," said James, who resumed dragging Trevor away from the line.

The young man looked at James and smiled. "Well, well, well! What is the infamous James Pidgley doing here?"

James turned to face the young man. He was James's age and height, but a few pounds heavier. His thin brown hair had a spiked look to it. The pin-striped suit gave him an air of authority. A crisp white shirt, which had been professionally laundered, was the backdrop to a flowery silk tie, knotted in the Windsor style and painstakingly positioned in the centre of his neck.

"Gary Hadley! And in a suit, with clean shoes."

"Not bad, eh?"

"So what are you doing here?"

"I work for a lawyer. Err, that's not quite correct. I'm finishing my training as a solicitor. I have to see a client. And you? Don't tell me they finally caught one of the Pidgley clan. Let me give you one of my cards." Gary produced a cream embossed business card from his inside pocket and gave it to James.

"We were trying to see a man who's here on remand," replied James, letting go of his hold of Trevor, "but you have to give seven days' notice."

"That's the system now. I haven't met our client yet. He only got caught in the last few days. Murder case."

"You aren't representing Brian Steel or Dave Lilly?"

"Brian Steel. How'd you know that?"

"Well, they are the only ones who have been caught in the last few days for murder."

"Right."

"And that's who we were trying to see."

"Why?"

"Because we believe they are innocent of the murder. Guilty of everything else and a lot more, but innocent of the murder."

"You should call my boss."

"We did."

"So, it was you who called. I've been instructed to tell Brian that someone might be able to prove he didn't murder the woman."

"That's why we need to see him. You couldn't get us in, could you?"

"Err, well, the pass is for two, and my boss is in court."

"You go, James I'll wait in the truck."

"If that's okay with you, Gary."

"If you have some evidence that will help our client, I don't see why not. And the boss said I was to try and get Brian to see you."

"See you later nice to meet you, Gary," said Trevor, who then half-walked and half-ran out of the prison forecourt.

"So what happens now?"

"Say nothing and fill in the same information as I do."

"Okey-dokey. Gary Hadley in a suit, ha!"

James followed Gary into the visitors' centre and was amazed how "snotty" Hadley had become. At school he was always the kid who was picked on because he smelt and farted at the most inappropriate moments. His clothes never looked washed, and his nose was always running. He was a likeable kid, but you always stood upwind of him! But now here was this debonair, professional man-about-town. It was incredible! As they waited to sign in, James couldn't keep his thoughts to himself any longer.

"What happened to you?"

"You mean how did a dirty, snotty-nosed kid like me become a handsome professional man with prospects?"

"Well, yes."

"Mom won the lottery."

"Really?"

"Yeah. Her and me Dad had divorced. He left her with nothing. Even threw her and me out of the house so his mistress could move in. Three weeks after the divorce was final, Mom won eight million pounds!"

"Good for her."

"Dad went ape-shit and tried to sue for some of the money, but the judge ruled he was no longer entitled. He had to pay Mom's court costs as well as his own. His mistress left him the day after."

"So what happened then?"

"Mom bought a new house, and I decided I needed to get a proper job. She sent me to college, and here I am."

"As my friend Trevor would say, 'Wow.'"

"Friend? Do you mean boyfriend, as in gay?"

"No, Trevor's just someone who's helping me, and I'm helping him finish his film."

"He's a film-maker. Have I seen any of his films?"

"I don't think so, but one day you will."

"Did you marry?"

"Not yet. What about you?"

"Oh yes, lasted all of three months, just after we left school. You remember Karen Smythe, lived on Turves Green Road near our school?" James nodded acknowledgement.

"Claimed she was pregnant, the longest pregnancy in the world. The baby still hasn't arrived! Then I realized I was gay, so I told Mom, she just said, 'Okay son, now what do you want for your tea?' I've been living with this bloke for about a year. He's older than me, but I like him, so that's that."

Gary filled out the paperwork in the visitor book, and James copied what he had put. "So what happens now?"

"We wait. We will be taken, searched, and then sent on to the main prison, just off the visitors' area. We will be placed in a room with a huge glass window. Then the prisoner on remand will be brought to us."

"So how long does this take?"

"Usually we see them within an hour, but I have been kept waiting for as long as three hours."

"Let's hope that this is not one of those days."

"So what do you have that may prove my client is innocent of murder?"

"I'm not sure until I've asked Brian some questions, and then it depends on his answers. Sorry, I can't really tell you any more."

"Does Brian know you?"

"Well... if he remembers."

"What?"

"He stole my car, and when I went to Dave Lilly's house about it, Brian was there, but he was drunk and drugged out of his head."

"Oh, I thought you might have been one of his customers."

"What, buying drugs?"

"Not only drugs. Brian is a known male prostitute."

"I see. Hence your question about me being gay."

"And it seems he has some very influential customers. One of them is paying for his defense."

"He doesn't look gay."

"These days we don't go round advertising it, and as a prostitute he would have to be very discreet, especially if he is also dealing in drugs."

"Sorry, I should have known better than to stereotype."

"That's okay, we all make those mistakes. So how did you get mixed up in this?"

"My father was arrested for the murder, and we own the house it took place in."

"Oh yes, I remember. I was wondering at the time if he was related to you, when I heard the name."

They sat in the visitors' centre and watched as the wives, girlfriends, boyfriends, lovers, and others arrived. "What if one of Brian's family has arrived to see him?"

"They won't see him. Remember it takes seven days to get an appointment."

"No exceptions?"

"No exceptions. We, of course, have a certain amount of unlimited access, because we are preparing his case."

"Do you get copies of all the police evidence?"

"We're supposed to, but all we have at the moment are the autopsy report of the murdered woman, some crime photos, and the arrest document."

"You don't have a copy of the confession?"

"Not yet. That is supposed to be with us later today."

"Anything of interest in the photos?"

"I don't know I haven't looked at them yet. I just picked them up on my way here." Gary took a large manila envelope out of his brief case and opened it. Inside were the autopsy report and a set of crime-scene photos. He looked at the photos and unconsciously handed them to James. James looked at each picture very carefully. He didn't know what he was looking for, but something might spring out at him. The first picture showed the entire room. The others were of the body from different angles. He went back to the first picture and looked at every part of it.

He knew he was missing something, but for the life of him he couldn't think what. He gave the pictures back to Gary, with frustration mounting inside. As a child, he had become angry with himself for not being able to grasp the obvious. Gary handed him the autopsy report. Elizabeth had died from a stab-wound to her chest, which had entered her heart. She had lost a great deal of blood.

"Can I see the photo of the room without the body?" Gary handed back the photo of the room minus the corpse. "There doesn't seem to be much blood on the floor where the body lay. The carpet's quite light, so it should have shown up."

"Really?" said Gary, taking the picture back and looking at it.

"Sometimes it's what's not there that's important. What was it Sherlock Holmes said?"

"'Because the dog didn't bark.'"

"Something like that, but that's the point. I have seen something that proves your client didn't do it, but I can't remember what it was."

"You saw something?"

"Saw, heard, read I'm not sure. All I know is, they didn't kill her. They may have knocked her out, but they didn't kill her."

"Is that why at school we all called you 'Weirdo'?"

"No, that was Tony Smith being prejudiced."

"You know he is in a wheelchair now."

"No, I didn't what happened?"

"Car accident two years ago. He was drunk and ran a red light."

"You reap what you sow."

A prison officer approached them. He was about their age and had already developed the hard-man guard look. "If you gentlemen would like to follow me."

Inside a windowless room, the prison officer checked Gary's attaché case. Then he searched Gary. As the officer ran his hand between his legs, Gary gave a little squeal. The officer ignored it and indicated to James to prepare himself for a search. Afterwards without looking at either of them, he said, "This way please."

The officer walked fast, and Gary had difficulty keeping up with him. They crossed into the main prison and were shown into an interview room off the main visitors' hall. The officer closed the door behind him as he left.

"Don't get your hopes up, we could be here for several hours. They just wanted us out of the visitors' centre before the next group arrived."

James sat and looked out on the visiting area. Gradually the women and men he had seen waiting outside were shown in. They each found themselves a table and waited for their prisoner to arrive.

At the beverage machine, a young girl fed her money in, but the coffee didn't pour out. She began hitting the vending machine. One of the prison guards standing at the side of the room walked over to her and stepped in between her and the machine. She became very angry and started to shout at the guard. He ignored her outburst and put some change in the machine. The plastic cup fell into place and filled with coffee. The girl took the coffee, and without saying anything to the guard, returned to her table.

Gary took the pictures out of the envelope, placed them on the table, and began reading the autopsy report again. James turned from the window and looked at the pictures. He put the one showing the whole room with the body and the one without side by side. He looked from one to the other very quickly, then put his index fingers, one on each picture, and moved them in parallel over each picture, hoping that would reveal the something he was seeking.

"No, this isn't going to help."

"What?"

"These were taken on the same day of the murder. Well, at least after the body was found. I need to look at one before she was murdered."

"We don't have any. No crime had been committed, so no pictures were taken."

"Yes, but I do. When she was showing me around the second time, I took lots of pictures, including one of the entire room."

"How will that help?"

"I'm not sure."

The door opened and a prison officer entered, followed by Brian Steel. He was in prison clothes and slumped into a chair opposite Gary. The sides of his Mohawk haircut had begun to grow. The top of the haircut lay lifeless and flat. The officer closed the door and stood inside the room.

"Could we speak to our client in private, please?" The officer didn't answer but left the room, closing the door.

"Got a fag?" asked Brian, not looking at either of them.

"Sorry, I didn't bring any," said James. Gary produced a pack and slid it over to Brian.

"What you want?"

"I have several questions regarding your defense. And this gentleman wants to ask you a few questions. He believes you and Dave Lilly didn't murder the woman."

"I didn't, it was Dave." He lit a cigarette and took a long drag. "He's mad!"

"But you were there?"

"So were others."

"Who?" asked James.

"I ain't telling that, I'm no snitch."

"Mr. Steel, when the police found you in the bunker, the place was full of prescription drugs. Were they yours?"

"Err, no. As I told the police, we went down to get out of the rain and someone locked us in."

"I see. So the fingerprints on the boxes aren't yours either?"

"Err, no."

"I see. What about the tape recording the police have of you and Dave Lilly confessing to the murder?"

"I don't know nothing about a tape."

"One last question. Where were you when Elizabeth Friedman died?"

"Who's she?"

"The woman you are supposed to have murdered."

"Oh, her! I was at home with me poor old mom. She's not well, you know."

"She has already told the police you weren't there."

"She's lying."

"Why would your mother lie?"

"Because she always does. Give her some money and she'll say I was there."

Gary went to speak, but James interrupted. "Please tell me what happened on the night of the murder. You were at Thirteen Crowhurst Road with Dave and Willie."

"How'd ya know Willie was there?"

"Dave told me. He says you murdered the woman."

"Well I didn't! We went to check something out."

"To see if the drugs were still okay?"

"Sort of. Dave and Willie had gone to look at the stuff, I think."

"In the shed in the back garden."

"Yeah. Dave told ya that, did he? I was in the kitchen when this woman appears at the back door. She asked me what I was doing in the house."

"What did you tell her?"

"I said I was just looking for a place to sleep. She asked me how I got in. I said the door was open. She said she was going to call the police. At that point Dave came into the kitchen from the hallway and hit her on the head and killed her. Willie, no not him, the other bloke checked to see if she was dead. He said she was, so we moved the drugs."

"Over the road to Willie's house?"

"Who was the other bloke?"

"Ain't saying."

"Why not? You know Dave will tell us if we ask."

"Then you'll get your answer, won't you!"

"Just tell me Brian was it Willie?"

"We already know he was there."

"Okay, it was Willie. But I'll kill ya if you say I said it."

"Then what happened?"

"Then we locked up and left."

"You left the woman in the kitchen?"

"Yeah."

"Who stabbed her?"

"No one. Dave hit her on the head."

"What did you do with the knife?"

"We didn't have a knife. I told ya Dave hit her on the head and killed her. Not unless Willie did it."

"Why would he do it?"

"When Dave and I left, he went back to the house. Said he was going to make sure it was locked up."

"Do you think Willie did it then?" Gary asked James.

"Maybe. I found a bag in the loft."

"A bag and a suitcase," said Brian.

"In the bag there were two videos. One of you and Dave having sex…"

"Really? I'd like to see that," said Gary, his interest aroused.

"The other video was of a party fifty years ago. Where did it come from?"

"The video of me and Dave having sex with the girl," said Brian, emphasizing the girl; "I took that one."

"You're not having sex together?" asked Gary. Brian and James ignored him.

"And the other one?"

"I found it. What about the money?"

"What money?"

"The money in the bag and suitcase."

"There was no money in them, just the videos."

"Shit, who took it? I bet it was Willie."

"Where did you find the other video?"

"Oh, that? It was in the woman's handbag."

"The woman who found you in the kitchen."

"Yeah, her."

"I was wondering what happened to her handbag."

"Willie took it for his Mom."

"I see. Where's Willie now?"

"I don't know, but if he's got my money, then he would have done a bunk."

During all this Gary had been taking notes. Now he looked up at James, then at Brian. "Anything you would like to add, Mr. Steel?"

"I was wondering, could you help me and Dave to escape? We'd make it worth your while honest. We were making a bundle selling the stuff. And I could look after you, you know, sex." Gary didn't answer, but the corner of this mouth curled very slightly into a smile.

"So let me get everything clear," said James. "Dave hit Elizabeth Friedman on the head in the kitchen. You left the body there and neither you, Dave or Willie stabbed her?"

"That's right. And if anyone's saying we stabbed her, they are liars. There'd be blood, and I hate the sight of blood."

"You didn't move the body?"

"No. Do you think you could help us?"

"Only if you've told me the truth."

"I have."

"Was anyone else there with you?" Brian Steel sat silently and looked into the busy visitors' hall.

"The gentleman asked you if there was anyone else there. If there was, it would be a good idea to tell us before the police find out."

Brian looked at Gary and then at James. Lowering his head, he quietly said, "Bobby Coates came over, but Willie sent him away. But I'm not sure if he left, because I thought I heard someone upstairs."

"You think he saw what happened?"

"I dunno. Bobby's a queer nutter." Gary gave James a questioning look. He responded with a shake of his head.

"Hey, can you get me sister to visit me? She won't even answer me phone calls."

"I can ask her. You know your mother is in hospital."

"Why?"

"Because you stabbed her."

"Stabbed her?"

"Yes, just before you went with Dave into the bunker," said James.

"Oh shit, I don't remember that."

"Why don't you write a letter to your mother, Mr. Steel?"

"Me, write?"

"It might help. I don't have any more questions for you at this time, Mr. Steel."

"Nor do I," said James.

"Do you have anything you would like to ask or say, Mr. Steel?"

"No, not really, just get me out of here. Why won't they let me see Dave?"

"I can't answer that." Gary rose from the chair and knocked on the door. It opened immediately, and a prison officer entered, took Brian out, and closed the door behind him. "They will search him now. So we have to wait. Well, did it help?"

"Err, yes. Brian and Dave didn't murder Elizabeth Friedman, and I believe that Willie didn't either."

"Willie who?"

"William Coates. He lives with his mother and his brother, Bobby, in Crowhurst Road."

"You seem to know a lot about the whole affair. Could you give me a statement?"

"Sure, once I've solved the mystery."

"You can come to the office."

"Were you one of his customers?"

"No, he is not my type. Rough trade."

They were interrupted by the prison officer who with a nod indicated that they could leave. He held open the door for them.

As they stood outside the prison, James looked for Trevor or his truck, but he couldn't see either.

"Well James, I must get back to the office. You will stop by and make a statement?"

"Yes, when I get to the bottom of all this. Gary, it's nice to meet you again. The new you! And thanks for letting me come in with you. I believe your client is innocent of the murder. I hope I'll be able to give you proof of that when I come to your office."

"Great! Make it soon."

"Soon as I can."

"Bye then." Gary ran across the road, narrowly avoiding a speeding car, and got into a new black BMW. James stood and watched as he drove off. That's proof, thought James. You should never judge anyone. You never know how they may turn out in life.

He began to search for Trevor's truck, it was nowhere to be seen. Walking out of the prison forecourt onto the main road, he looked up and down. Still no sign of the truck! Crossing to the opposite street, he didn't pay much attention to the man dressed in a grey tracksuit on the opposite pavement. He became anxious when he realized that the man was matching his pace exactly. He looked about to see if there was anywhere he could run to. There was an alleyway between two houses just ahead. James made a dash for it. The man ran after him. As James reached the alleyway, a man dressed in black police taskforce clothing got quickly out of a parked car, made a rush at James, and forced him into the alleyway. James ran ahead but stumbled over some black plastic bags and boxes. The track suited man joined the other man. They picked James up and held him against the wet wall of one of the houses. Water from a broken drainpipe was running down the wall and had created a small area of green slime. James now felt this penetrating his clothing and the back of his head. The policeman type grabbed James around the neck. His grip tightened like an iron clamp. The track suited man punched James in the stomach. He squealed and tried to control his breathing. It was not easy with the hand around his throat.

A third man joined them from the car. He was wearing a black Armani suit and very thick-lens glasses. His light, mousy hair was receding, and he had combed whatever remained over the bald patch. His brought his face very close to James's, the smell of his Indian lunch impregnating James's nostrils.

"Listen, if you know what's good for you, you'll stop poking your nose into that murder," he said in a Glasgow accent. "If the guys say they killed her, then they did, ya ken?" He slapped James on the face. "You got the message?" He slapped James again, this time a little harder.

James didn't answer. He was still trying to get his breath back after the punch in the stomach. "Now I won't tell you again, so don't mess with me and my friends. And if you see that Willie Coates, tell him Mr. McMason is looking for him, and if he knows what's good for him, he'll find me."

The man then slapped James on the face several more times before returning to the car. The track suited man punched James again. The man dressed like a policeman released his grip and kicked James as he fell to the ground, catching him painfully in the side of his chest. James gasped for air, desperately trying to control each breath. The man dressed like a policeman bent over and punched James in the face several times. Then just as he was leaving kicked James who had curled up into the fetal position. Lying on the ground for several minutes James expecting some other act of violence. When nothing happened he lifted his head to see where the men were. They had gone. The car was also no longer parked at the entrance to the alleyway.

James slowly raised himself to his feet and staggered out of the alleyway just in time to see Trevor's truck driving by. He was in too much pain to make any attempt to get Trevor's attention. He put one hand on the wall of the corner house. The cold brick felt like ice to his hand. He steadied himself, trying to get his breathing under control. The blood from his nose and mouth dripped on his clothes. His gut wrenched and heaved, and his stomach contents were now a painting on the pavement. He retched several more times, but very little vomit came to add to the original picture. An old Sikh man passed him. He looked at James and then at the vomit, then crossed to the other side of the street, avoiding Trevor's truck as he pulled into the roadside.

"James! What happened? Do you need to go to hospital?"

"I'll be fine once I get my breath and stop vomiting."

"What happened?"

"I'm not sure, but three men just warned me not to try and prove that Brain and Dave didn't kill Elizabeth Friedman."

"Why?"

"I think it may be to do with the drugs." A woman dressed in a bright green sari came along the pavement. She pushed her three children ahead of her, avoiding the vomit, and once they were passed, she began to run, telling the children in Punjabi to follow her.

James's face was white, and he looked as though he were going to faint. Trevor felt helpless and wasn't sure what he should do. "So what happened?"

"Trevor, less of the questions for now. Can you get me some water and paper towels?"

"There's a shop on the corner." Trevor ran to the small family-run shop. James watched him disappear before he vomited again. A few moments later, Trevor returned with a bottle of water and a large box of tissues. James drank some of the water then spat it out into the gutter. He wet several of the tissues and washed his face. His nose bleed had stopped. Once he had cleaned himself up, he took several deep breaths before speaking.

"I think we have stumbled onto something."

"Yeah, but what?"

"I'm not sure, but they obviously want Brian and Dave to stay inside."

"Do you know who it was?"

"No, never seen them before."

"What happened?"

"I was trying to find where you had parked when this man jumped out of a car and pushed me into the alley. The others came and beat me up. The one in the suit told me not to interfere."

"Shit, I'm sorry."

"It's not your fault."

"It is. If I had been with you, it might not have happened."

"Oh, it would have. They were really serious, and nothing would have stopped them."

"Let's get you home." They climbed into the truck, unaware of the unmarked police car parked up the street. The two plain-clothes officers sat in silence, making notes. Trevor helped James into the truck, and as he walked to the driver's side of the vehicle, he turned to check the street. But the two officers had slipped down in their seats.

He eased the truck into traffic. The police car followed at a safe distance. He dialed the farm on his mobile. "Hey Mom, James and I are on the way. He's been beaten up... No, just shaken... In about half an hour, if the traffic's not bad."

James lay his head against the head rest and closed his eyes. He awoke when Trevor hit the brakes hard. Police cars were surrounding the truck. The passenger door was violently opened and a policeman dragged James out onto the pavement and pushed him up against the truck. Another officer had opened Trevor's door, but just stood by it.

Inspector Mark Smith walked slowly over to James from a police car, a smirk on his face. He scratched at his backside before unconsciously putting his fingers to his nose to smell them. "Looking a little scruffy, Mr. Pidgley, especially for visiting someone in jail. Or was it because of your run-in with the McMason brothers? Well, I don't know what your connection with them is, but they are not the best of company."

"I don't know what you're talking about, Mr. Smith."

"Inspector Smith to you, Gypsy boy! No, I didn't expect you to understand plain English."

"Oh, I understand the Queen's English, but they don't teach police slang in state schools!"

Inspector Smith ignored James's comment and turned to a policeman who had just arrived. The officer spoke very quietly to the Inspector, who nodded his head. "I hear you're going to prove that Steel and Lilly didn't brutally murder poor, defenseless Elizabeth Friedman. Well, let me tell you, Pidgley, they did it, so don't bother to find out anything else."

"But what if they didn't do it?"

"They did. I have a taped confession."

"I know."

"What do you mean, you know?"

"I got that confession for you. I got it because you were convinced my father had murdered her, and I had to prove you were wrong. But they didn't do it either. And if you don't, or won't, find out the truth, then I will, regardless of you or the McMasons' threat."

"Big talk, Pidgley! But I warn you, dig any deeper and mess up my case, and I'll run you in for interfering in police business."

"What are you scared of, Mr. Smith? You just want to frame two innocent men of murder because you are too lazy? Or is there some other reason you don't want to do a proper job?"

"Just you watch what you're saying."

"Can't take the truth, Smith? I wonder how many others you've framed!" shouted James. Inspector Smith suddenly became aware that James was playing to a large crowd who had gathered. Before he could reply, James continued. "It's what we, the poor public, expect from the police these days. Corruption."

Someone from the crowd shouted, "Yeah pig, corruption!"

Inspector Smith came closer to James and whispered into his face. "I'm warning you to back off this case or I'll fix you. And I'd be very careful who I mix with. The farmer's boy is very much mixed up in this affair, and I'm going to have his arse on a plate by the time it's all over!"

A slow chant had begun from the crowd. "Pigs, pigs, pigs, pigs!" Several police officers had begun to push the crowd back when a fight broke out between them and the crowd.

"Let's go. I've finished with him. For now," said Inspector Smith. The police dispersed as quickly as they had arrived.

James climbed into the truck, and he and Trevor drove away from the crowd, who were still very agitated. "Wow, you got him riled! If Brian and Dave didn't murder her, then who did?"

"Willie may have. But I need to find him, and quickly, before the police or the McMason brothers do."

"McMason brothers? What have they got to do with this?"

"I don't know, but according to Smith, they're the ones who beat me up."

"You mean the police watched you get beaten up but did nothing?"

"Looks like it. So who are they? Do you know?"

"Kenneth and Anthony McMason. They are originally from Glasgow, but run the drug show in Edinburgh, and they've just moved down here. They've become the biggest suppliers in the Midlands, if not the biggest outside the London families. No one messes with them."

"We will! But don't tell them." James looked at Trevor and began to laugh. Trevor, unable to stop himself, joined in.

"Okay, we go back to the farm, clean up, and then try and find Willie."

"Where do we start?"

"I think I know," said Trevor, feeling a little more self-assured. "I may be slow on the uptake sometimes, but I get there in the end."

Into The Woods

J ames and Trevor entered the small forest, which
was part of the Lickey Hills. It had once been a
very large forest, but as Birmingham expanded it
shrank until now it was hardly more than a wood. The
smell of rotting vegetation and pine trees was almost
overpowering and burned the scent-hairs in their
nostrils.

James had grown up playing games of hide-
and seek in these woods. Creating a myriad of
mythical creatures to while away the long, lonely
summer days. His brothers and sisters never wanted to
play his games, so he spent much of the time on his
own. This worried his parents. He was contented and
remarked whenever they said something, "I like to be
on my own. No one can boss me about." Deep down,
however, he bore a slight resentment towards his
siblings, feeling they had abandoned him.

The steep climb to the top allowed him time to
think things over, although the trees interrupted his

thoughts. There were just too many of them, and in some places it was difficult to get over or passed them. He and Trevor eventually came across a well-worn path and began to follow it.

"I hope no one is following us."

"I don't think so, but we must be careful. By the way, where were you when I was seeing Brian Steel?"

"At home."

"Oh!"

"I was looking at the video of the house. You were right. Something was missing. I had seen it so many times, I had even filmed it, but when it was gone I didn't notice."

"So, what was it?"

"An umbrella."

"A yellow umbrella! Yes, it was there when I first looked at the house, and I've seen it somewhere else, but I can't remember where."

"Why would someone take an umbrella?"

"In case it rained?"

"Yeah, but to kill someone and then remove an object that most people who have been in the house would have seen doesn't make much sense." Trevor slipped on some leaves and grabbed at a tree to stop his fall.

"It could have been anyone. It's one of those supermarket freebies. There must be thousands of them all over the city. I remember the campaign: 'Spend twenty pounds or more and get a free umbrella.'"

"Yeah, me Mom got one and gave it to me Dad. Once, at the pub, all his mates laughed at him. Until they went to leave at closing time and it was pouring! Last laugh was on them!"

"I think it's important, but I don't yet know why." They continued to climb the hill. The trees were now sparser and the path less steep. As they reached a plateau, the trees suddenly ended. Growing around a grass picnic area were small bushes and bracken. Wooden benches and tables were strategically placed so that each set of picnickers wouldn't interfere with the next.

There was a group of picnickers there, enjoying a feast of sandwiches and what looked like hot soup, at one of the tables. Trevor and James crossed the green oasis, passing the group, and saw an infamous yellow umbrella lying on the grass next to a girl. Trevor pointed it out with a nod of his head to James and they both smiled. Thinking the smile was for her, the girl smiled back. On the other side of the picnic oasis, the path continued, surrounded by dense bracken that slowed them down a little.

"This is a long way around to where I think Willie might be, but I want to make sure we are not being followed. You've made too many enemies lately for us not to be cautious."

"Me, make enemies! I don't think I can help it if certain persons seem to have taken a dislike to me."

"Fair enough." The undergrowth abruptly stopped, and a road, the old Birmingham Road, dissected the natural beauty of the hills and forest. The tarmac on the road was cracked, and potholes filled with water stretched as far as the eye could see.

"Did you know the Romans built this road?"

"Yes, and I think they need to repair it!"

The bracken was very dense on the other side of the road, and James knew from childhood pranks that this could be dangerous. It was so easy for someone to hide in the undergrowth, unseen until they pounced. Several different types of fern grew in the area, and James had always been amazed at how the leaves, so tightly rolled up, unfolded as they grew. A young girl about twelve years old suddenly jumped out and ran past them, laughing. A boy of thirteen or fourteen stood up out of the bracken, his jeans and boxer shorts pulled down to his ankles. He looked at them, shouting, "Sod off perverts!"

Trevor gave his nervous little laugh. "I wish I had my camera. It would make a good scene for a horror movie."

"Then you would have been a pervert."

"No, it's art! Didn't they teach you the difference between art and porn at your school?"

James suddenly grabbed Trevor and pulled him into the undergrowth, placing a hand over his mouth before he could speak. Two Park Rangers rode by on beautiful brown horses, from their manner obviously searching for someone. After they had gone, James stood up slowly, listening intently to the sounds around him.

"I didn't hear them coming."

"I heard the hooves."

"Next you'll tell me you smelt them!"

"Oh, I did." Trevor gave a James a disbelieving look. "We have to be extra careful from now on. As you jokingly said, I've... no, it's not just me, we have made too many enemies, or at least enough people who want us not to find out the truth."

Silence enveloped them as they continued, both having different thoughts. Again Trevor found himself unexpectedly pushed into the bracken. A group of hikers passed by.

"You heard them or smelt them?"

"Heard. The breeze is taking the smell away from us."

"You're serious, aren't you?"

"Yes. When we were kids, my grandfather taught us how to listen to the sounds around and what to look for, and yes, different smells. For him, it was self-preservation and Trevor, that's what it is for us now."

Reaching a flat ridge, which looked out over Birmingham, the view was expansive. Years of urban sprawl had ruined what once must have been breathtaking. "On a clear day, you can see the University Tower. When we were kids, my dad used to play a trick on us. He would secretly look at his watch, then tell us it was three o'clock or whatever time it was. We would ask him how he knew, and he would reply he could read it on the University Tower clock. One of us would look through the telescope over there, and that would be the time it was. We were well impressed!"

"Wow. If you had done that to me now, I would have believed you too."

"Trevor!"

"Anyway, we'd better make our way down to the old fairground site."

"You think that's where we'll find Willie?"

"Let's see. We would play there as kids, and Willie would always say the Lickey Hills was his favorite place in the whole wide world."

"He didn't travel much then. He should have gone to the Malvern Hills."

"I've been there," said Trevor, slipping into a thoughtful mood.

Taking the path, which ran down the hill with its twists and turns as it descended. The bracken became less dense and trees began to appear, not giving them much cover in case they had to hide. The old fairground with its rotten wooden shell and rusted metal towers appeared as a long-lost ghost town. Abandoned and falling apart, it had always been a fun area for the many boys and some of the girls who grew up nearby.

"He isn't here, but I didn't expect him to be. Down the hill a little way is a man-made cave. When we grew up, Willie always said it was his cave. He even told us his father had made it. We didn't believe him, but it was always called the Coates Cave."

Circling around towards the cave, James listened intently to the sounds floating on the air. Trevor crouched behind a small bush and pointed at the hole in the rock face. Its blackness seemed sinister. No one knew why it was there, but hundreds of children had made a claim to it over the years.

"I'll go and see if he's there. If he sees you, he may panic." Trevor crept closer to the entrance of the cave. He had never really liked the place, it always smelt of urine. Once he was beside the entrance, he waved to James, then disappeared inside. He reappeared moments later and beckoned James to join him. James approached very cautiously. It was at moments like this that he felt things could still go wrong.

"He's not here."

"Has he been?"

"No, I don't think so. Someone has, but I don't think it was Willie."

James poked his head inside, but the smell of urine made him pull back and take a deep breath. "By the smell of it, I think it may have been Brian Steel." Trevor laughed. But the crack of a gun and a chunk flying off the rock next to him choked his laughter.

"Run," shouted James, grabbing Trevor's arm and heading off downhill towards cover, dodging the bullets being fired at them. It was hard to tell if there was one sniper or two. Racing between the trees, they reached a pathway with a narrow stream running alongside and cascading over rocks into small pools before pouring into a lake. Several hikers were shouting at them, but what they said drifted away in the wind. Faster and faster they ran as the pathway got wider and the gunfire continued.

They sped alongside the lake, scattering the ducks, much to the annoyance of the people feeding them. Trevor tripped and grabbed at James to steady himself before they continued. Passing a tearoom and the entrance to the golf course. Several other people who were enjoying the country park began to shout at them, not realizing that someone was discharging a gun.

Reaching the main road, Trevor began to slow down. James continued and was about ten feet ahead of him when he turned and saw a rifle protruding from the back window of a Range Rover with dark-paned windows.

"Trevor, down!"

Trevor threw himself to the ground as the gun discharged. Several people who were walking along the street did the same. The Range Rover sped away, almost crashing into a parked car. James ran back to Trevor and helped him to his feet. They jumped the low wall between the pavement and the woods, scurrying into the darkness and safety of the densely packed trees and thick canopy of leaves. About six feet inside, a path ran parallel with the pavement. Trevor and James ran along it until it all but disappeared and then came to an unexpected end behind a line of shops and arcades.

Out of breath, Trevor stopped and steadied himself against a tree. "What's going on, James? You really must have upset someone this time!"

"Someone is trying to scare us."

"You mean kill us!"

"No, scare us. If they'd wanted to kill us, they could have done it easily by the cave."

"What now? We can't stay here."

"No."

"Look," said Trevor, pointing to a poster on the side of an arcade. "There's a vintage car rally in the park. We'd be safer there, among a crowd of people."

"All we have to do is cross the road."

"Ah, yes."

"I know! The old tram terminal is over there. We can use the buses that turn and stop there as shields, and the old terminal building too."

"Okay, let's go." A bus was just arriving and began the turn into the terminal. Trevor and James dashed to it and then ran alongside it, hiding from the traffic. Once the bus had stopped by the old terminal shelter, they skirted around the back of it and into the shelter, which was less than thirty feet from the entrance to the park. The shelter was an old whitewashed brick building. The waiting area had been vandalized with graffiti, and the wood bench seat destroyed. Trevor looked around for any suspicious vehicles. He tapped James on the shoulder, and they both ran into the park and down the hill to the vintage car rally.

They stopped by a 1950 Austin Princess. The car was in immaculate condition, and the owner got rather agitated as James and Trevor leant against the car. It took a few minutes for them to get their breathing under control. Trevor looked like he was about to faint. James helped him to his feet and pushed him into the exhibition, leaving the Austin Princess owner anxiously inspecting the car's for damage.

James went straight to a tea wagon and ordered a bag of freshly cooked doughnuts and two hot chocolates. Trevor had found a table and was sitting down when he saw James walking towards him. "Are we crazy?"

"Possibly. Why?"

"Well, you buy doughnuts and cocoa as though nothing had happened, and only a few minutes ago someone was shooting at us!"

"My grandmother used to say, 'You can't think on an empty stomach.' I'm starving, and I don't think anyone will try to shoot at us in this crowd."

"Let's hope not." Trevor took a bite out of one of the doughnuts and looked at James, maybe his grandmother was right.

Chomping quietly on their doughnuts and looking at the people around them, they heard a loud bang. Without stopping to find out what was making the noise, they ran for cover, Trevor into a group of trees, James to an old hut inside a small garden with a wall around it. As he crouched behind the wall, he remembered the place. His father had told him this was where a woman they called Lady Jane had lived for many years. People thought she was a witch because of her unruly hair and very long fingernails. But she was just a homeless old lady who had found somewhere to end her days. Behind him he heard the hut door open. He turned and saw Willie's face peering nervously out at him. The door shut again quickly. James crawled up to it and tapped it lightly.

"Willie, open the door." There was no answer he tapped again.

From inside a voice said, "Go away."

"I can't, Willie, until I've talked to you."

I don't want to talk to you."

"Why not?"

"Because you're one of them."

"One of whom?"

"You're gonna kill me."

"No, Willie, I don't want to hurt you at all. I want to help you. Okay, don't open the door, but just tell me a few things."

"Why should I?"

"Because Brian and Dave are telling the police you stabbed the estate agent."

"I never."

"How do I know that?"

"Because I say so."

"Why did you pick this place to hide?"

"An old lady used to live here, she was my auntie, and I would come and see her. She told me where she kept her key, and no one knew I was related to her."

"Tell me what happened, and I'll tell the police for you."

"Let me think about it." In the pause that followed, James looked over the wall. He couldn't see Trevor anywhere. He did see a crowd gathered around one of the fairground rides. The light bulbs on it were popping explosively. It must have been that, not gunfire, that had sent them running!

"You on your own?"

"Yes, Willie."

"I'm not sure I can trust you."

"Why not, Willie?"

"Because…"

"Because you're scared. But if you don't tell me, how are we to know you didn't murder the woman?"

"I'm scared."

"I know, Willie

"Okay, I'll tell you what happened."

James stooped by the door so that he could still see over the wall if anyone came near. "You know about the drugs?"

"Yes."

"Well, me, Brian and Dave went to see if the drugs were still at the house. Dave disappeared upstairs, to hide something I think."

"Yes?"

"I was in the living room. Brian was in the kitchen when the woman walked in and asked him what he was doing there. Dave came in from the hallway and hit her on the head, killing her. That's what really happened. It was Dave who killed her."

"What happened after that?"

"We moved the drugs to my house. You remember when you first came and I had all them boxes in the outhouse?"

"Yes."

"Well, that was the drugs in them boxes." Willie gave a sob, then began to cry.

"It's okay, Willie."

"I want me Mom," cried Willie, opening the door a little so James could see his fraught face the tears running down the cheeks.

"Oh Willie." The boy gave another sob.

"What happened at the house after Dave hit her on the head?"

Willie didn't answer, but sobbed, looking out at James. His face pulled into a grotesque mask, frozen in time.

"Willie, you have to pull yourself together. Tell me what happened, then I can help you."

Willie gave a deep sob and several sniffs.

"Dave and Brian left and told me to lock up."

"Did you?"

"Well, first I went upstairs. I wanted to find out what it was Dave had hidden, but I couldn't find anything."

"So what did you do then?"

"Nothing. No, that's not right. I heard someone downstairs. I thought it was our Bobby, but when I crept down, I couldn't find him, or anyone. So I left by the front door."

"And that was it?"

"Yeah, except for the smell."

"What smell?"

"When I was coming down the stairs I could smell something."

"What sort of smell?"

"Flowers, nice flowers."

"Perfume, you mean?"

"No, it was flowers. A bit like Mom's lavender, but it wasn't lavender."

"Anything else?"

"No, I ran home and hid."

"Willie, the police and I think the McMason brothers are looking for you."

"The McMason brothers! Oh shit, I'm dead."

"Then maybe you should go to the police and tell them what you have told me."

"I don't know. If Dave and Brian are blaming me, the police will think I did it."

"Not if I can help it. Dave and Brian didn't do it..."

"Nor did I."

"I know that, Willie. I'm trying to find out who did, but if I were you, seriously, I would give myself up, and quickly."

The light bulbs began to pop noisily again. Willie closed and locked the door by drawing a bolt.

As James looked over the wall, a bullet hit it, sending fragments into his face. He sank down behind the brick wall. The gunman was still on his trail!

"Willie, stay inside there for the moment. There's someone shooting at me, but I don't think they know you're here. Then go to the police. Willie it's your only chance."

James crept to the gateway and peered out. Where was Trevor? He looked carefully into the mass of people who had come into the car rally area. Another bullet hit the wood of the gate, and James saw where the gunfire was coming from. High on the hill by a group of trees there was a flash just before the bullet hit the wall.

James rolled over the wall away from the gunman and crept along until he was behind the hut. He weighed up his options. He could run back into the crowd at the vintage car rally or try to make it over to the line of trees that ran behind the hut. Looking back at the rally crowd, he couldn't see Trevor, so he made a dash for the first tree. As he reached it a bullet hit just above his head. He ran to the next tree and then the next as another bullet grazed its trunk.

Ahead was an area of the park where the city council grew its Christmas trees, but it was at least fifty yards away, and there was only one more tree for protection. He waited for a few moments to gather his breath and nerve, then ran as fast as he could. The bullets came thick and fast. This was certainly no longer a game, if it ever had been. The sniper was trying to kill him. The fifty yards seemed like several miles, until at last he jumped over the wire fence and dived into the thick cover of the trees. He felt his heart was about to explode.

Hidden in the trees, he dialed Trevor's mobile number. It rang four times and the answer phone message came on. What was going on? Where was he? With a shudder, James suddenly recollected what Inspector Smith had said: "Careful who you mix with!" indicating Trevor.

James's head began to spin. Maybe Trevor was one of the McMason gang, and that's the only reason he was being so helpful. A bullet suddenly snapped one of the treetops near him. They had only shot to scare them over by the cave, when the two of them were together. But now that he was by himself, they were shooting to kill him.

He moved further into the tightly packed trees, making his way towards where he hoped the road was, his heart pounding. He turned over in his mind all the things that had happened. If Trevor was with the enemy, why had he stayed so apparently friendly for so long? No, this was silly! Trevor had shown his loyalty dozens of times. And yet…?

Lost in thought, he found he had walked into a clearing. He ran back into the cover of the trees and sized up the situation. In front of him were the road and a bus stop, and one of the few buses of the day was just arriving. He sprinted out of the trees, over the wire fence, and onto the bus, surprising the driver, who hadn't seen where James had appeared from. As the bus pulled out, he looked out of the window to see if anyone were following. He couldn't see anyone, so he sat down with a big sigh.

"You gonna pay?" said the driver.

"Oh yes. Which way do you go?"

"Barnt Green on to Bromsgrove."

"Err, Bromsgrove." James gave the driver a pound coin.

"I don't give change."

"That's okay," said James, returning to his seat. He looked into the park, but couldn't see Trevor or the sniper. The bus slowed as it approached the roundabout. There were police and ambulance men rushing all over, but James couldn't make out what the kerfuffle was. All he and the rest of the bus passengers could see was a vehicle sticking out of the building in the middle of the roundabout.

He returned to his thoughts about Trevor, he couldn't be wrong about him, surely? He, James Pidgley, was always a good judge of character, wasn't he? But how come Trevor managed to be somewhere else when the bullets were definitely for real? The bus stopped to let on a passenger. James looked out of the window and realized he was close to the Fishers' farm. He pressed the button and left the bus at the next stop.

James watched as the bus drove away, then he crossed into the lane that ran up to the farm. Walking up the lane he kept close to the hedge, just in case he had to hide quickly. At the farmhouse, he couldn't see Trevor's truck in the yard. Joe Fisher was driving a tractor and waved at James. He waved back and continued towards the farmhouse. If he could get into Trevor's room, maybe he could find a clue to the truth. He knocked on the kitchen door, and Irene Fisher opened it.

"Hello, James, on your own?"

"Err, yes. Trevor said he'd meet me here."

"Fine, come on in. Are you hungry?"

"Not at the moment."

"Okay, maybe you will be later when Joe has his tea. You want to wait in Trevor's room?" James couldn't believe how trusting the Fishers were.

He sat on the bed and looked around the room. Where would Trevor hide any secret stuff? He quietly began to search the room, opening several of the drawers and cupboards, but he didn't find anything out of the ordinary. James wondered what he was looking for. He felt he would know when he found it. He opened the desk drawers under the computer and looked underneath to see if anything had been taped there. He found nothing and again sat on the edge of the bed. He sprang up and went on all fours looking under the bed. Just some dirty clothes, which he put into the laundry basket Irene Fisher had placed by the door. Several videos, which had titles like *Once a Virgin* and *In the Beginning a Virgin,* but nothing that would help James fathom if Trevor were truly the friend he seemed.

Again he sat on the bed and looked around the room. Where would he hide things if this were his room? The only place he hadn't looked was in the large old walnut wardrobe. He opened the door. It was very neat, with all the clothes on hangers and several pairs of shoes placed on the floor. He closed the door and stood back looking at the wardrobe. Trevor's room was a complete mess, so why did he keep the wardrobe so neat? To keep someone out, so that they didn't move things or try and clean up inside? James opened the door again, something was wrong. He checked the walls and the back of the wardrobe. Maybe there was a secret way to Narnia! He laughed at the thought. He climbed on a chair and looked on top, nothing but dust.

He was about to close the wardrobe door when he had a brainwave. Picking up the shoes he felt the floor of the wardrobe. The wooden board lifted out easily. Here was Trevor's secret hiding place. Inside was a pile of photos of girls, mostly naked. Several notebooks and one large address book. James opened one of the notebooks. It was a diary. Trevor had made an entry for every day, but this particular book was several years old. James looked until he found the present one. The last entry had been a few days ago:

Tonight I met a really nice guy. At first he seemed a bit of a wanker, but I think Brian and Dave beat him up and dumped him in one of our fields. He thought he was at the Gates of Hell; anyway, I took him home. He has a nice place. I wish I had friends like him. Mom and Dad really like him, said he was class.

Brian and Dave called several times. Something's up, I want out I have to get out.

As he looked at the entry, he wondered if he were being paranoid because of what Inspector Smith had said. He put the notebook back into the hiding place. The only other thing to check was the address book. He replaced the board and shoes carefully and closed the wardrobe door.

He sat on the bed and flipped through the book. It was mostly girls' names and phone numbers, some with film names by them and dates. When he came to "S" he stopped and looked in disbelief: "Sharon Smith! Father a copper, but great look and can act." Next to this entry was a date. Maybe this was why Inspector Smith was so against Trevor. James went to the wardrobe and reopened the secret hiding place. He took out the notebooks and looked at the one corresponding with the date in the address book. It read, "Filming going well, Sharon is a natural she is doing a great job, her father arrives and storms into the field and takes her home, telling me he will prosecute me for porno, may not be able to finish the film."

James replaced everything and closed the wardrobe. Of course Trevor was innocent. He felt awful that he'd ever had bad thoughts about him. He should trust his instincts. That's what he had been taught as a child, and now here he was, ignoring them.

Irene entered the room, and James looked up like a boy caught doing something he shouldn't.

"You hungry yet?

"Yes, I am."

"Then come on and have something to eat. I don't know where our Trevor could have got to. He usually phones when he's going to be late."

James followed her downstairs and into the kitchen. Joe was already sitting at the table.

"Hello James, you been stood up?"

James nodded with a smile and took a seat at the table.

"I was just saying to James, our Trevor would normally phone if he was going to be late or something had happened."

"Well, he can't this time, he left his mobile in the office, recharging."

That explains that! Thought James.

"But he's late, and he said he was going to met James here."

"He didn't say we'd meet exactly. I just expected he would come here."

Irene dished out the food and they sat in silence, eating. When they had finished, Joe took out his pipe and filled it with tobacco, but didn't light it.

"So James how is your father? I haven't seen him for at least thirty years. He was a clever kid. He knew everything about the countryside. Could tell you all the plants and trees. I remember once he caught not one but two hares. He gave me mom one. She was so pleased, she loved jugged hare."

"Dad's okay. A few aches and pains, but I think he is really doing fine."

"He married young Sarah Welch. She was the prettiest girl around. They had two weddings, Irene, one in church, and the other was a Gypsy one, and it was beautiful. Made me wish I had been born a Gypsy."

"Except for the prejudice," said Irene.

"Oh, well, that's always been there. People are so scared of what they don't understand. That's right, ain't it, James?"

"I think so. I know my Dad suffered, but us kids haven't really had it too bad since we became home dwellers. But I know some who still travel have a dreadful time, especially since the Thatcher days. The prejudice still there, and I don't think it will ever go away."

"Maybe you're right."

The phone rang. "That'll be our Trevor now," said Irene.

Joe answered the phone. After a few seconds the color drained from his face and he sat down. "Which hospital?" Irene dried her hands and also sat down. "I see. We'll come straight away." He replaced the phone on the cradle. "Our Trevor's had an accident. He is in Selly Oak Hospital."

"How bad is it?"

"They didn't say. Let's go."

All three rose and left the kitchen as it was.

CHAPTER SEVENTEEN

Persons Unknown

The drab green walls of the hospital waiting room were covered sporadically with discernibly color-drained pictures of country scenes. Grey metal chairs lined the room; years of being pushed against the wall had created an indentation. A frieze to the pain and suffering loved ones experienced fearing the worst. Each time the room had been painted, the indentation was painted over, and it was now a feature of the room.

James sat opposite Joe and Irene. When they had arrived, they had been told to wait until someone came and explained what was happening to Trevor.

Silence hung over the trio. Joe twiddled his thumbs and sighed deeply. James looked at him. What a good man he was, he loved his wife. He had worked hard all his life to bring up his family as best he could. Irene and James looked at each other. She gave him a weak, worried smile, her large arms folded across her chest and resting on her ample breasts. She was staring at the wall in front of her when someone dropped a metal pan in the corridor. She didn't react. Her cheeks were blushed, and small droplets had gathered in the corner of each eye. Her normally perfect lipstick was smudged, and the bridge of her nose was shiny.

She suddenly spoke, not moving her gaze from the wall. "Joe, you'd better phone our Neil again, please luv." Joe stood up to go to the pay phone out in the corridor.

"Please use my mobile," said James, handing it to him.

"James, thank you, that's really kind of you," said Irene. "I'm glad you're here. It's so nice to know he has such a good friend" She stopped talking and started to cry. James moved over to the seat next to her and put his arm on her shoulder. She sobbed loudly, and taking a clean white handkerchief out of her outsized bag, wiped her eyes. "I'm sorry."

"Irene, there's nothing to be sorry about. But we don't know what's happened to Trevor yet."

"That's true, but I can't stop myself thinking the worst." Joe dialed Neil's number and was listening for someone to answer.

The door to the waiting room opened, and a young Asian man entered. He was in blue hospital clothes and had a stethoscope around his neck. Joe closed the mobile. "Mr. and Mrs. Fisher?"

"Over here," said James, realizing how futile he must sound, as they were the only ones in the waiting room.

"Is he alright? Please tell me he's alright."

"My name is Doctor Mossavar, and I've been attending to your son. I'm afraid he has a broken leg and a small fracture in his arm, but I'm pleased to be able to tell you that everything else is fine."

"Thank God," said Irene, who began to cry even more.

Joe sat down next to Irene and put his arms around her. "Now now, my love, he is going to be okay."

"From what the police tell me," continued the doctor, "he is lucky to be alive. If he'd had a passenger, they would not have been so lucky."

"Do you know what happened?"

"The police have said, oh, they are with your son at the moment. They have said that someone cut the brake-fluid pipe."

James sat down, feeling sick. He should have been that passenger. Joe and Irene said nothing, but continued to hug each other.

Feeling a little awkward, the doctor said, "We will keep him in overnight, but he should be all right to go home tomorrow."

"Oh, that's good. What time can we pick him up?"

"Once the doctor on the ward has done his rounds, provided there are no complications."

"Can we see him now?" asked Irene.

"You should be able to see him in a moment. Let me check to see if the police have finished, and I'll take you through."

"Oh thank you, doctor," said Irene, as Doctor Mossavar left the waiting room. "What a nice man he is, kind. I can't understand why there is so much animosity towards them."

"Irene, my sweet, like James and his family, who have suffered from it, prejudice is everywhere, but it's only ignorant people who discriminate in that way."

"True, luv. Did you get through to our Neil?"

"No, I left another message. Irene, luv, it's market tomorrow morning…"

"Oh yes, Joe, I forgot about that."

"So maybe we can ask the hospital to fetch our Trevor home in an ambulance."

"No problem. I'll pick him up and bring him back to the farm," said James.

"Oh James, you really are a love."

"No, son, we really couldn't…"

"There's no argument. I'd be delighted to do it, for you and for Trevor."

The doctor returned and beckoned them to follow him. They walked down the green-painted corridor to a cubicle in the emergency department. The doctor pulled back the curtains and there was Trevor, sitting up in the bed, his leg in a plaster cast. He was talking to a young police officer. Trevor smiled when he saw his parents, and the smile grew bigger when he saw James standing behind them.

Irene gave a little run to the bed and threw her arms around him, giving him several kisses and hugs. The police officer moved to the side, and after looking in his notebook, said, "I think that's all for now, Mr. Fisher, but we would like to get a proper statement from you later, if that will not be too much trouble."

"Right, later, thanks," said Trevor, dismissing the police officer.

As the officer began to leave, James moved in front of him, blocking his way. "What happened? The doctor said someone had cut his brake-pipe."

"Are you family, sir?"

"Yes, he is," said Joe, who had moved closer to hear what the officer was saying.

"From our preliminary investigation, it looks like someone was trying to cause harm to whoever was in the vehicle."

"You mean someone was trying to kill our lad and whoever was in the truck with him?"

"Yes, sir, you could put it that way."

"Well, who would do such a thing?" asked Joe.

"I can name three people," said James.

"Who would those be, sir?"

"The McMason brothers or Inspector Smith."

"Our Inspector Smith?"

"The very same."

"And why would Inspector Smith try to kill this young man?"

"Because Trevor and I are on the way to proving that Brian Steel and Dave Lilly didn't murder Elizabeth Friedman."

"Are you?" asked Joe, surprised but pleased.

"And this shows we are very close to solving the whole thing."

"I really don't think that is any good reason for suspecting Inspector Smith of being implicated in this."

"Maybe not, but he did threaten me earlier today in front of a great many witnesses."

"You must have misunderstood, sir. I know the Inspector personally, and he is a gentle, kind, family man. And you should really leave police work to the professionals."

"He is a bigoted, prejudiced idiot," said James. "Now if you have nothing else to tell us, we would like to visit Trevor uninterrupted."

The police officer was eased out of the bedside area, and Joe closed the curtains on him. Joe and James returned to Trevor, who became very excited and was about to ask James a lot of questions. James put his finger to his lips to stop him. Irene, seeing the excitement on Trevor's face, thought he was in pain. "Where does it hurt, darling?"

"I'm not in any pain, Mom, because of the pain killers they gave me, it really doesn't hurt at all, but it will tomorrow, they said."

"So what happened, son?" asked Joe.

"After James and I got split up, I decided to go back to the truck. I thought I could drive around and find you. I suddenly saw you and the problem you were having, so I planned to drive across the grass and pick you up."

"Thanks," said James, feeling even guiltier at what he had been thinking earlier.

"Anyway, I made it to the truck and began to drive down the hill, but then this car cut me off and I hit the brakes, except there were none, and I ploughed into this building at the bottom of the hill. James, if you had been with me you'd have been killed. That side of the truck was completely crushed."

"It's okay, at least you're safe."

"The doctor said you can come home tomorrow, and James said he will pick you up."

"He hasn't got a car any more, Brian Steel stole it. That's how all this started."

"I'll borrow one from my brothers, they have a second-hand car place."

"Does he do trucks?" asked Joe.

"Yes, I think so."

"Good. We know where to get Trevor a new one, once he is fit to drive again and we get the insurance money."

The curtains opened and a nurse looked at them with an astonished face. "I'm sorry, but that's all for now. Mr. Fisher needs his rest. You can come back tomorrow."

Irene gave her son another hug and several kisses. As they were leaving the cubicle, James nipped back and said quietly to Trevor, "I'll see you tomorrow and tell you all the news then." Trevor nodded and James gave a wink.

As they stood in the corridor trying to work out the way to the exit, the double doors at the end burst open and Anne came running down the corridor, straight into James's arms. "Is he alright? Why didn't you call me immediately? What kind of friend to Trevor are you?"

"He's fine. Have a look for yourself, he's just in that cubicle. But be quick, the nurse isn't the nicest in the world."

Anne rushed into the room. The nurse who had asked them to leave could suddenly be heard shouting, "I must ask you to leave!"

"I will not leave until I have seen my fiancée!" shouted Anne back.

"I'm sorry, but you must go."

"Listen, you loveless old woman, Trevor is my husband to be, and not you or anyone else is going to stop me seeing him!" The nurse came running out of the room and down the corridor.

"Who's that?" asked Irene.

"That's my sister Anne. The family bitch. Although I think they like each other."

"You mean romantically?"

"Well, I wouldn't go that far, but there is hope."

"Is that the one he has the date with?"

"Yes, God help him!"

"She seems very forceful to me," said Joe.

"Nice, yes, and very pretty. And such a nice way of speaking! Doesn't let people boss her around. Oh yes, Trevor couldn't do better. I think we should invite her over for tea. Don't you, Joe?"

"Irene, they haven't been on a date yet. Give the poor lad a chance."

"Look, if you two want to get off home, I'll wait for Anne and get a lift from her. And don't worry, I'll be back in the morning to pick Trevor up."

"Okay, and thanks for your help, James," said Irene, who gave a James a kiss on the cheek.

"Yes, thanks, son," said Joe.

Anne took James home. She talked incessantly about Trevor and how she hoped he would be alright. This was in between the constant attacks as to why James hadn't called her. She never told him how she knew Trevor had been in an accident.

After she drove away, James circled the block of apartments before entering up the back stairs. He cautiously opened his front door, and once inside he locked it. He checked each room before sitting on the edge of his bed. Alone again, he took stock of the situation. Whatever his confident assertion to the policeman at the hospital, the mystery of who had committed the murder of Elizabeth Friedman was still unsolved. How was he going to solve a fifty-year-old murder if he couldn't get to the bottom of one that happened only a few days ago? But his instincts were telling him that the answer was there, somewhere among all the information he had amassed. He lay back on his bed, staring at the ceiling. His mind kept returning to the same thought. He was missing something or someone. As this thought engrossed his mind, he fell asleep.

Morning came, and after showering and a cup of tea, James took the bus over to his brother Bryan's used-car showroom. Bryan had already prepared a car, which stood on the forecourt ready to drive away. Bryan threw him the keys and returned to the phone call he was on.

James drove to Crowhurst Road and parked outside Number Thirteen. He felt the answer to the mystery was either in the house or very close by. He checked his watch, he didn't have to pick Trevor up until about eleven o'clock, so he had three hours. A knock came on the passenger side window. He jumped slightly, then saw Bobby, Willie's brother, grinning at him. He was still wearing the same clothes he'd had on for the last two days. The light green sweater was back to front. James rolled down the window just enough to speak to him.

"Hello. You got a new car!"

"Yes, do you like it?"

"No, the color is wrong."

"What color should it be?"

"Blue. I like blue cars. You seen our Willie? He's run off."

"No. Do you know where he is?"

"May do. What's it worth?"

"Oh, nothing. I don't want to see him."

"He said you were looking for him."

"So, you have seen him."

"No, he telephoned our mom. She weren't half mad at him. She said she'd kill him when he gets home. No point coming home if ya mom is gonna kill ya, is it?"

"I suppose not."

"I know who killed that woman."

"Which woman?"

"The one in the ground they just dug up. Me mom told me. It was her husband or her lover, that's what me Mom said."

"Really. What else did your mother say?"

As they talked, the woman with the yellow umbrella, whom James had met outside the phone box the night it rained, passed and smiled at Bobby. She had a smart beige woolen coat with the belt pulled tightly around her waist. Her shoes were a deep beige color.

"Hello Daisy," said Bobby, grinning back at her.

"You know her?"

"Should do, she lives just there," said Bobby, pointing to one of the houses in the road.

"What's her name?"

"Daisy Marsh. She lives with her brother. Haven't seen him for a long time until last week, now he's back. There he is, talking to her."

James looked out of the windscreen and saw Daisy talking to a young man. He was the same height as her, but about two stone heavier. His head was down, as though he were looking at the ground or the way a little boy would when being scolded for doing something wrong. His clothes were from a different age, hand-me-downs from the 1940s. He must have been in his twenties, but had been dressed as though he were a boy of twelve.

"Hey Bobby, where has he been?"

"Nuthouse, so Mom said. Not sure which one."

"What's his name?"

"Jeffrey. I like him. He gave me sweets, and we play games up the Grove."

"What games?"

"You know, naughty games."

"Naughty games?"

"Yes, we take our clothes off and do things."

"Bobby, that's wrong."

"No it's not. It's fun," said Bobby, who then ran off down the road.

James turned to look at Jeffrey and Daisy. She wasn't angry, but seemed upset about something and was trying to explain it to Jeffery. When she had finished speaking, she walked away from James, not looking back. Jeffrey kicked the air and strolled towards James. His head was still down, looking at the ground. As he passed, James heard him muttering, "Bugger, bugger, bugger, bugger."

James didn't turn around immediately to see where Jeffrey had gone, but waited a minute or so before looking in the mirror. The road was empty. James turned around to check, but there was no sign of him. Turning forward again, he was shaken to see Jeffrey staring at him through the windscreen. Jeffrey then walked around the car, looking in all the time, then ran off in the direction of his sister.

The missing link, thought James. He watched Jeffrey run down the road, then disappear around the corner. He even ran like a twelve-year-old. He began to wonder why Jeffrey had never been mentioned before. What did he know about the other residents of Crowhurst Road. He needed more information, and he knew just where to get it.

Knocking on the door of the Coates house gave him a sense of "been here, done that!" He hoped Willie's mother was in, but when Bobby opened the door, his hope dropped. Bobby had changed his clothes and grinned at James. "Yeah?"
"Bobby, is your mother in?"

"Maybe."

"Can I see her?"

"Maybe."

"Could you ask her? I need to talk to her."

"What about?"

"You."

"Me? What have I done?"

"Who said you have done anything?"

Mrs. Coates came to the door and opened it wider. She had heard Bobby being belligerent and hit him on the head with the palm of her left hand.

"Ah Mom!"

"Don't be so rude to the gentleman. Now sir, what can I do for you?"

"I was wondering if I could have a private chat with you."

"Is it about...?" She didn't finish the sentence, but poked her head out of the door, looking out onto the street.

"Partly."

"You'd better come into the living room." James followed her, and she indicated for him to sit on the sofa. He looked around the room and noticed how clean it was. Quite a transformation since the last time he was there. "Have you seen our Willie?"

"Yes. Last time I spoke to him he seemed okay, but very scared."

"He said you'd seen him when he phoned, and you'd told him to go to the police."

"I think he would stand a better chance with the police than with the McMason brothers."

"You know about them?"

"We've met."

"I knew their mother. She was a money lender. Huh! Thief more like. You could borrow one hundred pounds from her today, and this time next week you'd owe her four hundred eighty! And if you didn't pay, she'd come to your home with her boys and take anything she wanted. They are a real bad lot, make no mistake."

"Willie needs to protect himself."

"Maybe you're right. The police would be the best bet."

"Now I need your help, Mrs. Coates. I would like to know about the people around here."

"You mean those who live in the road?"

"Yes. Tell me about 'the good old days,' as my father would say."

"Well, I'm not one to gossip, but we were the fifth family to move into this road. In those days, you could leave your door open and your windows unlocked. Everyone would help you if you had a problem. But not any more."

"So, which families were here then and are still here?"

"Oh, that's easy. Us, the Marshes and the Woolleys, and around the corner, the Salters. You know, we had a party for the Queen's Coronation a week after we moved in. Such fun and dancing. Lots of food for the kids as well. Fifty years later and no one wanted a party to celebrate her fifty years on the throne. Such a shame. There was one family they were Gyppos, who came to live in a house. Number thirteen it was and they seemed to like it as well. Well, the husband, nice man, he could sing, dances, and tell jokes. He would have you laughing for hours. A very funny man he was."

"What happened to them?"

"Oh, he died a few years back, and the wife about ten years ago, I think."

"What about the Marshes?"

"Well, Jack, the father, he's still alive, but you don't see much of him these days. His wife what was her name? Anyway, she ran off with the milkman, so they say. Not that I believe everything I'm told."

"What happened to him? Jack Marsh, I mean?"

"Oh, he still lives in the house. Daisy, the daughter never married. She had a lot of boyfriends, just like her mother, but now she looks after him. And sometimes Jeffrey is there; otherwise, he's in the loony bin. It's not that he's mad or anything. He's just soft in the head. Well, that's what they tell people."

"I've never seen Mr. Marsh around."

"Not these days. Because of his legs. He worked for the council digging ditches, or was in the parks department? I can't remember, but he worked hard."

They sat in silence for a few moments, until Bobby interrupted. "Can I put the telly on, Mom?"

"No."

"Mrs. Coates, who do you think the body in the road was?"

"Maureen. It were Maureen Marsh. Some around here reckon he did her in. They did at the time she disappeared, but they had no proof. But that's why I don't believe she ran away with the milkman."

"What made them think Jack had murdered his wife?"

"Well, for a start, she didn't tell anyone, and believe me, she would have told me. I was her best friend. "

"Tell you what?"

"If she was going to run away with the milkman, or any man. And another thing, she didn't take any clothes, and she loved her clothes. No, I reckon he did her in."

"Mom, can I put the telly on?"

"No, Bobby, and if you are not quiet, you can go to your room. But I don't think he killed Elizabeth."

"Elizabeth Friedman you mean, the estate agent?"

"Yes. She was his niece, you know. Her mother and Maureen Marsh were sisters."

"No, I didn't know that."

"Oh yes. For a time some thought Jack was her father, but Margaret, that was her mother, managed to prove he wasn't. There was always a little bad blood between Elizabeth and Daisy. Jealousy, I think."

"Do you know if Maureen was seeing other men at the time of her disappearance?"

"Well, that's it. She told me the night before she disappeared that Margaret's husband, Ron, had made a pass at her, and she might have a little fling with him. But I don't know if she did."

"Well, thank you, Mrs. Coates, you've been a great help."

"That's okay, love. Do you think you could help our Willie?"

"That's what I'm trying to do. I don't believe Brian Steel, Dave Lilly, or your Willie murdered Elizabeth Friedman, but it's hard trying to prove it."

"You will. I can feel it in me bones. You're Matthew's son, aren't you?"

"How did you know?"

"Nothing gets past me. I liked your dad. He was a good kid, didn't speak much. He had a hard life, especially when he went to school. I fancied him once, but that was a long time ago."

"I'll tell him."

"Oh no, you mustn't do that. I don't think he would like it."

"Why?"

"Because I used to tease him. I'm sure he hated me."

"I doubt it. My father is a very forgiving man."

"Yes, and it's that look you've just given me that reminded me of Matthew! Very sexy."

"Wow! I think I'd better be going. Thanks again, Mrs. Coates."

James left the house and sat in the car, trying to work out how all this new information fitted into the mystery. One thing seemed certain, it wasn't Maureen Marsh in the film. She was already dead, buried in the road. So what was the importance of the video? He looked at his watch, ten thirty-five! Only twenty-five minutes to get to the hospital.

Trevor was sitting on the bed, dressed and ready to go. Beside him was a pair of crutches. He smiled as James entered the ward.

"Did you think I wasn't coming?"

"No, I knew you would. Anne just left, and she said you already had a car."

"Oh she did, did she! You really like her, don't you?"

"Err, sort of," said Trevor, blushing red.

"Mr. Fisher, you can leave now," said a nurse, who seemed anxious to get rid of Trevor so that she could get the bed remade for a new patient.

"Easier said than done! It's hard on these crutches."

"Take your time, and if you fall I might pick you up!"

James and Trevor made slow progress along the corridors of the hospital, but with each step Trevor grew in confidence and speed. In the parking lot, Trevor looked inquisitively at all the cars. "Which one is yours?"

"Only the best for you. It's the limo."

"No, seriously." James went to the limo and opened the door like a professional chauffeur. "Bugger me," said Trevor, as he negotiated his legs into it. James had already put the passenger seat back so that Trevor could stretch his legs. "Not bad!"

"I'm glad you like it, sir!"

"I do. Err, don't drive off just yet, I've something to tell you."

"What? You've already married Anne, and she's having twins?"

"No, it's a little more scary than that."

"Impossible!"

"The McMason brothers came to see me last night."

"What! In hospital?"

"Said they were me cousins."

"Nice! Did they threaten you?"

"No. I told them it was Brian and Dave who had ripped them off, and that Willie was just a stupid runner who thought he was a big shot."

"Did they believe you?"

"Not at first. But when I said the bit about Willie, they seemed to think I was telling the truth. It seems Willie's been telling everyone that he is part of the McMason gang!"

"Well, let's hope that means Willie's out of danger."

"As long as he keeps his mouth shut."

"I'll call his mom later and ask her to tell him what's been said."

"They told me to tell you that you're in the clear, and they are sorry for beating you up and shooting at you. They got a little carried away."

"So it was them!"

"Yeah. They did say someone else was shooting, but they couldn't see who it was."

"What about you?"

"Oh, me too. They never thought I was anything to do with the drugs, just a friend of Dave and Brian. But I think they have a little trouble with the police."

"Let's hope so."

"Don't mention any of this to Mom and Dad, will you? I don't want them to worry."

"I don't think that is what is on their minds."

"What ya mean?"

"Your mother is already planning the wedding, Brother-in-Law!"

"What! Anne and I have only just met!"

"I know that, but do your mother and your father? They think there should be two ceremonies: one church, and the other Romani."

"We haven't even been on a date yet!"

"Unless you count saving the damsel in distress."

"Did you hear her last night with the nurse?"

"Yes. So did your parents, that's why your mother likes her."

"Bloody hell."

"Hey, remember, you've got to ask my father for her hand in marriage."

"Oh yeah. Has Anne said anything about me?"

"Yes, but brothers don't tell."

"James! And I thought you were my friend!"

"That's why I'm not telling. Let's get you home. Your mother is probably cooking a feast."

"Good. I'm starving. Hospital food is… well…"

"'Nuff said!"

They sat in Trevor's bedroom, bloated after the huge and delicious meal Irene had prepared.

"So what happened?" asked James.

"When?"

"After we split up at the car rally."

"Oh, all hell broke loose. I managed to hide in some trees, and then I noticed it wasn't me they were trying to get, but you. They had a clear line, but they never fired one shot at me."

"I couldn't see you anywhere."

"I saw you, hiding by that little hut. I thought you were a gonna. That's when I thought that if I could get the truck, maybe I could get close enough for you to get in, and we could drive out of the park in the opposite direction. Anyway, I walked out into the open, and no one fired at me."

"No need. Because they thought they would get you with the cut brake-pipes."

"It wasn't the Mcmasons who cut the brakes. But whoever did that must have been watching us from the start, and I didn't see anyone following us."

"Me neither. Still, that doesn't prove anything. It could have been the McMason brothers or one of their people."

"They said it wasn't them, they called for help when they saw the accident."

"Inspector Smith?"

"He may be crazy and prejudiced, but I don't think he would have done that."

"So then you got in the truck, started off down the hill...?"

"Yes, towards the park. Then a car cut in front of me. I put the brakes on, and they didn't work."

"I saw the accident when I was on the bus. Of course, I didn't realize it was you."

"On the bus?"

"Yes. I escaped from the park and took a bus to here."

"I see. So who told Anne?"

"I didn't. That is why she is mad at me. She had found out you had been injured and I hadn't told her. I told you she is the bitch of the family."

"What are you, the family marriage broker?"

"Maybe," said James, laughing.

Irene entered the room carrying a tray. "Not more food, Mom."

"No. If you boys are gonna sit up talking, you'll need a cup of tea."

"Thanks, Irene."

"You're welcome, Son. Well, we are almost family."

"Mom!"

Irene winked at James as she was leaving the room. "I must get Joe's suit to the cleaners. He only uses it at funerals and weddings," Irene laughed.

"Oh, very funny. Thanks, Mom." After she closed the door, James poured the tea. "So you never found Willie?"

"I did. He was hiding in the little hut in the park, which used to be Lady Jane's house. I think she was some sort of relative of the Coates family."

"I didn't see him."

"He stayed inside. I told him to, so that it looked like I was just hiding there, when in fact I was talking to him. He was very upset. He tries to come across as a hard man, when in fact he's just a little boy."

"Clever that. It really looked as though you were just hiding by yourself. What did he say? Did he kill her?"

"No, I don't think so. I think we have got it all wrong."

"You mean Brian and Dave did murder her?"

"No, neither of them."

"Then who did?"

"I think it all has to do with the murder that took place fifty years ago."

"'The Body in the Road', great title for a film."

"Beneath the road."

"So the person who murdered the first woman murdered the estate agent too?"

"No. But the murders are connected."

"Stop, James, you're losing me. Can we start at the beginning?"

"Okay, fifty years ago, three days before the Queen's Coronation, Maureen Marsh was murdered."

"Who's Maureen Marsh?"

"That's the woman whose body was found under the road."

"Okay, continue. Who murdered her?"

"I'm not sure yet. Maybe her husband. But I think Elizabeth Friedman was murdered because she found out, that's a guess, but she found something out. Did you also know that Elizabeth was Maureen's niece?"

"Eh?"

"Did you know Daisy had a brother who had been in an institution?"

"Hang on a minute. Who's Daisy?"

"Trevor, where have you been? Daisy is the woman with the yellow umbrella who told me not to believe anything Bobby Coates said."

"Well, she's right about that."

"But that's the point is she? Maybe Bobby is telling the truth."

"She's the one with the yellow umbrella who keeps appearing when you don't expect her?"

"Yes. It could be her umbrella that disappeared. I don't understand why she's always there. She lives with her bother, Jeffrey, who has a mental problem."

"He's mad?"

"No. I think it's more like he gets out of control and forgets to take his medication."

"So Brian, Dave, and Willie were set up?"

"Not necessarily. They just happened to be in the wrong place, doing something wrong, and someone saw the opportunity to commit a murder and blame someone else for it."

"Okay, in all the films and television programs I've seen, the detective makes a list of all the suspects and eliminates each one as he proves they couldn't have done it."

"Let's start, then."

Trevor passed a notepad and pen to James. "You write, I'm still too weak."

"Right. Lazy, more like! Yes, you and Anne will get on just fine."

"What do you mean?"

"She hates slackers."

"I'm not a slacker, just a little tired, that's all. And may I remind you that I have a fractured arm?"

"Oh. You're left-handed, then?"

"Just write!"

"Okay, to start with, there's Brian and Dave. Oh, and we mustn't forget Willie."

"The McMason brothers, or one of their gang."

"You."

"Me?"

"You said all the suspects."

"Okay, you too."

"What motive?"

"Who knows what dealings you was having with that estate agent! She could have been your secret lover."

"I don't have one."

"So you say. Maybe you were desperate for a relationship, Elizabeth rejected you, and you killed her."

"Your idea or Anne's?"

"Anne's."

"Figures. She really wants to know about my personal life."

"She thinks you're gay."

"She and a lot of others. I've had girlfriends, but this is taking us away from our list. I'll put myself down just to please you and Anne."

"Who else?"

"Jack Marsh."

"And he is…?"

"Husband of Maureen, father of Daisy and Jeffrey, uncle of Elizabeth Friedman."

"That's enough to put him top of the list!"

"Except he can't walk!"

"Ah! Says who?"

"Mrs. Coates."

"Maybe a cunning bluff."

"Okay, he's still on the list."

"Daisy."

"Maybe, but I don't think she could hurt anyone."

"In films, those types are always the worst. What about her brother?"

"Jeffrey? Too soft in the head, I think. If you shouted at him, he would fall to the ground and cry."

"Your dad?"

"What!"

"Well, he was around fifty years ago and he is here today. He must have known Maureen Marsh."

"That's true. Okay, if you're on the list, so is my dad."

"Anyone else?"

"Bobby Coates."

"Yeah, but only if his mommy tells him to."

"Then her as well."

"What about Phil?"

"Yes. I wonder what happened to him?"

"When I was in hospital, I found out he is very sick. The last lot of drugs he took was contaminated and almost killed him. He will live, but his short-term memory is affected. Add the McMasons. He's related to them or something. May not be a blood relative, but he was connected, and they hated the fact that he was using."

"Okay, let's start and eliminate a few."

"Dave?"

"He hit Elizabeth, and thought he'd killed her."

"So did Brian and Willie."

"Yes, but I don't think they did it."

"Why?"

"Because she was killed with a knife, and none of them ever mentioned a knife."

"Maybe Willie did it after Dave and Brian left."

"I don't think so. I think he would have given the game away if he had, when I spoke to him. What about Phil, could he have done it?"

"Maybe. He did most things Dave and Brian told him to do."

"So we keep him on the list for now. Next?"

"McMason brothers, or one of their gang? Long shot. Also, not really their style. They take people to the countryside and do it."

"Did they bring me here that night?"

"Yeah. Well, I think so. God, you certainly gave me a shock. Dave had just told me about you and the fact that you could be trouble. 'The Gates of Hell'!"

"Okay, don't laugh."

"Keep them on the list or not?"

"Not."

"Okay."

"You?"

"I could have, but I didn't."

"Can you prove it?"

"No."

"So, I keep you on the list."

"You too, then."

"My dad?"

"He could have done it, but from what Anne's said, take him off the list."

"What did Anne say?"

"She said he was a good man."

"Bloody hell! My sister sticking up for a family member."

"Mr. Marsh?"

"Leave him on the list. First, we have never met him, and second, it was his wife who was murdered."

"Daisy?"

"I don't think so. It would have been too hard for her to do all that work, the room change and all."

"Okay, I'll take her off the list for now, but that might be a mistake."

"Bobby Coates?"

"Only if his mother is involved."

"She was around fifty years ago."

"True. Maybe she had the hots for Mr. Marsh and did away with his wife so she could have him. Then Elizabeth found out, so she killed her as well."

"Sounds like one of your film scripts."

"Or a romantic love story!"

"No, cross her off, and I don't think Phil did it."

"Me neither."

James's mobile rang. "Hello, Anne. Trevor's getting all excited here. Haven't you rung the wrong number? ...What channel...? Trevor, put Channel Three on for the news. Thanks. ...No, he's fine, just resting. Okay, 'bye." He closed the phone, ignoring Trevor's hand, which was held out expecting to receive it.

"She didn't want to talk to me?"

"I don't know, she didn't say, just told me to say hi."

"That all?"

"No. Give her a call later."

"Thanks."

The television came to life. "Local farmer Earnest Bartlett found the body of a young man at eight o'clock this morning hanging from a tree. The police have now confirmed it was the body of William Coates of Longbridge, someone they have been looking for in connection with the murder of Mrs. Elizabeth Friedman at Crowhurst Road. Police have not ruled out foul play, and said they would be continuing their investigation into the tragic death. Back to you in the studio."

Trevor switched the television off. Stunned by the news, they sat in silence for few moments.

"Was it murder?"

"Yes," replied James.

"Who?"

"The same person who murdered Elizabeth Friedman. And I may have caused his death."

"How?"

"By going to see his mother this morning."

"So she did it?"

"No. I think now's the time to confront Mr. Marsh."

"Mr. Marsh?"

"Yes, I need some answers from him."

"I'm coming with you."

"Do you think that's wise, in your condition?"

"James, if you think I'm going to run out on the kill, so to speak, you are very much mistaken. Tell my mom we are going to see Anne. She'll accept that without asking any awkward questions, and anyway, afterwards, we will go and see her."

"If you say so."

"Okay, it's back to where it all started. Crowhurst Road."

CHAPTER EIGHTEEN

Dead Man Talking

James and Trevor stood on the doorstep of the Marshes' home. The paintwork on and around the door had peeled, and bare wood was exposed. Trevor, on his crutches, had difficulty keeping his balance and leaned against the brickwork. James had run the doorbell several times before the door was opened by Daisy. She smiled at them. She was wearing a light summer dress with a white apron tightly tied around her wait. Her manner was like a hotel receptionist, as though she were removed from the worries of the world. "Hello, I was expecting you. Why don't we all go into the front room?"

James helped Trevor up the step and into the hallway. The stench of rotting food could be smelt as they stood waiting for Daisy to show them into the room. "Sorry for the smell. It's the drains. They keep clogging up, and you can't get a reliable plumber anywhere these days. I've called so many times, and he never shows up."

She showed them into a smallish front room. All the houses in Crowhurst Road had been built to the same plan, with a long living and dining room combined. At some point the Marshes had apparently had it converted into two separate rooms, with the fireplace being in the back room. This room had very little furniture. Daisy sat precariously on the arm of a winged chair and indicated that Trevor and James should sit on the brown, imitation-leather sofa.

"Now, how can I help you?"

"We'd really like to see your father."

"Daddy? Oh, he never sees anyone these days."

"He's not ill, is he?"

"No, he just doesn't like meeting people any more. When you get to his age, you just want to watch television and sleep. Now, what were you going to see him about?"

"I want to ask him about what happened fifty years ago."

"Fifty years ago?"

"Yes, when your mother disappeared."

"She ran off with the milkman."

"No, Daisy, she was murdered. And her body was found under the road a few days ago."

"They don't know for sure if it was Mommy. Daddy said she was a slut and a prostitute who had sex with many men."

"Maybe if we could see your father, he could tell us."

"I told you. Daddy sees no one."

"Well, if Daddy won't see us, then we'll go to the police and tell them what we know."

"What do you know?"

"We know who murdered your mother and your cousin Elizabeth."

"Who?"

"I'm not telling you, only your father."

"Let me see if Daddy will see you." Daisy left the room, carefully closing the door behind her. James stood up and began to look around the room. There were no pictures or knick-knacks, just basic furniture and heavy brown velvet curtains pulled closed.

"Anne is so like you. Pushy?"

"Persistent."

"That's what you call it!"

"Oh, Anne's worse. Trevor you don't know what she is really like."

"You're enjoying this, aren't you?"

"What am I enjoying?"

"Your sister and me."

"Oh yes, this is going to be fun. Not because of you but all those taunts from Anne. I can now pay her back."

"What do you think of Daisy?"

"That she's trying to hide something."

"She's been gone a long time."

"I know. Maybe she left the house."

"No, I can hear her talking in the next room."

"What do you think that smell really is?"

"I'm not sure, but whatever it is, it's bad."

The door opened, Daisy had taken off her apron and brushed her hair. She smiled at them. "Daddy said he'll see you, but only for a few minutes, as he is feeling very tired. Can I offer you some tea or coffee?"

"No thanks, I think we are okay."

"Daisy, you don't have any pictures of your mother, do you?"

"No," said Daisy, looking at Trevor. "Did you have an accident?"

"Err, yes, a small one."

"You are lucky, car accidents can be very dangerous."

"Yeah, tell me about it!"

She turned to James and stared at him. "I've seen you before. Oh yes, you were a friend of cousin Lizzy."

"I wasn't a friend. I was buying the house from her."

"Is that right? When I was a little girl, Gyppos lived in that house. Dirty people, Daddy told me. Let me see if he is ready to see you." She left the room again, closing the door very carefully.

"She seems very calm, as though she is acting a part in a film."

"It's definitely an act, Trevor; I'm sure of that."

"I didn't say I was in a car accident."

"I know, which means she knew about it."

"Could she have caused it?"

Before James could answer, Daisy returned, the smile still fixed on her face. "Daddy will see you now. The room doesn't have much light. It hurts Daddy's eyes. And his voice is very weak, so if you can't hear him, I'll tell you what he says. Please follow me."

As James and Trevor entered the back room, the stench of something rotting became stronger. Trevor heaved, only just managing to control the wrenching of his stomach. The back room had been converted into a bedroom. The bed itself was piled high with clothing, and several chairs were set facing it. A cat sat on the edge of the bed eating a bone of some sort. The window was draped with heavy burgundy-colored velvet curtains.

Mr. Marsh sat in a winged chair with the only light in the room behind him, making it very difficult to see his face. Trevor positioned himself against a wall just inside the door so he could lean against it and take some of the pressure off his leg.

"Daddy, these are the two men who want to talk to you."

"Hello, Mr. Marsh. Sorry to hear you're not feeling very well, but what I have to say must be said."

A soft voice replied, too soft for James and Trevor to hear. Daisy put her ear close to the old man. "Daddy said thank you and how can he help you?"

"Mr. Marsh, do you know who murdered your wife fifty years ago?"

Again Daisy put her head close to the old man. "Daddy says he didn't know she had been murdered. As far as he knew, she had run off with Stan Cooper, the milkman."

A gloved hand emerged from under the blanket covering Jack Marsh, it touched Daisy's arm. She lowered her head to listen again. "Daddy said, if she was murdered, then the police should find the milkman, Stan Cooper."

"The police don't think she ran off with anyone, but that someone closer to home murdered your wife."

"Like who?" shouted Daisy.

James remained calm and said quietly, "Like your father or your uncle."

"My father would never hurt a fly. It was Mommy. She was a slut and a prostitute. That's right, isn't it Daddy?" The old man nodded his head.

"Was your wife having an affair just before she disappeared, Mr. Marsh?"

"With the milkman!" shouted Daisy.

"Anyone else?" asked Trevor, who repositioned himself so that the light from behind Mr. Marsh was not directly in his face.

Daisy bent her head lower to listen again. "Daddy said she had so many lovers it was hard to keep up with them."

"Did you have any lovers, Mr. Marsh?"

"Daddy would never cheat on Mommy! It was her. That's right, isn't it daddy?"

"Did you, Mr. Marsh?"

"End of meeting," snapped Daisy.

"Your father didn't say so."

"I said, end of meeting. I can tell when Daddy's had enough. You have to leave now."

"Oh please, Daisy, one more question."

The old man spoke again. "No Daddy, the meeting is over." The gloved hand grabbed at Daisy's arm. She squealed in pain as it gripped tightly.

"Your father is prepared to answer one more question, Daisy. What are you scared of, that he might say something he shouldn't?"

"Daddy's very tired and not very well, but if you insist, one last question. But only one."

James looked at Trevor, gave a little nod, then asked, "When did you die, Mr. Jack Marsh?"

Daisy screamed. "What?"

The old man sat up in the chair. "Bugger, bugger, bugger."

Trevor switched on the main light, a single bulb hanging from the centre of the room with no lampshade. Jeffrey smiled from beneath the wig and removed the blankets covering him.

"Your father's dead, isn't he, Daisy? That's what's making this foul smell." Daisy looked at them, anger building up on her face. "Where's the body?" Neither brother nor sister answered. Then, as if he couldn't help himself, Jeffrey glanced at the bed. Daisy shook her head, but it was too late. "On the bed? Is he under all the clothing?"

James pushed the squealing cat and the clothing on to the floor. The stench was overpowering, and there was clearly the shape of a body under the covering. Gingerly, James took the corner, raised it, and pulled it slowly back to reveal an old man, dressed in his underwear, with stab wounds visible on his chest. The cat had been gnawing at his right foot, and ripped flesh and bone were exposed.

"Leave Daddy alone. He is just sleeping," said Daisy in a quiet voice.

"He's not sleeping, Daisy, he's dead, and either you or Jeffrey murdered him."

"Bugger, bugger, bugger," said Jeffrey, and then began to giggle.

Daisy suddenly drew herself up to her full height and said in a very strict, commanding voice, "Jeffrey, these men are going to tell the police about our little secret. I want you to stop them like you did before." Jeffrey began to rock back and forth in the chair.

"Okay, Sis." He stood up and produced an eight-inch chopping knife from down the side of the chair. With a roar he lunged at James, who managed to swerve out of the way just in time.

Daisy began to sing in a high-pitched voice, "La, la, la, la, lupe loo, la, la, la."

Jeffrey swung round and attacked James again. The knife thrust forward again and again. Trevor had moved in, and as Jeffrey took another stab at James, he hit him on the arm with one of his crutches. Jeffrey fell to the floor, crying in pain. The knife fell to Daisy's feet. She picked it up and screamed as she charged at James.

Trevor tripped her up with his crutch. James grabbed her arm, prying the knife out of her hand. Regaining her feet, she began hitting and scratching him. He took hold of her wrists and pushed her back to one of the chairs. She fell into it.

Jeffrey continued to cry, a howling noise, like a dog. "Can't you stop him?" Trevor asked Daisy.

"Shut up, Jeffrey, or I will put you to bed again, and you know what that will mean." James looked at Trevor; they both wondered what she meant. But Jeffrey obviously understood and began to calm down. His crying became a sob and then a sniff.

"Thank you. Now, Daisy, before we call the police, you are going to tell us what really happened fifty years ago and what happened just a few days ago. When your mother and cousin were murdered."

"How can I? I wasn't there fifty years ago, and I know nothing about Elizabeth's death."

"You may not have been born fifty years ago, but you know what happened."

"I don't know what you're talking about."

"Yes, Sis, he's talking about Daddy killing Mommy because she was a slut." Jeffrey climbed into a chair and curled himself up into a ball.

"All right! Daddy told me he caught Mommy having sex with another man. He couldn't take it any more, so he killed her."

"Then what happened?"

"Daddy and Uncle Ron, who was Elizabeth's father, put her in the trench and covered her up."

"Why did Ron do it?"

"Uncle Ron was a deserter from the war, and Daddy told him that if he didn't help, Daddy would tell the police. Everyone knew she was a flirt, so when she went missing, Daddy told everyone she'd run off with the milkman."

"What happened to Uncle Ron?"

"I'm not sure. Daddy told me he had been murdered by a gang of soldiers and his body hidden somewhere up in the Lickeys."

"You mean your father murdered him and hid the body?"

"Maybe."

"Did your father have an affair with your mother's sister, Elizabeth's mother?"

"I don't know. Daddy said he did, but he kept changing his story."

"Daddy was good at telling stories."

"Quiet, Jeffrey! We never knew if Elizabeth was my sister or my cousin."

"So your father killed your mother. Okay, let's move on to the next murder. Elizabeth Friedman."

"Cousin Liz was murdered by those drug men."

"No. They may have knocked her out in the kitchen, but they didn't kill her. Someone else murdered her. We want to know everything that happened."

"Tell him, Sis, it's okay. He should know everything. Maybe he will understand and help us."

"Quiet, Jeffrey, I won't warn you again. My Auntie Maureen, Lizzie's mother, always believed my father had killed Mommy. She never really said anything, but she always gave that look as though she knew something."

"Maybe she did."

"I don't think so. Anyway, after she died, Lizzie started to say things."

"Like what?"

"Things about my Daddy. At first it was silly things. Then she said he'd raped her. He didn't! She may have wished he had, but Daddy told me he hadn't."

"He tried to, I saw him. Like I saw him do it to you, Daisy."

"Be quiet, Jeffrey! You don't know what sex is. So be a good boy and shut up."

"I do know what sex is. I do it sometimes too, with the other boys."

"Jeffrey, don't talk rubbish."

"Carry on, Daisy, you were saying?"

"Lizzie started to tell everyone Daddy had murdered his wife. Of course, no one believed her. Then she left and went to London. I think she got married. We weren't invited to the wedding, not that I would have gone."

"When did she return to Birmingham?"

"Last year. She never said a word about Mommy, but I found out she was asking questions."

"Bobby told me that. Bobby's my lover, you know."

"Jeffrey!"

"Is that why you put Jeffrey back inside the hospital?"

"I had to. She was asking too many questions, and if she had spoken to Jeffrey, he would have told her everything. He's not homosexual. He just talks that way to get attention. We don't have any of them in our family."

"So what happened then?" asked Trevor, ignoring her comment.

"Somehow she got hold of this video from the street party. It was an old film, and Mr. Carpenter from around the corner had it transferred onto video so everyone could see it. I was scared it would show something."

"I never saw it. I like videos."

"Jeffrey, shut up! I won't tell you again! I knew the drug men were hiding stuff at the house. She told me she was scared of them. Or was it she was scared she couldn't sell the house because of them?"

"So what happened that night?"

"I went there to look at the place. When the Gyppos lived there, no one was ever allowed inside. I wanted to see the place. I heard someone coming, so I hid. It was the two drug men plus Willie Coates from across the road. He was helping them. They were planning to move something, because Lizzie had sold the house. Also, they were worried about the police snooping around after they found Mommy's body. Anyway, Lizzie came in while they were there."

"Then what?"

"I think one of them knocked her out, she was in the kitchen. I heard them move the stuff. It took them a long time. The drug men left, and I watched as Willie Coates looked around the place. I think he saw me, but I'm not sure."

"He told me he heard you, and he knew it was you because of the perfume you wear, Sis."

"Willie locked up and I went downstairs. Lizzie was still on the floor, but she was waking up. Jeffrey came in from the garden. He had just gotten out of the hospital. He hasn't been well, have you, Jeffrey?"

"No, Daisy, I was really doing poorly. I had to go to hospital."

"Lizzie woke up and asked why we hadn't called the police about the drug men, and then she told me she was going to tell them about Daddy."

"Daisy told me that Lizzie mustn't tell anyone about Daddy, and I was to make her be quiet."

"So what did you do?"

"I cut her. I like cutting things." Daisy sat back in the chair, silently looking at the floor. Trevor, who had been standing by the door, now sat on a hardwood chair, which he had pulled closer to the door with his crutches.

"How did you cut her, Jeffrey?"

"I stuck my knife in her. She screamed and made more noise, so I stuck it in her again and again until she stopped. That's right, isn't it Daisy?" Daisy sat silently.

"What happened then, Daisy?"

Daisy spoke, but didn't look up from the floor. "We moved her into the living room. Someone had been making a dirty film there, so it was very clean. Anyway, someone came back as we were putting Lizzie on the floor. Jeffrey had started to clean up the blood in the kitchen, and we had to hide. It was the filmmaker. He had a girl with him, and when she saw the body, she screamed and fainted. I think he slapped her on the face first. Anyway, he had to carry her out."

Trevor sat with indignation all over his face at her suggestion that his films were dirty. James looked at him and gave a weak smile.

"We made it look like a film set so everyone would think it was something to do with the film. We found this bag of very fine dirt, so I told Jeffrey to put it all over the carpet—it would hide any foot marks we had made. We finished cleaning up the kitchen and then left. As we were leaving, I saw my yellow umbrella in the corner. Lizzie had borrowed it. I couldn't leave it for someone to find, so I took it. When Jeffrey and I got home, I hid him. Daddy was drunk and saw us, and he said was going to tell everyone that Jeffrey had come home. When they found out Lizzie was dead, Daddy said he knew it was Jeffrey because of all the blood on his clothes that night, and he was going to tell the police."

"Bugger."

"I told him Lizzie said she knew he had killed Mommy, and that's why Jeffrey had to do it. He was drunk, and kept saying I was like Mommy and trying to kiss me."

"I didn't like that," said Jeffery. "Daddy should only kiss Mommy like that. Then he tried to do other things to Daisy."

"So what did you do, Jeffrey?"

"I had to stop him. Daisy asked me to stop him, didn't you, Daisy?"

"So what did you do?"

"I cut him. And he screamed like Lizzie did."

"So you kept cutting him until he stopped screaming?"

"Yeah. It was funny. I like doing it."

"But it was wrong, Jeffrey."

"No, no, it wasn't wrong. He was going to hurt Daisy, and that's wrong." Jeffrey once again began to rock back and forth in the chair.

"Stop that, Jeffrey! You know I hate it when you do that," shouted Daisy.

"What happened next, Daisy?"

"What do you mean?"

"Well, it didn't end there, did it?"

"All right. I found out you and him was trying to find out what really happened. So Jeffrey tried to stop you."

"How? What did he do?"

"He took Daddy's rifle, and we watched you in the woods trying to find Willie. I wanted to find him so he wouldn't tell you what he had seen."

"What then?"

"We followed you up the Lickeys and saw that there were some other men watching you too. When you got near the cave, Jeffery fired at you."

"No, I didn't. I can't shoot. But you can, Daisy. She's really good at it, she won all the prizes at the fair."

"Then the other men fired at you," continued Daisy.

"So you were the ones in the Range Rover?"

"No, we were behind it in Daddy's old Ford Cortina. Then you went into the park. I knew I had to stop you, so I kept shooting, but you got away."

"What about my car brakes?" asked Trevor.

"That was easy, we just cut the pipe. Daddy had shown me. He used to work at the Austin Car Factory after he got laid off from the council, and he knew everything about cars."

"You almost killed me."

"I know." She gave a Trevor a manic smile.

"Why did you have to kill Willie?"

"I didn't. It was Jeffrey who did that."

"You told me to, Sis."

"No I didn't, Jeffrey. You must stop saying that. These men will think I tell you what to do all the time."

"You said Willie has a big mouth and he'll tell everyone about you being in the house and that. And then you said I was to shut his mouth for good."

"Jeffrey, don't tell lies to these nice men."

"I'm not telling lies, and these aren't nice men. You said they were from the devil." Jeffrey changed his position in the seat. He had become very agitated.

"Jeffrey told me he had found Willie hiding up in the Grove and helped Willie hang himself."

"You told me to hang him. You put the rope around his neck."

"So you and Jeffrey murdered Willie?"

"Not quite. He was dead before we hung him. Jeffrey did it."

"So Jeffrey, what happened with you and Willie?"

"He was scared of me and kept saying he'd tell his mom about Bobby and me, so I put my hands around his throat and squeezed until he shut his mouth. Then Daisy and I put him up in the tree to dry out." Jeffrey began to rock again and started to make a strange humming sound, which grew louder and louder.

Daisy became very distraught, "Stop it, Jeffrey!" She stood up, screaming, "Stop it! Stop it! Stop it!" Jeffrey continued humming and rocking.

Trevor picked up one of his crutches in case he needed a weapon. James watched. It was the first time he had seen madness at first hand. Jeffrey was so much under the control of Daisy. But who was the madder?

She stopped screaming, turned back to the chair she had been sitting in, and grabbed something out of a bag that was stuffed down the side of the chair. She swung around and lunged at Jeffrey. The grey knitting needle penetrated his chest. He gave a squeal before falling silent. James grabbed hold of Daisy, who fought to get free, kicking him and biting. "Trevor, I need something to tie her up." Trevor looked around the room, frantically opening drawers and sideboard doors in search of something. James was moving around the room as Daisy struggled with him. He tried to keep her at arms' length as she kicked at his legs and scratched and bit and screamed.

Trevor eventually found several silk ties in a drawer and handed one of them to James. It was very hard to get it tied to her wrist whilst she was struggling so violently, and Trevor wasn't much help on crutches. James suddenly had a brainwave and put his feet on top of hers to stop her kicking him.
"Wait until I tell Daddy. He'll kill you!"

Between them they finally managed to tie one wrist and then bind both wrists together. James pushed her into the chair. He removed the knitting bag. Taking her feet, and after a fierce struggle, he bound her ankles together with one of the other ties.

Trevor had maneuvered himself next to Jeffrey, who still sat silently in the chair, the knitting needle sticking out of his chest. He checked to see if Jeffrey was alive. His pulse was faint, but he was still in the land of the living. Trevor picked up the phone from the small table next to the chair and dialed 9-9-9.

"Yes. I need the police and an ambulance to come to one Crowhurst Road. No, I don't live here, but... Trevor Fisher. Look, we have a dead body and a man with a steel knitting needle in his chest. Yes, he is breathing, just, but please hurry. ...Yes, the woman who did it is here now. She's tied up. Yes. Thanks."

James sat on the arm of the chair watching Daisy, who had quieted. He took the tape recorder out of his pocket and switched it off, unplugging the small microphone pinned to his jacket. He rewound the tape and played some back. Everything that had been said seemed to be there.

"What happens now?" asked Trevor.

"Once the police have taken over, we will go and make a copy of this tape. Like the last one, I don't want to give them the master copy, just in case Inspector Smith decides to lose it."

'They won't hang us, you know," said Daisy suddenly. "They don't hang people any more. Jeffrey is mad, and I didn't actually do anything. No, really, it was all Jeffrey He has been like that since he was a little boy, haven't you, Jeffrey?" Jeffrey sat still, his body rigid. Only his eyes moved, from James to Daisy. He gave her a very weak smile, and a single tear rolled down his face.

A knock came at the front door. James went to open it. The police officer on the doorstep smiled as the door was opened. "I believe you have a small domestic problem, sir?"

"I think, officer, when you have seen what is inside this house, you won't be taking that stupid, patronizing tone."

"Is that so, sir? I'd better take a look then, hadn't I? Oofff!"

"What you smell is a decomposing body."

The officer continued into the house, placing a hand over his nose and mouth. Outside in the street the ambulance had arrived. James left the front door open while he showed the police officer into the back room. The officer looked at Daisy, then at Jeffrey. He nodded to Trevor, who raised the sheet to reveal Mr. Marsh lying on the bed. The officer stood for a moment transfixed, and then he bolted out of the room straight into the front garden and vomited over a dead rose bush.

The paramedics entered the room and began checking Jeffrey. "I think he is alive, but he does have a mental problem," said Trevor. One of the paramedics left the room to bring a trolley to transport Jeffrey to hospital.

"Untie me at once. I need to look after my brother," demanded Daisy.

"Quiet!" said James, "You've done enough damage."

"Don't you speak to me like that! When my father hears about this and all that you have done to me, he'll hit you so hard it'll make you cry." The paramedic looked at her, then at James, before returning to attend to Jeffrey. His colleague returned with the trolley. They carefully placed the now placid Jeffrey onto it.

"I think you should know he has murdered three people - or is it four? So it might be advisable to restrain him."

"Right. Who stabbed him?"

"His sister."

"No I didn't liar, it was Daddy. He never liked Jeffrey, because Jeffrey's queer."

The paramedic looked at James, eyebrows raised. "We'd better look at the guy on the bed next."

"Don't bother, he's been dead for at least four days." The men nevertheless took a look.

"Shit! What's been eating him?"

"The cat."

James followed the paramedics out to the street. A crowd had gathered, and there was a deal of speculative chatter when people saw Jeffery lying on the trolley with the knitting needle sticking out of his chest. Mrs. Coates walked across the street to see what was happening. Her face was drawn and white. She had been crying, and several of the neighbors gathered around to comfort her.

As the ambulance drove away, she approached James. "What happened?"

"Hello, Mrs. Coates." He could see the deep pain in her face. "I am very sorry about Willie."

"I feel so ashamed."

"Don't. Willie didn't hang himself."

Her facial expression changed, and a glimmer of hope began to cross over her face. "What do you mean?"

"Willie was murdered. By Jeffrey."

"Murdered? Why?"

"Because Willie knew too much. At least, Daisy and Jeffrey thought he did."

"Oh, my poor Willie."

"I knew it wasn't suicide, dear," said one of the women, comforting Willie's mother.

The young officer had gathered himself together. "Inspector Smith is on his way."

"Huh! A fat lot of use he will be!" said James. The officer seemed stunned by the remark. A sergeant arrived and spoke briefly to the officer before approaching James.

"So what happened, sir?

"This house belongs to a family called Marsh. You will find a body on the bed in the back room. That is the father, Jack Marsh. His son, Jeffrey, who has just been taken to hospital with a steel needle in his chest, has committed several murders at the behest of his sister, Daisy."

"I see. And you are?"

"Pidgley; James Pidgley."

"Can you prove any of this, Mr. Pidgley?"

"Oh yes."

"So, what murders did they commit?"

"They murdered Elizabeth Friedman, the estate agent, who was a cousin. Then they murdered their father, who for his part murdered his wife, Maureen, fifty years ago. And finally they murdered poor Willie Coates."

"Does Inspector Smith know all this, sir?"

"Inspector Smith knows nothing, sergeant, because he's too bigoted to see beyond his own stupidity. But I think even he will acknowledge the truth when I give my statement."

"Where is Miss Daisy Marsh now, sir?"

"Tied up in the back room."

"Why is she tied up?"

"Because she stabbed her brother with a knitting needle and then kept kicking me."

"We'd better go and see."

They entered the back room. Trevor was standing. "Oh good, you're back. I need to get some fresh air." He hobbled out of the room.

"Officer, would you untie me and arrest these men? They have kidnapped my poor, ill father and held us hostage, haven't they, Daddy?"

The officer followed her look and saw the uncovered body on the bed. "Oh my God! I think we should get her out of here." He went to the door and called down the hallway, "Jenkins!"

The young officer entered the room, a handkerchief over his face. "Yes sir?"

"Let's get her out of here and into one of the cars. Is there a female officer around? We should put her into handcuffs." The young officer removed the tie from Daisy's legs.

"Oh thank you, kind sir, you are such a gentleman. My knight in shining amour, come to save a damsel in distress. Will you fight all my battles?" The officer didn't reply, but removed the silk tie from her wrists.

He took a pair of handcuffs from his belt. "What are these?" asked Daisy.

The sergeant quickly replied, "They are gold bracelets for you, milady."

"Oh, how delightful! Please, won't you put them on for me?"

"Be quick about it, Jenkins."

"Do not hurt me. I am a queen, you know." And then, as if someone had flicked a switch or changed the channel on the television, "Get these bloody handcuffs off me, you bastards! What the hell do you think you're doing? My father is going to fucking kill everyone of your buggers."

"That was close," said the sergeant.

"I think she's been like this for some time. I'm not sure if it's multi-personalities, but she is crazy." Daisy hit out at the young officer as he helped her up from the chair. She kicked him several times and spat at the sergeant.

"Jenkins, get her out of here."

As she passed James, she put her tongue out at him and said, "I'm going to murder you."

James watched her go, and for the first time noticed a picture hanging on the wall. It was a young Jack Marsh, standing by a vintage Austin Princess. Daisy struggled by the door and kicked out at the sergeant, hitting the wall. The picture fell.

James picked it up, the glass had broken, and the photo had slipped to show another picture underneath. He opened the back and carefully removed the picture. It was of Maureen and Jack Marsh in front

368 | EDWARD ARNO

of their house. Coronation decorations were hanging from a lamppost and in the window of the house. Jack was dressed in a demob suit and Maureen in a very pretty flowered dress. They looked a very happy couple. Next to them was a pram an old-fashioned pushchair, and just peering around the edge of it, a little girl.

James turned the picture over, written on the back was "June 1952. Jack and Maureen Marsh by their new house." Someone else had written, "To my sweet, my love for ever." James placed the picture on the sideboard and left the house.

Outside, Daisy was screaming and shouting. It was taking several officers to get her into a police car. "She spat at me," said Trevor.

"That's nothing, she told me she was going to murder me! Shall we go before Smith arrives? I don't think I could face him just at the moment."

"Likewise."

"Sergeant," called James. "We will come down to the station to make our statements, but I think I should get my friend home first. He has only just got out of hospital, and Inspector Smith is taking a long time."

"That'll be okay, sir."

"Oh, and please tell Inspector Smith I have another confession tape for him."

James and Trevor slowly walked to the car. Mrs. Coates came over to them. "Thank you."

"I'm so sorry we couldn't save him. I did try, but he wouldn't go to the police when I told him to."

"You did your best, he was always a stubborn boy."

"How's Bobby taken it?"

"Won't stop crying. He loved, no, worshipped, his brother. I'd better get back to him."

"Take care, Mrs. Coates."

They climbed into the car. "I really feel bad about Willie," said Trevor.

"Trevor, there was nothing we could have done. Look, here's Smith arriving. Let's go."

They drove down the road, waving to Inspector Smith, who stood on the pavement looking at them open-mouthed.

CHAPTER NINETEEN

The Good Book

The living room in James' apartment was stacked with cardboard boxes. Some filled, others waiting for the last few items. James had decided to move. He needed fresh pastures and had persuaded his brothers to buy some land in Malvern and build new houses. They already owned an old manor house that had been converted into apartments. It was one of these apartments that James was thinking of moving into, so he would be near the building site. It was a new venture for the Pidgley Property Company, but he was convinced it was the right thing to do. Old houses had too much of a history, and you never knew what skeletons you might find in the closet.

He made one last cup of tea. He would miss the place, his place. Sitting at the kitchen table, he picked up the letter from Mrs. Coates. Bobby had finally told the truth, and the whole story would come out in the court case against Daisy. The police had decided not to charge Jeffrey, but to have him committed to a hospital for the rest of his life. Mrs. Coates and Bobby were going to visit her sister in Doncaster. The letter said they had not had a holiday for a very long time, and this gave them the opportunity. She finished by thanking James for all he did.

James wondered if he could have done more to save Willie. The look on Willie's face at the little hut would haunt him for a very long time. He closed the letter and slipped it into the box lying on the table. He sipped at the tea. Why was he procrastinating in packing? He had been the driving force to the new venture, and here he was not wanting to leave. He picked up the small Bible he had found at Thirteen Crowhurst Road. He had never really talked to his father about its contents. He opened it and began to read. His father had written in such detail about the abuse his own father had given him. For the first time James understood why his father didn't talk about his childhood. It must have been horrible.

He flipped through a few more pages and read. It was the night before the Queen's Coronation, and Crowhurst Road was a hive of activity. Matthew Pidgley had, as always, hid in the unfinished house, watching the road and the people who lived in it.

The party committee had gathered on the small stage for a photograph. Dad organized them pushing Mom to the side so Mrs. Coates could stand next to him. After the picture was taken they all cheered and hugged and kissed, Mrs. Coates and dad kissed for a very long time.

James turned a few more pages.

Mr. Coates stood in front of our house and painted "Gyppos live here" on the front door and wall. Later when Dad and Mrs. Coates came back, Dad was mad and started to shout and wake up the neighbors.

James put down the Bible and sipped some more tea. 'So it was Mr. Coates who did the graffiti, and while he was in prison it stopped,' thought James. He went back to the book.

Mr. Marsh and his brother had a fight. Mrs. Marsh still not around and the road has now been filled in. Dad brought some men back with him, so I stayed out all night. Mr. Marsh putting another bundle in his car, I think it was his brother, I saw a hand sticking out of the sacking.

James closed the book. His father had seen it all, even written it down. Why hadn't he told someone? He phoned his parents' house.

"Hello."

"Dad, its James."

"Hello, son. You packed yet?"

"Yes. Just a few things to do, and then wait for Trevor and Anne."

"They left about an hour ago."

"Well, it's love. They possibly stopped on the way."

"Knowing Anne, to look at furniture."

"Dad, I've just been reading the Bible."

"Really? I didn't know you were into religion."

"I'm not, the Bible you wrote in when you were a child."

"Oh, that Bible."

"Dad, I now understand what happened. I'm sorry. We kids must have given you such a hard time when we kept asking about your childhood."

"It's okay, that's history. As I said recently, we have to move on with our lives."

"Dad, in the book you wrote about the murder, grandfather and Mrs. Coates. The graffiti, you knew who did it."

"Son, knowing and telling someone are so far apart in my mind. I was a child worried that my father would kill me. I didn't tell anyone anything. Also, remember, we were regarded as 'dirty Gyppos.' Who was going to believe a child?"

"Why didn't you tell me when this all started?"

"I had forgotten it. I blanked out my childhood. That way it couldn't hurt me. Then, when you wanted to buy the house in Crowhurst Road, I had to make a decision. Come to terms with what had happened and not let it hurt me. Your Grandfather's dead. He could never hurt me again, so why let the memories hurt?"

"I don't understand, we could have solved the murder so much more quickly."

"Maybe, but I had to protect myself. You had a beautiful childhood. Your mother and I never hit you or shouted at any of you. Why? Because we didn't want you to suffer. If only more people would take the time to talk to their children, I think there would be less problems in the world."

"But…"

"Son, let it go. You did your best, and that's all that matters. You also found your sister a boyfriend."

"Yeah, poor man. Dad, I think I can hear a truck. Maybe it's them."

"Okay. We will speak more about this if you need to."

"Thanks Dad."

He closed the phone and placed the Bible in one of the boxes. A knock at the front door made him jump. He was still nervous.

"Open the door!" The guard chain stretched as Anne tried to push her way in. "James, let me in."

"Stand back and I'll take the guard chain off."

"Why have you got a guard chain on? Scared someone will come in and rape you? Don't make me laugh. You haven't even got a girlfriend." He opened the door wide, Anne was standing impatiently with Trevor, who was piled high with boxes behind her. "I hope you're ready and packed. We have to get you out so I can clean the place before I move my stuff in."

"Hello Anne, nice to see you too. Hi Trevor." Trevor nodded and took the boxes into the bedroom.

"James, you haven't finished. Why are you dilly-dallying. You've not gone sentimental and decided not to move?"

"No."

"Then get a move on. I want to be in by tomorrow, and I still have to clean this filthy place.

"It's not filthy."

"It is to me. Trevor, is this place filthy or not?" Trevor looked at James and then Anne. "Trevor…"

"Anne, shut up and make James and me some tea while we start moving the heavy furniture first." Anne looked at him, smiled, and then went into the kitchen.

James nodded. Trevor gave one of his corner-of-the-mouth smiles, which he had perfected since going out with Anne.

It took them several hours to move James out of his apartment. Anne didn't say a word and kept them supplied with tea. She washed and packed the teacups and took them down to the truck, leaving James alone to have one last look around his apartment.

He stood staring at his empty living room. Trevor entered and made a little coughing sound. "Sorry James, but Anne is a little agitated."

"Yeah, I hope you can handle her."

"She shuts up when I tell her to."

"Maybe that's what we should have done for all those years of suffering her."

"Did you ever find out if your Dad knew what really happened? Anne said he wrote it down in a little Bible."

"No. I asked him, and he said he couldn't remember. The Bible is so hard to read, I think it must be in some sort of code."

"Pity."

"Yeah, but that's life."

"Let's go. I'm not sure if me telling Anne to shut up will always work."

"If she gets really out of hand, call her 'Piglet'. She hates that."

"Really? I must remember that."

"Thanks for everything."

"Hey, what are friends for?"

"I'm sorry we couldn't help Willie. He didn't deserve to die."

"Yeah, he was okay, just a little misguided."

"I think you all were."

"I'll go down and tell Anne you're just coming."

James stood by himself, pondering whether telling Trevor a lie was wrong. No it was not. He was protecting his father. He would hide the Bible so no one would ever know what happened.

He turned the key in the lock of his apartment for the last time.

MUSIC THAT INSPIRED THE WRITING

Les Yeux Noirs

A Band of Gypsies/Balamouk /Live

Edward Elgar

Enigma Variations

Adam Faith

The Very Best of Adam Faith

Adam & the Ants

The Essential Adam Ant

Wet Wet Wet

Popped in Souled Out

Beautiful South

0898

BBC Concert Orchestra

The Last Night of the Proms

Various Artists (Road of the Gypsies)

L' Épopée Tzigane

ABOUT THE AUTHOR

Edward Arno was born in a field in Frankley Beech, Birmingham, England. His father was a milkman and his mother was a house parlor maid. They met during a bombing raid at the end of the Second World War. Growing up on a council estate, he attended the local public schools. The Issigonis Mini auto plant at Longbridge was the symphonic sound of his childhood. He moved to America to pursue a screenwriting and directing career.

He resides in Burbank, California . *Coronation Souvenir* is his debut novel. He is also an active member of the Mystery Writers of America.

www.edwardarno.com

THREE RING CIRCUS

Circus clown Brinarno finds the report of his death funny until his credit card and bank account are frozen. Someone had gone to a lot of trouble to declare him dead.

James Pidgley has moved to the quite hillside town of Great Malvern to develop a small piece of land. Trouble with the locals about his caravan forces him to move into the circus winter quarters adjacent to his land.

The circus owner's boyfriend is found murdered and then clown Brinarno is found dead. James starts to investigate on behalf of Mabel Morris, the circus owner. His Romany ancestry makes him a welcome ally of the circus travelers.

James is shocked at the misinformation given out by the local police. Brinarno's employment for the British government on classified military projects complicates his search for the killer. The unlikely combination of skinhead circus tentmen and Chinese acrobats aid James in solving this three-ring circus mystery.

A BRIGHTON CALM

Pidgley Properties is expanding its empire and its next project will convert a Victorian hotel into luxury apartments. James Pidgley has been sent to the seaside town of Brighton to oversee the project. The building had been abandoned for several years. An unscrupulous security firm is hired to vacate the premises. They send their employees, operatives recently returned from a tour in Iraq, to remove squatters from the hotel. Drugs, sex and smuggling had been the recent business of the dark damp corridors.

A high profile supermarket tycoon's son is murdered in the old hotel's once prestigious blue room. James and his new girlfriend are drawn into the investigation and face a stone wall of silence from the local criminals. James reveals the secrets of the hotel and its hub of activity for the English south coast underworld

AUTHOR LINKS

It's my heartfelt hope that you've enjoyed Coronation Souvenir. If you have a question you'd like to ask, or an opinion to express, I'd be delighted to hear it and respond.

Your reviews, comments, questions and opinions are invaluable and appreciated. There's a variety of ways to engage;

Face Book
https://www.facebook.com/edwardarnoauthor

Reach out to Victory Rose Press directly at;
victoryrosepress@gmail.com

My web site has latest news and links to my titles;
www.edwardarno.com

Twitter
https://twitter.com/EddieArno